Gator Bait

Doug Fletcher book 9

Dean L. Hovey

Print ISBNs
BWL Print 9780228619222
B&N Print 9780228619239
LSI Print 9780228619895
Amazon Print 9780228619246

BWL Publishing

Books we love to write
Authors around the world.

http://bwlpublishing.ca

Copyright 2021 by Dean L. Hovey
Cover art by Michelle Lee

Dedication
To Nancy and Jim Finkbeiner

"It is a capital mistake to theorize before one has data. Insensibly one begins to twist facts to suit theories, instead of theories to suit facts." – Sir Arthur Conan Doyle

Chapter 1

The crowded bar emptied as the after-work crowd left and singles paired up. Madison Wirth sat alone in a booth. Having turned away several men who'd tried to strike up a conversation, she frequently checked her cell phone, obviously awaiting a text or message in the waning moments before last call.

A woman who'd been sitting alone at the bar slid into the booth. "Hey, looks like you're trying to avoid the vultures too." The woman glanced around the room, glaring at one young man who tried to make eye contact.

Madison swirled the brown liquid she'd been nursing. "Yeah, my idiot boyfriend stood me up again."

"Again?"

"He sometimes gets called out just before the end of a shift. But he usually texts me." Madison glanced over her shoulder at the door. "How about you?"

"My friends took off for a party. The guys who invited us looked a little questionable and dropped some hints about better living through chemistry. I have to work tomorrow, and I don't need my brain fried." The new woman put out her hand. "I'm Jesse."

"I'm Madison. My friends call me Maddie."

Jesse looked at the door. "Is your boyfriend one of the uniformed guys who just came in?"

Maddie turned toward the door and searched for the uniforms. Jesse dropped a white pill into Maddie's drink. After a few seconds Maddie turned back. "Those guys are firemen. They sometimes come in after their shift."

Jesse nodded and sipped her drink. "Sorry. I thought maybe…"

Maddie shook her head and pushed her drink aside. "He won't show tonight. I think I'll just go back to my apartment."

Jesse put up her hand. "Hey, let's finish our drinks and I'll walk out with you. I don't like walking to my car alone this time of night."

"Yeah," Maddie said, tipping her glass back and finishing her drink. "This neighborhood isn't bad, but I don't like walking around alone after midnight."

They slid out of the booth and threaded their way through the tables to the front

6

door. Maddie bumped into a middle-aged drinker sitting next to the door and excused herself. The humid Florida night had a fresh, floral fragrance.

"Where are you parked?" Jesse asked.

Maddie nodded to the right. "Down this way." They walked away from the bar and within a few steps Maddie stopped and leaned on a storefront. "Whoa, I didn't think I'd had that much to drink."

"Maybe you shouldn't drive," Jesse suggested. "My car is right here. I'll give you a ride home."

Maddie staggered to the car and leaned against it as Jesse opened the passenger door. Maddie nearly fell into the front seat, grabbing at air as she fell back.

Two women walked past and watched with obvious disdain. "Drunks."

Jesse buckled Maddie in, then unlocked the driver's door. She looked around to see if anyone else was watching, then got in her rental car. Maddie's head lolled and Jesse smiled before taking out her phone and typing in a text. Then she drove west, toward the Everglades.

* * *

Caden Roush had been with the U. S. Park Service for three years. He loved being outdoors and felt pride when wearing his green and gray uniform with Smokey

Bear hat. He'd led hundreds of tour groups on the Anhinga Tour, one of the easiest walking trails in Everglades National Park. The flat pathway attracted the most tour groups, and often included handicapped people in motorized wheelchairs and scooters. His handicap today was a pair of newlyweds who'd told the group of twenty-two hikers they were on the third day of their honeymoon. They lagged behind while holding hands and stopping to stare into each other's eyes. Caden pointed out wildlife and great photo opportunities, but they ignored his commentary. In short, they were driving him crazy.

"Jim and Vickie, we're picking up the pace a little," he said, hoping to get them back into the group.

Vickie, a petite blonde, nodded and pulled Jim along as they caught up with the last of the tour group. Jim, a slender man with dark hair and glasses that made him look studious, stopped to take a photo of a vulture perched on the handrail.

Caden stopped the group, who'd already taken their vulture pictures. As Jim approached the large bird, Caden backtracked. "Vultures don't have any predators or natural defenses. However, they will vomit a stream of partially digested carrion on you if they feel threatened. I've only seen it happen twice, but the recipients would've rather been sprayed by a skunk."

The comment froze the honeymooner, who'd been so focused on the image on his phone display that he didn't realize he was only three feet from the big bird.

Vickie tugged at his hand. "Pay attention. You're not in Iowa anymore."

Fifty yards further down the boardwalk Caden stopped the group and pointed out a group of vultures fighting over a carcass on a hump of vegetation. "Alligators and vultures are nature's garbage collectors. The alligators prefer live prey but aren't picky if they're hungry and the meal is easy to catch. The vultures aren't predators. They often clean up after the alligators are through eating."

Vickie pushed ahead while Jim shot more photos of the vultures. "That's a big carcass. What are the vultures eating?"

Caden loved questions. It gave him an opportunity to show off his knowledge of Everglades biology and ecology. "The largest prey animals in the Everglades are deer and wild pigs. I imagine the vultures are working on one of those two."

Jim took a pair of pictures, then froze. "Look at the black log. It just moved."

Caden shifted his gaze in the direction Jim was looking and smiled. "That's a big gator. He'll probably chase the vultures off the kill."

As predicted, the vultures flew away as the alligator approached. When they flapped away, the tour got a view of the carrion the vultures had been on. The group watched as the alligator slowly swam across the small opening.

Vickie pointed, momentarily unable to speak. "That's not a deer, it's wearing jeans."

Chapter 2

My wife and law enforcement partner, Jill Fletcher, was riding alongside me in a U.S. Park Service pickup as we patrolled the North Padre Island beach. On this southbound leg of the trip, the passenger saw the dunes, covered with sea oats and brush. Jill's view had been unchanged for an hour. We turned around at the Port Mansfield channel and Jill watched the Gulf of Mexico on the return leg of our drive.

Jill had been the Flagstaff, Arizona park superintendent when we'd met. Her life had been hectic and demanding. "You know, this life as a park service investigator is pretty boring."

I smiled. "Hours of boredom and seconds of terror."

"I thought pilots said that."

"Pilots, firemen, and cops," I replied.

"Boring makes for long days."

"And being shot at can end your life."

Jill glanced at me. She knew I'd been shot at as a soldier in Iraq and had been in several gunfights as a cop. Since becoming a law enforcement officer and now an investigator, she'd been involved in two gunfights. She'd performed fearlessly, but each experience rattled her. We'd talked at length after each encounter, leaning on each other, expressing our fears and regrets, and embarrassed by the news reports painting us as heroes.

Our last investigation hadn't involved shooting but ended when I'd broken my collarbone. Jill was scraped and bruised after sliding down a hillside while apprehending criminals. After the investigation, the criminals were prosecuted and given short jail sentences. All were out of jail before my arm was out of the sling.

Jill turned to face me. "Both our families are in South Dakota. I suppose we should plan on spending either Thanksgiving or Christmas with them again."

I was about to make a profane comment about barren prairie, blizzards, and horses, when Jill's cell phone trilled. She fumbled with the phone and answered before it rolled over to voicemail. She listened for a few moments, answering, "uh huh," a few times.

I looked at her and saw a smirk, then a smile. "Hang on. I'll tell Doug." She put her hand over the phone. "Matt got a call from Everglades National Park. They'd like us to fly to Miami and assist with the investigation of a body recovered near a popular trail."

I read her smile. "You want to go."

"It beats driving up and down the beach twice a day."

"It's August. The temperature and humidity will be unbearable."

Jill's smile spread until her dimples showed, then she uncovered the phone. "When do we leave?"

She listened for a few more minutes, then she ended the call. "Matt will have the details by the time we get back to the visitor center."

* * *

Matt Mattson was busy on his computer when we knocked on the doorframe. He looked up and gestured for us to close the door and sit.

"A ranger leading a tour group found a body in the swamp next to the boardwalk. He called in help, and they had to chase off a couple alligators so the recovery crews could get to the remains. They took the body to the local coroner who identified the remains as a young woman. No one has reported her missing, and there wasn't any identification with the body."

I leaned back. "What was the cause of death?"

Matt tapped his pencil. "At this point, it's listed as undetermined. Jane Doe was badly decomposed and there had been depredation by alligators and vultures."

Jill glanced at me, awaiting my next question. "What are we supposed to do?"

Matt smiled. "Pull another rabbit out of the hat like you did in South Dakota. Figure out who she is, how she died, and the manner of her death."

"You know, one of these times we won't solve the mystery."

"The big bosses are convinced that you two are their golden children."

Jill smiled at me. "Think of it as a Florida vacation."

"Bullshit. We both know it's going to be hotter than hell, long hours, probably involve wading in a swamp, we'll get eaten by mosquitoes, and…"

"And it'll be better than driving the beach twice a day staring at sea oats and irritating sea gulls."

Jill knew I wanted to go, and her frank statement made me smile. I looked at Matt, trying to appear resigned to accepting the assignment. "When do we leave?"

Matt pulled a sheet off his printer. "You're flying out tomorrow morning. Here's your itinerary. Mandy's going to pick you up at six and drive you to the airport."

I looked at the itinerary with irritation. "You booked us before we said yes." Then I realized our return flights were non-refundable and scheduled two weeks later.

"Matt, it's going to cost hundreds of bucks each to rebook these flights if we're through with this in a day or two."

Matt stood up and opened the door. "I guess you'd better pack your sunscreen and swimsuits."

"But…"

Matt smiled and put his hand on my shoulder. "I can't authorize rebooking fees, so you'll have to figure out a way to stay busy in Florida."

"I kind of like the beaches better here. They're not as crowded."

Matt chuckled. "Take a dress uniform along."

I froze. "Why?"

"Because you get dragged in front of a television camera everywhere you go, and I want you in a uniform this time."

"Sorry. I'm getting forgetful and hard of hearing."

I'd taken two steps when Matt yelled after me, "That was an order, not a suggestion."

I kept walking and waved my arm. "Can't hear you."

I felt Jill's hand on my back, so I walked down the hallway to my office. She sat in a chair by my desk. "You don't know when to shut up, do you?"

I handed her the itinerary. "I don't like big cities and we're booked into a hotel just outside Miami."

Jill shrugged. "I've never been to Florida. I think this'll be fun."

I tried my best glare but got a dimpled smile in return. "Let's go home and pack. Luckily, your dress uniform is back from the cleaners."

"*If* there's a news conference, you can go. I'll sit by the pool and drink something with an umbrella sticking out of it."

"Quit being a pain in the butt. You took the job, now do it. All of it."

"This is nothing but a wild goose chase. I'm sure they've got a qualified medical examiner who's already determined that the body can't be identified, and the cause of death can't be determined. What are we going to do except trip over what's already been done? And we'll be doing that for two weeks."

Jill pushed the office door shut and leaned her elbows on my desk. "Listen, Fletcher. I'm looking forward to a change of scenery and something more interesting than watching sea oats. Stop being a Debbie Downer and suck it up."

"Florida's different, and I find it uncomfortable. I like Texas because it feels Midwestern. Florida has a different vibe, especially the Miami coast."

"You can be a chameleon. I've seen you shift from tough cop to South Dakota hick to polished professional going toe-to-toe with FBI bureaucrats from Washington.

16

You do that much better than I can, and you're good at it."

"There's a difference between being good at something and enjoying it. I don't like putting on a façade and pretending to be something I'm not."

Jill stood up. "You better figure it out pretty quickly because tomorrow we'll be regular South Beach hipsters."

"Hipster? Remember who you're talking to."

I locked the office and trailed Jill to her pickup in the parking lot. She had the engine and air-conditioning running when I got in. She turned to me. "Are you okay?"

"What are you asking?"

"You usually jump at the chance to do an investigation. You're balking."

"Like I said, south Florida is different. There was a gang shootout after a bank robbery. The gang members had fully automatic weapons and the cops were out-gunned."

"That's it? The guns?"

"Our last few assignments were pretty mundane. This has the potential to be something more…"

"Risky?"

I shrugged. "I guess."

"You're usually up for anything."

I took her hand and squeezed it. "I didn't have as much to lose."

"You're worried about me?"

I nodded. "You're a South Dakota ranch girl who spent the middle part of her life in northern Arizona corralling young rangers with raging hormones. This has the potential to end dramatically."

"Honey, the investigation in Wyoming had a wild ending and I held my own."

"Have I told you why I like my pilots and doctors to have gray hair?"

"I don't think so."

"Gray-haired pilots and doctors have experienced a lot of things and they're better prepared to deal with an emergency situation."

"Unlike rookie cops."

I nodded.

Jill frowned. "I've held up okay."

I squeezed Jill's hand. "You've been fearless, and that's not always a good thing for a cop."

I saw the revelation sweep her. "You don't think…"

"When that crazy guy ran out of the garage shooting, everyone was ducking for cover. You took a step out from behind the log house and fired at him. That was fearless, but not necessarily the smart thing to do."

"You and the sheriff told me I probably saved lives."

"You most likely did—by risking your own life." I paused and let my words sink in. "Promise me you'll take one extra fraction of a second to assess the situation before you put yourself in danger."

She leaned over and hugged me. "I will, but only if you're out of danger. Deal?"

I tipped my head back and drew a breath. "You're as stubborn as a mule."

"And as protective as a mother grizzly."

"I'm not a bear cub."

Jill released my hand and shifted the truck into gear. "You're right. Sometimes I think a bear cub has more sense."

Chapter 3

Our flights to Miami were quiet. We didn't get upgraded to first class, nor did we have to deal with a drunk assaulting the flight attendant, as we had on our July flight to Minneapolis. I felt the humidity as soon as the plane's exit door opened. Although Corpus Christi is steamy in summer, it has its own distinctive Gulf of Mexico smell. The feel and smell of Miami are very different.

We claimed our bags and looked for someone from the park service, but no one seemed to be awaiting our arrival. The government-preferred car rental vendor was out of mid-size sedans. I declined a minivan and agreed to a no-charge upgrade to a premium full-size Nissan Altima. Jill took control of the onboard GPS and we left the airport, driving toward Everglades National Park headquarters in Florida City. Within minutes we hit a toll booth.

"You're kidding! They're charging us for the privilege of driving on a road built and paid for by the federal government?"

Jill dug in her backpack and pulled out a handful of change. She handed me the coins I needed. "Take it easy. It's just the way it is. There's nothing we can do about it."

I threw the change into the bucket as cars whizzed past in a lane for prepaid tolls.

"Catch the next ramp," Jill coached without looking up from the GPS.

"I hate this traffic. It's the mid-afternoon and it's worse than rush hour in Corpus Christi."

Jill glanced up at the road ahead. "You've been living in the boonies too long. At least the traffic is moving."

Almost immediately the traffic stopped. Seeing her sheepish grin, I shook my head. "You had to say it, didn't you? How far do we go in this parking lot?"

She looked at the map. "Maybe eight miles."

I closed my eyes. "At this rate, we should get to the park headquarters sometime tomorrow."

"The woman they found won't be any more dead tomorrow than she is today."

The traffic moved ahead, and a car nosed into the space ahead of me, trying to gain a half car length. "I'd have to see a therapist for anger management therapy if we lived here."

"Just keep your hand off your pistol and we'll be okay."

I looked around at the grim faces of the other drivers. "I wonder if this is like Wyoming where every driver has a gun."

Jill looked around. "The difference would be that Wyoming folks grow up shooting and respect the lives of the animals they kill. Here, I suspect the people on this road have no idea what a gun does except for what they've seen on television cop shows."

"Some of them probably live in neighborhoods where there are more gang shootings than deer killed during a Wyoming hunting season."

Jill sighed. "I hope that's the cynical cop talking and not the result of some online research."

The traffic speed picked up when we passed an accident. I quickly learned that leaving a car's length stopping distance ahead of me only invited some idiot to pull into the space and jam on his brakes to warn me I was too close.

"Sonofabitch! Did you see that?"

"Take it easy. You'll get used to this traffic."

"I don't want to get used to it. I want to turn around and catch the next flight out of here."

"We're less than a half hour from the park. It'll get better."

The traffic eased the farther we got from the airport. I stopped squeezing the steering wheel like I was trying to kill it. Jill seemed to be enjoying the scenery. "You're amazingly relaxed. Are you taking Valium?"

"I think I'm running on less testosterone than you are. Ease up. This will be okay."

I took a deep breath and after a few minutes felt my blood pressure drop to near normal levels. Jill had been glancing at me.

"What?" I asked.

"You got quiet."

"So."

"It's out of character. The more you stress out the more you talk."

"I'm okay."

"You're not okay. You've been resistant to this whole assignment, and you exploded over a traffic jam. What's up?"

"I don't know."

"You haven't been the same since Iowa. I don't think the broken collarbone did you in. Did I miss something?"

"Talking with Jamie got me thinking about my life…our lives," I said, flashing back to the Iowa discussions I'd had with my Navajo Nation Police partner and friend.

"What about our lives?"

I watched the traffic. "I don't know if I can verbalize what's in my head."

"He and Liz live a more uncluttered, simpler life, in a quieter environment."

"It's not that. I guess he got me thinking about our mortality. I've been…"

"You've been a reckless cowboy who runs toward the sound of gunfire instead of away."

"I guess that's part of it."

Jill shifted and turned toward me. "Honey, that's what good cops do. They put their lives on the line to protect innocent people."

"I…we don't have to live that way."

"Doug, you stepped away from it when you retired from the St. Paul PD. After working the antique dealer's murder, you told me you missed the thrill of the chase. Has that changed?"

"I hate talking about touchy-feely things."

I saw Jill's smile out of the corner of my eye. "It's the testosterone thing again. Only women can talk about their feelings, is that it?"

"I don't know what I'm feeling."

Jill glanced at the GPS. "Take the next exit." She guided me down a short piece of highway until I saw the Everglades National Park sign. We followed smaller roads until we got to the headquarters building. I parked and we clipped our badges to our belts as we walked across the parking lot.

Jill fell in step beside me. "We're not through with our feelings discussion."

I wove through the parked cars and stopped to let an RV with Pennsylvania license plates pass. "*I* think we're done with that discussion."

Jill stepped ahead of me and opened the entry door. "No, we aren't. It's just on hold."

The superintendent's office was down a short hallway. We found two men in ranger uniforms sitting across a desk from each other. Both stood when we entered the office.

The ranger behind the desk put out his hand. "I'm Jack Adler, the Everglades National Park Superintendent. This is Larry Marconi, my law enforcement ranger."

Adler was a middle-aged bureaucrat with graying hair and a bit of bulge over his belt. Marconi looked military, with a thick neck, wavy dark hair, broad shoulders, and a narrow waist. I was intrigued by the thick gold chain inside his uniform shirt. Neither of them smiled.

We sat and Jill jumped right to the elephant in the room. "You don't seem pleased that we're here."

Marconi clenched his jaw and thought for a second. "We've recovered the body and brought it to the medical examiner. He can't identify the remains or determine the cause of death. Nobody saw the body before it was reported by the tour group, nor did they see anything suspicious that would lead us toward the timing or cause of her death."

25

Adler leaned forward. "Can I see your credentials?"

Jill and I handed him the leather folders with our picture IDs. "I've never met a park service investigator before." He examined them and handed them to Marconi. "I assume you have experience that qualifies you beyond being regular law enforcement rangers."

I took out my St. Paul Police Department (retired) ID and handed it to Adler. "I was a police detective."

Marconi looked at me. "Have I fucked up and need two babysitters?"

"I wasn't told to babysit you. I was asked to consult on your investigation. As far as I'm concerned, it's your investigation and we're here to help. If we're not welcome, we'll leave."

Jill jumped in before the situation got confrontational. "You look military."

"Army. I was deployed twice in Iraq. Went back to New Jersey and got a job with my hometown police when I mustered out."

Marconi got up and closed the office door. "Doug, you said you were here to help me, right?"

"Have you led a murder investigation?"

"This could've been an accident," he countered.

"Are you missing any visitors? Are there cars in the parking lot that have been left for weeks?"

Adler looked at Marconi before answering. "No to both those questions."

"Then you probably have a murder."

Marconi took a breath, let it out, and seemed resigned.

Adler waved him to a chair. "Let's talk about what's next."

"I'd like to see a copy of the post-mortem," I said, trying not to be pushy, but making it clear we weren't backing down.

Marconi looked irritated with me. "I didn't see the need to get a copy when we thought it was an accident."

"Did the medical examiner have any comments at the autopsy?"

Marconi's eyes narrowed. "I didn't go to the autopsy. Remember, we thought it was an accident."

"I'd like to talk to the medical examiner and get a copy of the examination."

"I already told you, the results were inconclusive. He couldn't determine her identity or the cause of death."

Adler leaned forward. "What do you hope to accomplish, Fletcher?"

I could tell Jill was getting irritated by being excluded from the conversation. She leaned back, crossed her arms and legs, and let me answer. "We know absolutely nothing right now. I'd like to ask the medical examiner about his observations. The ME usually observes things they don't put in their report because they don't want to defend their opinions in court. I want to know if your ME had anything that isn't written down. I'd also like to look through the woman's clothing to get a sense of her age, her style, her persona. Was she dressed for a cocktail party, or did she just get off a horse?"

Marconi interrupted. "She was wearing jeans. What do you need to know besides that?"

Jill maintained her antagonized posture. "Were they Levi or Jordache? Size four or fourteen? Worn out or new? Boot cut or tapered? Distressed kid jeans or farmer denim? Low cut hip-riders or high waisted?"

Adler glanced at Marconi whose face was turning red. "Can you answer any of Jill's questions, Larry?"

Marconi shook his head. "They were jeans."

Jill's eyes narrowed. "If we know the answers to those questions, we narrow our search down. How many agencies have you called?"

"The ME is checking."

I looked at Adler. "Checking what?"

Adler shrugged. "What's he checking, Larry?"

"To see if she fits the profile of any missing women."

Jill shook her head. "How broad of a net is he casting? Has he checked the database for missing and abused children?"

28

"I s'pose he has."

"But you don't know?" Jill asked.

"I've only been on this case a few days," Marconi countered.

Jill leaned forward. "Let's leave the superintendent to do his job while we review your call logs. I don't want to duplicate steps you've already taken."

I could tell from Marconi's expression that he hadn't called anyone.

Adler saw it too. "Doug and Jill, there's a break room at the end of the hallway with a coffee machine. Why don't you have a cup and Larry will join you in a minute."

I closed the door and hesitated as Jill walked toward the break room. "What the hell have you been doing, Larry?"

I couldn't hear Larry's reply, but Adler was right back at him. "Damn it, Larry. We look like a bunch of hicks. You get your ass down to the break room and act like you appreciate the help those people are offering because it sounds like they're going to save your butt, or at least try to."

I walked away before I caught any more of the conversation. Jill met me next to a coffee pot and handed me a paper cup of black coffee. "What did you hear?"

"Larry is either going to be madder than a wet hen, or peaches and cream."

"You're hoping for peaches and cream?"

I checked to make sure Marconi wasn't walking down the hall. "I prefer wet hen. At least I'll know where we stand with him. If he's too nice, we'll be watching our backs the entire time we're here, waiting for him to stick it to us."

Jill sat down and frowned. "Maybe you were right. We should've stayed in Texas."

Marconi walked in a minute later with his cell phone in hand. "I called the ME. He has time to talk with us in half an hour."

I couldn't read his expression. "Are we cool, or are we stepping on your toes?"

"I was told to help you any way I can."

I pushed a chair toward him. "Lay your cards on the table and let's figure out how to deal with this."

Marconi didn't sit, which was a bad sign. "Listen, I didn't ask for your help, and I don't want your help. Adler says I have to give you a hand, so I will."

Jill stood and threw her empty coffee cup at the wastebasket. "Get in your truck, patrol the campgrounds, and ticket litterers. We've got this, and if you're not going to be part of the team, we'd rather work without you."

"Adler says..."

Jill leaned on the table. "Do you have any vacation time?"

Marconi looked confused. "What?"

"If you have accumulated vacation time, now would be a good time to take it. Get

30

the hell out of here and lay on the beach for a week."

Marconi glared at her as I stood up. "What Jill's saying is, the train is leaving the station and if you're sitting on the bench, stay out of our way."

"Adler said…"

Jill got a menacing look I'd never seen before. "Listen Marconi, I was a park superintendent for twenty years. I've dealt with people like you, mostly by firing them. Get the hell out of here and leave us alone. If you can't do that, I'll call the regional superintendent and have your status changed to unpaid leave pending dismissal."

"You can't…"

Jill pulled out her phone and started punching in numbers. Marconi watched, unconvinced of her ability to follow through on the threat.

"Marcia? Hi, it's Jill Fletcher. I've got a personnel problem. We're in Everglades National Park on an investigation, and the law enforcement ranger here is interfering with our work. I want him terminated. List the cause as impeding a federal investigation pending the U.S. Attorney filing formal charges."

Jill listened for a moment, then replied. "No, you don't need to contact the U.S. Attorney's office at this time. If he continues to impede us, I may change my mind and ask for charges to be filed." Jill listened quietly again, then held the phone to her chest. "Human resources needs your badge and federal identification numbers for the forms."

The color drained from Marconi's face. "Hold on. We don't need to do this."

"We asked you to play nice and you refused. We're done."

Marconi put up his hands. "Hang on, you've got no authority…"

Jill lifted her phone. "He's declined the information." Jill listened, nodding. She ended the call and looked at Marconi. "Go to Adler's office. He's getting a call right now. You can give *him* your badge and firearm."

"Jesus! You're serious?"

"Serious as a heart attack."

Marconi spun around and rushed away.

"Are we bluffing?" I asked.

Jill pocketed her phone. "He's on terminal leave pending completion of approvals. We should probably sit here and wait for Adler."

I poured two more cups of coffee and sat down across from Jill. She took a few deep breaths and stared at me. "I'm sorry. I just can't put up with behavior like this anymore. I used to work through it and handhold people trying to get them to change, but I just don't have the patience."

"He'll lose his job, his pension… lifestyle."

Jill shrugged. "He chose to act like an ass. All I did was call him on it. The employment manual is explicit about defiance of orders. A law enforcement ranger refusing an order is grounds for immediate termination."

I nodded. "We'd have to add dereliction of duties as well. He hasn't done anything to investigate this woman's death."

Footsteps preceded Adler's appearance in the break room. He pulled out a chair and sat down with us. "I just had a call from Washington."

Jill nodded. "I know. I called them when Marconi refused an order. I told them to terminate him."

Adler ran his fingers through his hair. "Larry is the only permanent law enforcement ranger I have."

"I'd say you made a poor choice when you hired him. He's not suited for the job."

"He was a cop."

I leaned forward and pushed my coffee cup away. "He's had a possible murder case sitting in his lap for days and hasn't done anything but call the ME. On top of that, I don't trust him. He's arrogant and has given us the impression he's not willing to engage with us. I can't work with someone I don't trust. He's armed and I need to know the sworn law enforcement people I work with will back me up. I'm not convinced he's going to do that. I'm not even sure he'll be around if I need him."

Adler drew a deep breath. "Larry's in my office. I locked his badge and pistol in my file cabinet. He's had a 'come to Jesus moment' and his attitude has been adjusted. Please give him another chance. He's a good man."

I looked at Jill who had crossed her arms and leaned back. "Listen, Adler, from the little we've seen and what Marconi's said, he's going to hinder, not help, this investigation." She looked at me. "Doug?"

"We're not a couple of seasonal rookies sent here to snoop around. We're experienced park service investigators who were sent here by headquarters. We didn't volunteer for this; we were told to come here because someone in your chain of command was unhappy with the way this death investigation is being handled." I paused. "Adler, your job is on the line here, too."

That comment shook Adler. "What makes you think my job is at risk?"

"You've dropped the ball on this investigation. You accepted Marconi's assessment of this woman's discovery. He's done nothing. Nothing. And you've stood behind him and let the investigation languish based on his one phone call to an ME."

Jill leaned forward and her voice softened. "We were sent here because *you* dropped the ball. You're the boss and the buck stops with you." She paused, then added, "Think about what it means to have the U.S. Park Service send two investigators to help your investigation. Then consider Marconi's reaction to us."

Adler ran his hands through his hair again. "We talked about it. He's pissed that you were sent here to second guess him. I listened to what he said about the coroner's report and didn't disagree with his assessment that there was nothing more to investigate."

I let his words hang for a minute. "Okay, let's back up and talk about his investigation. What he's done so far is either criminally negligent, or…I hate to say this, but he's so casual, I wonder if he's complicit in the crime and is covering his trail by closing the case."

"You're accusing Larry of a crime?"

Jill jumped in. "I told the Park Service Human Resources Department he's impeding an investigation. They suggested involving the U.S. Attorney."

Adler's eyes went wide. "The U.S. Attorney?"

"That was their suggestion."

"You said okay?"

Jill shook her head. "I told them what I saw was negligent, but not criminal. They accepted that, but I wouldn't be surprised if they called the Inspector General and requested him to start an investigation of Larry's inactivity."

"Geez. You two are going to get me fired."

I leaned close. "Marconi's actions, or inaction, is what will get you fired. We're just the ones who discovered it."

Adler stood. "Let's go back and have a heart-to-heart talk with Larry. He was in over his head. I want to start fresh with him and move ahead. He understands that he's dropped the ball and I'm sure he's ready to accept any help you offer."

We walked to Adler's office, and I stopped him before he turned the doorknob. Marconi was having a heated phone discussion with someone, and we listened.

"...and this retired cop shows up with this dyke and they start asking questions about me. Like I'd screwed up somehow. All of a sudden, they threw me under the bus. The dyke tells the park service to fire me because I didn't investigate the death of some woman who wandered off the trail."

Jill's face was red, and she was seething. I put out my hand to stop her, but she pushed open the door and burst in. "Sorry to interrupt your conversation, but your boss asked the *dyke* to give you a second chance and she came down to hear what you had to say for yourself."

36

Marconi fumbled his cell phone, "Immy, I gotta go." He ended the call and pocketed the phone.

Adler closed the door and stood blocking it. "Larry, that was stupid."

"I was having a private conversation with the door closed!"

I put up my hand. "You have no right to privacy when you're talking on a cell phone and on park service property. Your conversation was audible to anyone in the hallway *and* what you said was misogynistic and derogatory. We came back here, at Adler's request, to give you a chance to explain your change of heart. Instead, we heard you disparaging Jill and me."

"I was venting to my wife, that's all. I didn't know anyone was listening."

Jill sat in the superintendent's chair and leaned on his desk. "So, your issue was being asked to work with someone you thought was a lesbian?"

"I was just shooting my mouth off. I didn't mean anything by it."

Jill leaned back and crossed her arms, preparing to verbally shred him.

I glared at Jill and shook my head slightly, trying to warn her that she was only deepening Marconi's prejudice.

Adler stepped between them. "Larry. Jill is married to Doug. She was a park service superintendent when you were still in school. Her credentials are legendary, and

37

her sexual orientation is none of your damned business. Your characterization of these two...park service professionals is out of bounds. What the hell is the matter with you?"

Marconi glared at Jill. "It was just New Jersey *guy* talk."

"Any woman who isn't wearing makeup and stands up to you is a dyke? Is that it?"

Marconi waved his hand dismissively. "I was just venting."

We waited in silence for a moment, waiting for Adler to take the lead, but he just stared at Marconi, who was hanging his head. "Are you going to say something, Larry, or should I call someone to escort you out of the park?"

Marconi looked up at him and shook his head. "I guess I fucked up."

Adler shook his head. "That's all you've got to say?"

"What do you want me to say? I told you I fucked up."

"Larry, that's hardly an apology."

Marconi looked from Adler, to me, then to Jill. "You came in here to make me apologize?"

Jill leaned on the desk. "Your boss thought you'd want to apologize. I don't *want* you to do anything. Maybe the best thing you could do right now is leave and wait for the inspector general, or the U.S. Attorney, to call and ask for your statement about your inaction on the death investigation. I could give them a call and suggest adding harassment and creating a hostile work environment to the discussion."

Marconi looked at Adler. "You're with them on this?"

Adler blew out a breath. "You've got me over a barrel. My career is on the line because I haven't reined you in and nothing you've said has made me think that taking your badge and gun is the wrong thing to do."

"I did everything my experience told me to do."

Jill leaned back. "Does your experience tell you to call your colleagues dykes?"

Marconi threw up his hands. "What's with you guys? I get mad. I swear and call people names. I do it with my family. I do it with my friends. I do it at the bar. It's what normal people do. We vent, yell, swear, wave our arms around, and let fly. Then, we're done. Everybody shakes hands, hugs, and moves on."

"I bet your family Christmas celebrations are a riot," Jill said with a sneer.

"Oh, shit, somebody's swearing at someone all the time. It rotates through the whole family. Last year Nonna teed off on my brother Nick because she didn't get a thank you note for the five dollars she sent for my nephew's birthday. She threatened to write him out of her will and was close to throwing an ashtray at him from her wheelchair. An hour later they were laughing and hugging."

Adler looked at Jill. "Where are you from?"

"I've worked in seventeen parks."

"No, where did you grow up?"

"Spearfish, South Dakota."

"Doug, how about you?"

"St. Paul, where I worked as a cop."

Adler nodded. "I think we have a culture clash. Midwesterners are unaccustomed to Larry's Italian/New Jersey style."

Marconi glanced at Jill. "I never knew you were even irritated until you were on the phone with human resources. I thought you were joking around. Hell, you never swore at me, pounded your fist, or anything."

Jill turned red. "You didn't know I was mad because I wasn't swearing at you?"

"Yeah. You were just kind of quietly listening and asking questions. All of a sudden, you're on the phone trying to get me fired. I thought you were yanking my chain."

"What the hell do you think constitutes a hostile work environment? Calling your co-workers dykes is hardly office banter."

Marconi rolled his head. "Yeah, well, you weren't supposed to hear that."

"I did hear it, and it pissed me off. It was unprofessional and inappropriate language for any park service employee." She glared at Adler. "We're done here. Doug and I are going to meet with the medical examiner."

Adler put up his hand. "Larry, do you have any more to say?"

"I'm sorry you heard the conversation with my wife."

Jill stood. "That's not an apology, you arrogant ass. You just apologized for getting caught."

Adler opened the office door and gestured for me to take Jill into the hallway. Jill was still seething. "I can't believe it! I've never been treated with such disrespect in my entire career!"

I put my finger to my lips and pointed to Adler's door.

"C'mon, Larry, get your head out of your ass! Those people are senior park service law enforcement officers and they've just had you fired for being a jerk and not doing your job. Then, you call the woman a dyke and tee off on her. What the hell is wrong with you?"

Marconi's answer was unintelligible.

"That's no excuse! They were waiting for an apology, and you even effed that up! Don't you know how to say you're sorry? You said you were sorry you were caught. Hell, you couldn't even look the woman in the eye and say you were wrong. You deserve to have your badge pulled!"

The phone rang and Adler had a quiet conversation. I heard the phone click as he hung up. "The paperwork has been started. The only thing you've got going for you right now is that the wheels of the park service move slowly. You've probably got three days to pull your ass out of the fire before it's too late to stop the termination process. So, what's it going to be? Are you playing nice or are you going home to start looking for a job?"

We couldn't hear Marconi's answer. I pointed to the break room. We sat down at a table and waited for Adler. Jill was still fuming. "I don't care what Marconi says, I can't unhear what he said."

"Hey, you're letting the past affect your judgment. The names you were called in high school have nothing to do with what's going on here. Marconi is an ass, but he didn't know you'd been called a lesbian. You're still lean, with short hair, and you're in khaki pants and a button-down shirt. I know you're all woman, but Marconi made a bad assessment of your sexual orientation and let's leave it at that."

"My gender or sexual orientation has no bearing on my job performance. He should know and respect that. It's the twenty-first century and the Me-Too movement is all over the news. Does he live in a cave or is he just too stupid to understand that he's a Neanderthal?"

Adler walked into the break room. His face was red, and his armpits stained with sweat. He didn't speak but nodded us toward his office.

Marconi was sitting in a chair he'd moved to the farthest corner of Adler's office. His arms were crossed, and he looked unhappy. "We got off on the wrong foot and I'm sorry for what I said and for the way I reacted to you showing up here. I thought I had this investigation under control, and when you started asking questions, well, it pissed me off. Part of it was you sticking your noses into my investigation, and part of it was because you were making a fool of me in front of my boss."

Marconi paused and collected his thoughts while we watched silently. He looked up, like he was awaiting Jill's acceptance of his apology. When none was forthcoming, he went on. "I dropped the ball. The things you suggested were spot on and I feel like an idiot for not thinking of them myself."

Marconi looked at Adler, apparently expecting him to step up to defend him. When that didn't happen, he clasped his hands in his lap and stared down. "Jack showed me video of press conferences after your Black Hills and St. Croix

43

investigations and you guys have your shit…stuff together. Jack and I think I could learn some things from you. I'd like to be part of your investigation…if you'll have me."

I looked at Jill who was shaking her head. "Larry, I don't trust you. I don't know that you'll have my back if we get in a pinch. I'd rather go ahead without you than worry that you won't be there when I need you."

Adler stared at Marconi, waiting for his response. "I'm a good cop and you've knocked the chip off my shoulder. Give me two days to prove I'll have your back."

Jill was still shaking her head, but I sensed his sincerity. "Two days, starting now. If we're not happy with everything you say and do, we let the paperwork continue through the system and you find a job somewhere else."

Marconi nodded.

Jill crossed her arms and leaned against the wall. "If I ever hear you call me or another woman a dyke, you can kiss your park service pension goodbye."

Marconi stood and put out his hand to shake. "What should I call you? Jill? Ma'am?"

Jill turned away from him without shaking his hand. "Inspector Fletcher for now, Ranger Marconi."

He pursed his lips. "I guess I had that coming." His cell phone trilled, and he picked it up. "That was the ME, we were supposed to meet him five minutes ago. We'd better get going. I can drive."

I hung back a step and stopped at Adler's door. "Write a note up and put it in his file. Even if he gets past this, I want it hanging over his head."

"Listen, Fletcher," Adler said as he stood. "This is my park, and I'll do what I think is appropriate."

"Superintendent Adler, that wasn't a suggestion. It's an order."

"You have…"

"I'm a GS-14 and the park service is a quasi-military organization. I outrank you, and I just issued an order. If you don't obey it, there'll be a note in your personnel file too."

Adler turned red but didn't reply.

Chapter 4

Marconi was silent as we exited the parking lot. "Where's the trail where the woman's body was found?" Jill asked from the backseat.

"The Anhinga Trailhead is the other direction. It's about four miles from the visitor center."

"Tell us about the trail."

"It's not a hard walk. The trail is a mile and a half. The middle portion is a boardwalk that cuts through a big slough. That's where they found the body."

"What else?"

"It's one of the most heavily utilized trails in the park because it's an easy walk and because of its proximity to Miami. It's named for the anhinga, a bird related to cormorants you may know from the Midwest. They don't have oil glands, so they perch with their wings spread, drying when they're resting. It's a birdwatcher's paradise, plus there are alligators and all the other regional animals. Visitors sometimes see Everglades deer, raccoons, turtles, and sometimes wild pigs. It's native habitat for the Florida panther, but they're pretty elusive. I don't think anyone's ever seen one except on game cameras."

"You said it was heavily used, so I assume the body was found the day it was dumped there."

"I talked with the guide who reported it and he'd seen vultures hanging around that spot the day before it was reported. He assumed it was a wild animal."

Jill sounded displeased. "And no one called it in?"

"Inspector, there are dead animals all over here. The gators catch fish, frogs, deer, pigs, and about anything else that moves including smaller gators. We see the vultures eating things all the time. All. The. Time."

The landscape went from Everglades to urban within a few miles. "Where is the medical examiner's office?"

"Damned near downtown Miami." Marconi glanced in the mirror. "Sorry, ma'am, I didn't mean to offend."

Jill waved it off. "I've heard swearing before. I choose not to use it myself."

I looked over my shoulder and winked at Jill. She didn't see the humor in being reminded of her own occasional tirades, usually reserved for a stubbed toe or after a call from our park service superiors.

"What's it like to live down here?" I asked.

"It's hot and humid nearly all year long. The winter cools down and I wear a jacket in the morning and evening, but the summers are like a pressure cooker. The heat and humidity are relentless, and it rains in the afternoon most days. The crime skyrockets as tempers flare." Marconi paused. "Where are you two located? I heard something about the Midwest and Doug was a St. Paul cop."

"We work out of Padre Island National Seashore, in Texas."

"That's about the same weather as here, isn't it?"

"The summer heat and humidity are stifling, but we get some pretty cool winter weather. We don't see the spring break crowd until late March and April. It's really not sunbathing weather until then."

We wound through urban areas and turned into a parking lot just after passing a massive hospital. Marconi led us to a utilitarian building across the street from a medical center that occupied an entire city block of downtown Miami. A middle-aged Hispanic woman looked up from her computer when we walked into an anteroom. Her laminated name tag identified her as Rosa M.

"Help you?" She asked with a mixture of Spanish and southern accents.

"Dr. Parks is expecting us. We're from the park service," Larry said.

48

The woman nodded toward a hallway. "He's in his office."

The medical examiner's office was the third door down the hallway. Dressed in scrubs, Ken Parks was busily filling out a form on his computer. He shut down the computer screen and turned when he sensed us standing at his door. Parks looked at Marconi's uniform, obviously not recognizing his face. "You're the park service guy I spoke with?"

Marconi stepped forward and offered his hand. "I'm Ranger Marconi and these folks are Park Service Investigators Doug and Jill Fletcher."

Polished and professional, with an entirely blank expression Parks said, "I'd like to see your identification, please."

Jill smiled and pulled out her ID. She handed it to the ME who examined it, then took mine. "I've never had anyone from the park service come in before. What can I do for you?" He gestured for us to gather around a small round table opposite his desk.

I was surprised that the office was so neat. Most medical examiners seemed to gather files while awaiting tox reports and notification of families. Park's office was immaculate, with a flowering plant on a stand next to the window and the requisite diplomas and society memberships framed and hung on the walls. "We'd like to discuss the Jane Doe found in the Everglades National Park."

Parks leaned back. "Sure. What would you like to know?"

"Ranger Marconi said you couldn't identify her or determine her cause of death."

Parks glanced at Marconi. "That's what I put on the death certificate."

"But?" Jill asked.

Parks shook his head. "That's it."

"What did you note that didn't go on the death certificate?" I asked.

Parks leaned back and looked at me. "I see a little gray in your hair, and I hear something in your question that tells me this isn't your first death investigation."

I shook my head. "I've been to a few post-mortem exams and spoken with a number of medical examiners and forensic pathologists. I'd like to hear about your observations that weren't recorded."

Parks took a pen out of his pocket and flipped it between his fingers like an experienced card player flips a poker chip. "Why are you asking?"

"We want to know as much as we can so we can do a complete investigation." I paused, then added. "I'm not recording this, and whatever you say to us won't be passed on to the U.S. Attorney before a trial."

Parks relaxed. "She was White and young. Not a teenager, but not in her thirties. Never had children. Had an IUD and was wearing a wedding ring so I assume there's a husband somewhere. She wasn't a manual laborer—her muscle development looked more like someone who worked out in a gym than in the fields. She was five-seven, dark-haired, and trim. Her last meal was hours before her death and was probably sushi or sashimi."

"How long had she been dead?"

Parks shrugged. "More than a day but not a week."

"Any trauma to the body?"

"You heard her left arm had been detached."

I nodded. "Cut off or torn off by an alligator?"

Parks came close to smiling. "In my professional opinion, it was wrenched off her body post-mortem. That would be consistent with an alligator attack."

"Was there other trauma?"

The pen flipping sped up. "Not anything I would point to as the definitive cause of death. She had a blunt force injury to her head that fractured her skull. It would certainly have rendered her unconscious."

"You said you couldn't determine the cause of death. What could you rule out?"

Parks smiled. "You know the questions, Fletcher. She didn't drown, didn't die of a gunshot or stab wound, wasn't strangled, and didn't die of obvious body trauma."

"Not stabbed?"

"There'd been animal depredation on the body that might've obliterated any shallow wounds, but no, there wasn't a deep wound that would've led to her death."

"Was there a lot of animal depredation?" Jill asked.

Parks blew out a breath. "The vultures can do a lot of damage in a short time."

"Meaning?"

"I don't know what your experience has been with bodies exposed to the elements. My residency was in Maryland, and rural murder victims are recovered from shallow graves after they've slowly decomposed. Florida vultures can strip a body to a bare skeleton in a few days."

"What did your external exam show?"

"Her right arm was missing, consistent with an alligator attack. The soft tissue damage was consistent with extensive vulture depredation."

Jill slid her hand across the table. "You said one arm was missing. How could you tell she didn't die from an alligator attack?"

"Alligators don't usually attack humans. When they do, they drag the person into the water and roll them over and over. The victim drowns, not from the trauma inflicted by the alligator. Jane Doe's lungs were dry. She didn't drown."

Jill nodded. "Tell us about her clothing."

"I've got it in storage if you'd like to see it. There's nothing very interesting from a forensic standpoint. Her t-shirt was shredded except across her back. It had a beer logo I didn't recognize. Her jeans were intact."

"What brand of jeans?"

Parks smiled and moved to his desk. He pulled up a report on his computer. "The brand was 'Rag and Bone.' According to the label, her jeans were slim cut, size twenty-five, low-rise, boyfriend fit with a twenty-eight-inch inseam."

I looked at Jill. "Rag and Bone? Size twenty-five?"

"I can't afford Rag and Bone jeans on my salary. And size twenty-five is not the traditional women's size, it's a waist size."

Parks returned to the table. "Like I said, she was slender. There was nothing in the pockets to identify her."

Jill looked perplexed. "Has her husband filed a missing person's report?"

"My staff have been watching the police reports. No one has reported a missing woman matching Jane Doe."

"Some women wear wedding rings to ward off unwanted attention," Jill said. "Are there any unmarried women who match this description?"

Park looked Jill in the eye. "Inspector Fletcher, think of Miami as the bathtub drain for the east coast. Everyone who's at loose ends, running away from home, being pimped out, or escaping an abusive relationship, gravitates here. Just because she wasn't reported missing here, doesn't mean she's not missing somewhere between Maine and Key West. On the other hand, if her husband killed her, he might not rush to the police to file a report, especially if he thinks the Everglades gators are going to destroy the evidence."

Jill nodded. "Is there anything else you noted that we're not smart enough to ask about?"

Parks leaned back. "She had a Panama City license plate."

"Huh?"

"Panama City license plate or tramp stamp. That's what the locals call a tattoo across the lower back. They were popularized by spring breakers up on the Florida panhandle and it's become 'a thing.'"

I envisioned a tattoo that said Panama City. "Are they all the same or is there a unique design that might be traceable?"

"It's a dolphin jumping out of her waistband. I see similar tattoos a dozen or more times a year. So, it's not anything special. No initials in it or anything distinguishing. I assume you'd see a hundred of them if you strolled South Beach in the afternoon." Parks walked to his desk, pulled up a computer file, clicked a couple times, and a picture of the tattoo on discolored skin appeared on the screen. "I'll print my whole file for you."

Jill glanced at the picture, then handed the coroner's report to Marconi, who passed the printout to me. I glanced through the file while Parks waited patiently. "Other than high blood alcohol, nothing else showed up in the toxicology screening. It appears the tissue samples told you something else."

The corner of Parks' mouth twitched with a split-second smile. I'd hit on something he hadn't expected a cop to catch. "Blood alcohol testing after a body decomposes for days doesn't tell us much because it evaporates through the skin. There was alcohol in her tissue that indicated she was intoxicated at the time of her death."

Jill had been flipping through the autopsy pictures and stopped. "High enough to kill her?"

Parks shifted in his chair. "It's hard to say. Alcoholics have an incredible tolerance; I'd say she was inebriated, but she didn't die of alcohol poisoning."

"You're equivocating," Jill said with a smile.

"If this were her first experience with alcohol, I'd say she was unconscious. If she were an alcoholic, I'd postulate that she was functioning. Odds are, she was somewhere in between those extremes."

I took the file back from Jill. "Your examination of her liver doesn't note any signs of alcoholism. It wasn't swollen or fatty."

"She was young. I don't often see someone her age with those conditions." Parks paused. "I'm going to speak off the record. I think she probably wasn't falling down drunk or passed out at the time of her death. That's my judgment, not a technical analysis. But it may help you understand the situation that led to her death."

I looked at Marconi. "How many bars are there between Florida City and here?"

Marconi leaned back and Parks smiled. "Whew. I'd only be guessing, but if we spread that out to South Beach, you're talking hundreds."

Jill looked at me. "What are the odds that a bartender or waitress will remember a dark-haired, young woman with a dolphin tattoo, who was intoxicated?"

Marconi put up a hand. "I'm not walking from bar to bar with a picture of a tramp stamp…" He looked at Jill and paused. "I don't think asking bartenders about a drunk woman would be a good use of our time. Unless she was dancing naked on a table, she'd be invisible to most of the servers. If she was out clubbing on a Friday or

Saturday night, she'd be one of a thousand drunk women who'd fit her description."

I looked at Parks, who nodded. "It's not a pretty sight, but Ranger Marconi is correct. The beach bars are alcohol and drug mayhem any night of the week. The weekends are even worse."

"I assume you ran her fingerprints and DNA."

"She's not on file, so she's never been arrested, in the military, or screened for a security clearance. We checked the DNA profile against the CODIS database of convicted felons and came up dry. That means it will only be meaningful if we find a relative for comparison. If we get a DNA match, we can do a dental comparison too."

I picked up the printed pages and looked at Parks. "Is there anything we'd learn from looking at her body?"

Parks shook his head. "You've got the tattoo picture. That's after my tech enhanced the image to bring it out of her degraded skin. No one is going to make a facial identification after the buzzards…"

Jill looked relieved that we weren't going to the morgue. "Can we look at her clothes and wedding ring?"

Parks got up. "Certainly. Rosa can take you to the property room."

We shook hands with Parks in the entryway and Rosa led us to a locked, screened-in room with a deputy sitting behind the door. "Guillermo, can you bring us the box from the Everglades Jane Doe?" Rosa handed him a slip of paper with a file number.

He returned carrying a shoebox, the entire belongings of a dead woman. "Sign here, then return it all when you're done. There's a table over there."

Marconi picked up the box and led us to the table. "You guys got a lot out of the ME. Hell, I didn't know what to ask."

Jill nodded, but didn't comment. Marconi cut the tape sealing the box, and we slipped on purple gloves before handling the contents. Jill lifted out the jeans and read the label. "Rags and Bone, just like the ME said. These cost a couple hundred dollars a pair." She held them up. "And yes, Jane Doe was a skinny thing."

The front pockets were already inside out, but Jill put her fingers into the back pockets. "This is very wrong. No woman is going out without at least keys, a cell phone, and a debit card. If she's young, she'd have an ID to show bartenders, too."

I picked up the t-shirt that was in tatters. There was an obscure beer logo on the back. Most of the front had been shredded. I put it back in the box.

Jill peeked into the box and took out a small, zippered plastic bag with a ring. She took out the ring and inspected it inside and out, then said, "A&J, and their marriage date last week." She looked up but seemed unable to speak.

"What's the date?" I asked.

"She was married eight days ago and died a few days later. She was probably on her honeymoon."

She let out a deep sigh and put the ring back into the baggie, then put the bag back into the box. "No panties, bra, socks, or shoes."

Marconi nodded. "That's what women wear clubbing."

"Women wear only a t-shirt and jeans to go clubbing?"

I looked at him. "Clubbing?"

"The young people go to the clubs without underwear. She was probably wearing sandals without socks."

"Really? No underwear?"

Marconi put up his hands. "It's not my scene. I've just heard people talk about clubbing and not wearing underwear. No panty lines and..." He saw my look of disgust. "I'll leave the rest to your imagination."

Jill shook her head. "Less evidence to accidentally leave behind if you have a hookup at someone's house while their significant other is away."

I looked at Jill. "She was a newlywed. She wouldn't be cruising the bars for a hookup."

Jill shrugged. "It's a different world, Doug. Think about spring breakers in Texas."

Marconi nodded. "Welcome to South Beach where it's spring break year 'round."

* * *

Marconi suggested we wait in the air-conditioned lobby while he brought the truck around. Jill took the file from me and flipped past the grisly autopsy pictures and stopped at the tattoo. "What are the odds some local tattoo artist is going to remember this art?"

I knew the question was rhetorical so didn't answer as she pulled out her cell phone. She punched in something then looked up. "There are over two hundred tattoo parlor listings in the Miami area."

"She could've been inked anywhere. Maybe the dolphin was her reminder of a happy place, and she had some guy tattoo her in Akron, Ohio."

Jill closed her search down as Marconi pulled up in front of the building. "He's still not bought in. Did he really refuse to canvass bars?"

I opened the building door and held it for Jill. The heat and humidity hit me like a wet towel. "Yeah, but he backtracked and made it a suggestion. He's trying to be constructive."

Jill shook her head. "His fuse is short. It doesn't make him the worst cop I've ever worked with."

"But not the best, either."

I put my hand on the door handle and paused. "Not many people measure up to you."

Jill's eyes sparkled. "You're trying to charm me. What's your ulterior motive?"

"We've got a hotel room somewhere, maybe with a view. We'll have a nice seafood dinner, maybe with a bottle of wine, and we'll need to be distracted from the coroner's report to be able to fall asleep."

Jill got in the back seat of the SUV and buckled in. "I'm glad no one suggested viewing the body. Looking at the pictures was bad enough."

Marconi pulled into the afternoon traffic. "I held a rifle in case one of the alligators got too curious about the recovery team. I saw her body then, and I don't need to see it again."

A thought jumped at me. "She's missing an arm. Did you discuss trying to find the alligator that ate it?"

Marconi shook his head. "There are half a dozen big bull gators who hang out in that area. We'd have to kill them all and open them up to see which one ate it, and it wouldn't tell us anything. Besides, the gators in that area are a big tourist attraction. Everyone wants to walk that trail and see a gator or two."

I looked at my watch. "It's quitting time. Let's go back to the park, we'll get checked into our hotel and pick up the investigation in the morning."

Marconi glanced in the rearview mirror at Jill. "I'm at your disposal. If that's what you'd like to do, I'm with you."

Jill's voice told me she wasn't convinced he'd turned over a new leaf, but she didn't shut him out. "I don't think we'll need the car tomorrow. Pick us up at our hotel in the morning at eight, and then I'd like to walk the trail where the body was found. We can strategize about our next steps while we're walking."

Marconi hesitated, making me think he was trying to dream up an excuse not to pick us up. "I don't want to sound contrary, but the Anhinga Trail is busy and we're not going to have a private conversation on that walk."

"Good point," Jill said from the back. "We can talk on the drive to the park. Tonight, think about what you'd do next, and we'll discuss it tomorrow."

"I'm coaching a little league game tonight, so I'm not going to think about the case a lot until after that."

"That's reasonable," Jill replied. "We're at loose ends here and we sometimes forget the rangers we're working with have home lives. We'll talk in the morning."

Chapter 5

We drove back to Florida City, located the hotel booked by the park service travel office, and checked in. The hotel was a major chain with a federal employee discount. Jill pulled up the hotel chain on her smartphone and asked for driving directions. "The big features on their website are in-room Wi-Fi and a free hot breakfast."

Aside from giving me directions to the hotel, Jill was unusually quiet the entire drive.

I parked in the half-full parking lot. "Is something eating you?"

She blew out a breath. "I may have overreacted to Larry. It's just when I heard him call me a dyke all the old feelings boiled to the surface."

"You didn't overreact. He was way out of line and his boss should've been the one to call him on it."

"Larry's trying, I'll give him that. He wanted to say he wasn't going to canvass bars, but backed off and said it wouldn't be productive, then explained why he felt that way."

We carried our bags into the lobby and checked in. Jill opened the drapes and sighed. "We've got a lovely view of the parking lot and highway."

I joined her at the window. "I imagine they save any rooms with an appealing view for guests who aren't booked in at the U.S. government discount rate. The guy ahead of us is paying sixty bucks a night more than us."

Jill turned and put her arms around me. "I love that you're analytical."

"You're the one with the soft, personal side, the yin to my yang."

"My soft personal side is telling me the pretzels I ate on the plane are long gone and it's time to feed me." She let go of me and opened her suitcase. "Let's hang up a few things and find a restaurant. I like your suggestion about seafood."

We consulted with the concierge who called for reservations. She put her hand over the phone, "They can seat you right now, or not again until eight. What's your preference?"

Jill didn't hesitate. "Now, please."

The concierge, a middle-aged woman with a name tag indicating her name was Margot, was wearing the same maroon jacket as the desk clerk. With the reservation made, she pulled out a map, and highlighted the hotel and the restaurant. "It's walking distance, but I'll give you a map for future reference."

Jill accepted the map. "Thank you."

The concierge smiled and stood. "You're from the Midwest."

"Did our accent give us away?"

She shook her head. "The locals are too busy to say please or thank you. Mostly I get sworn at for not getting a last-minute reservation or ticket to a sold-out sporting event." She leaned close. "I've been known to do the impossible, but not for someone who's calling me a bitch and threatening to have me fired."

I nodded. "Thanks."

* * *

The mostly retail area around the hotel was filled with people rushing past, probably on their way home at the end of their workday, at least that was my observation. Jill checked out window displays as we walked hand-in-hand.

A young guy rushed up with a backpack dangling from one shoulder. He seemed intent on walking between us and was irritated when I didn't let go of Jill's hand so he could pass. He gave me a withering glare. "Get a room," he uttered as he bumped my shoulder on his way past.

Jill glanced at him. "I'd like to see him try that in Spearfish. He'd be picking himself up off the sidewalk and wondering which truck hit him."

I watched the crowd. "A lot of these people have situational awareness. I assume that's because they've been preyed upon. I see a guy ahead in the doorway. He looks like a jackal looking for prey."

Jill looked at the guy as we passed. His hands were jammed in the pockets of his dirty shorts, and he wore a Hawaiian shirt with the tails out. He sized us up, glancing at the guns on our hips. When we made eye contact, he froze for a second, waiting for me to look away. When I didn't, he just watched us pass.

Jill glanced over her shoulder. "Did you see his eyes? They were dead. I mean, there was no emotion there. They reminded me of the guy in the backseat of the car we stopped in Texas with the kidnapped woman."

"He was a sociopath. He didn't care if anyone passing lived or died. He was looking for someone to pounce on."

"Why not us? We look like tourists."

"He sized us up and saw our guns. I'm sure he knew we were some kind of cops. He wanted easier victims."

"What do you mean?"

"Like lots of predators, he wanted someone alone and easy to overcome. Like a wolf going after the deer herd, culling out the old and injured."

We walked past a line of people waiting for tables at the seafood restaurant and approached the maître d. "Table for Fletcher."

The man smiled. "Margot called." He glanced past us at the dozen people in line, then pulled out two menus. He seated us at a table near the front windows and removed a sign that said, reserved. "Krista will be your server. Enjoy!"

I put up my hand. "You got us right in. I thought..."

"Margot sends us a lot of business. I treat her people right."

Krista was an anorexic-looking bleached blonde. She'd passed her thirtieth birthday but was still trying to look eighteen. She filled our water glasses from a pitcher. "Can I get you something from the bar?"

"A bottle of chardonnay, please."

She nodded, then paused. "Margot sent you, right?"

"Yes," I replied. "Margot the concierge."

Krista leaned down, like she was picking a crumb off the table. "Our house chardonnay tastes like horse piss. I'll get you a bottle of the good stuff."

Jill suppressed a smile. "Thank you."

Krista stood up and put her hand on Jill's shoulder. "And those magic words just got you a complementary plate of fried calamari."

Krista sped away, ignoring an overweight man who was trying to get her attention. Jill watched her for a second. "I wonder what her backstory is. She's pleasant but looks like she's been ridden hard and put away wet."

I chuckled. "You said that about the hooker in South Dakota."

Jill nodded. "It still fits."

Jill's phone trilled and she struggled to get it out of her pocket before it rolled over to voicemail.

"This is Jill."

There was enough noise in the restaurant to cover the other speaker's voice. I watched Jill's face, trying to guess who'd called. She made several supportive uh huhs, but never engaged beyond that. I shrugged, trying to get her to tell me who she was speaking to, but she chose to ignore me. After a couple minutes she handed the phone to me. "Your mom wants to talk to you about my Uncle Chet."

My mother moved to South Dakota a few weeks ago to help Jill's adopted Uncle Chet, a close family friend, recuperate after prostate cancer surgery.

"Hi, Mom."

"I hope I didn't catch you at a bad time. I can never figure out these time zone things. Is it six or ten o'clock there?"

"It's just after six and we're in a restaurant waiting for our dinner."

On cue, Krista showed up with a bottle of wine and unscrewed the cap. She poured some into a glass and slid it to me. I gestured for her to pour.

"I drove Chet to see the surgeon in Rapid City today. Everything is so far away here."

"How did the appointment go?" I asked, trying to move the conversation along.

"Chet's PSA levels are down to almost nothing and the surgeon said that was good. He doesn't have to go back again for six months."

"That's great, Mom."

There was an uncharacteristic pause. "There's something else."

"With Chet?"

"Chet's fine, but…"

"You're sick?"

"No, nothing like that. Chet asked if I'd move out of Rickowski's house and into his spare bedroom."

"Okay. What's the problem?"

"I didn't know if you'd approve."

Krista brought a sizzling platter of breaded calamari to the table. There was a bowl of red dipping sauce in the middle of the platter. I nodded and mouthed, "Thanks."

"Do what you want, Mom. You don't need my permission."

"I thought I'd ask. I'm not sure how this looks, and Chet thinks people might talk."

I looked at Jill who was munching on a piece of calamari, grinning like a Cheshire cat. I gave her a disgusted look that brought out the dimples in her smile.

"Look, Mom. Do whatever makes you happy. You're at a point in your life where you don't need to worry about what other people think."

"But…"

"You're not going to get pregnant and you're not going to sully your reputation with the family. Move in and move on with my blessing."

There was another pause. "You're sure?"

"Do it! Have fun! Say hi to Chet." I ended the call, handed the phone back to Jill, then took a piece of calamari. The squid was as tender and tasty as any I'd ever eaten. I looked at Jill who was still smiling.

"You're okay with your mother living in sin?"

"Is that what she called it?"

Jill nodded. "She called me because she wanted to make sure you wouldn't have a fit and yell."

"You're joking."

71

Jill shook her head. "That's what she said."

"What else did she say?"

"She thinks Chet is falling in love with her."

"But she's not there yet?"

"Not yet, but she said she hasn't ever been treated with more kindness in her life. She's still a little unsure of ranch life, but I think she's getting comfortable."

"I'm afraid she might break Chet's heart."

"So is she. That's why she called me. She reminded me that I said I'd shoot her if she broke Chet's heart."

Krista came back and topped off our wine glasses. "Are you ready to order?"

"What's the special?"

Krista glanced at the crowd and leaned close. "The chef has a couple grouper filets in the back. There aren't enough to put it on the menu, but he'd let me have them if I asked nice."

Jill smiled at her. "I'll take mine grilled with a salad."

Krista looked at me. "And you?"

"Same for me, with whatever salad or side dish you recommend."

She nodded. "Do you like anchovies on your Caesar salads?"

Jill grimaced. "Not for either of us."

I frowned. "I like anchovies."

"I don't like anchovy breath. So, no anchovies for you."

Krista smiled. "No anchovies on either salad." She leaned on the table and looked back and forth at us. "I don't want to pry, but one minute I could swear you two are co-workers, and the next you're told not to eat anchovies. That's the kind of comment a wife makes."

Jill nodded. "Good call. We're both."

"He looks like a cop. You look like you lead workout classes at the gym, but you're both carrying guns."

Jill grinned at me. "We're park service investigators. One of us works on staying trim and one eats whatever tastes good and exercises when he feels guilty."

Krista laughed and put her hand on Jill's shoulder, but looked at me. "You're a lucky guy." Then she sped off.

Jill snatched the last piece of calamari from my fingers. "I got the last piece, Lucky."

"How do you feel about Chet and Mom living under the same roof?"

"I think it's sweet. How do *you* feel?"

"I don't want to dwell on it."

"You don't want to think about your mother and Chet living under the same roof?"

I gave her my best glare. "I don't want to discuss this any more than you wanted to talk to your mother about the squeaking

73

springs in your South Dakota bed the morning after..."

"That was different," Jill said as our salads arrived.

Krista set them down and slid a tiny plate with four anchovy filets alongside my salad. "Eat them at your own risk." She emptied the wine bottle, topping off our glasses. "Another bottle?"

Jill shook her head. "I'm at my limit. We have to be able to walk back to the hotel."

I waved her off and pushed the anchovies aside.

"Good choice," Jill said. "Eating anchovies would've ended any hopes you may have had for romance."

"Okay, backing up to the bedspring discussion. How is the discussion about Mom and Chet different?"

Jill leaned across the table and put her hand on mine. "Honey, whatever happens between them is platonic. I'm not sure Chet will be making the bed springs squeak after his surgery. I think a prostatectomy will leave him impotent."

"I'm not sure of that, and it really doesn't make any difference. As I said when we were dating, I'd want to be in bed beside you even if I could never have sex again. I think Chet's head is there. I hope Mom catches up."

Jill let go of my hand and picked up her fork. "I hope so, too."

* * *

Krista treated us like royalty, and I left her a tip large enough to reflect our appreciation. Krista rushed over when we got up to leave. She hugged Jill and whispered something in her ear that made them both laugh. The maître d nodded and wished us a good night.

"What did Krista say that made you laugh?"

"She booked a six o'clock reservation for us tomorrow. They're getting some red snapper from a local fisherman that'll be to die for."

"I've got to hand it to her. She knows how to please her customers. I felt special."

Jill took my hand as we walked back to the hotel. The sidewalk had changed over from rushing commuters to a younger bar-hopping crowd. "I think Krista needed that tip. She's working hard to get by."

"I think she's doing okay. I bet she made five hundred bucks in tips tonight. Being a good waitress at a successful, upscale restaurant is probably a fairly good paying gig."

"I bet she has a lot of years in greasy spoons to get here. I'm thinking a broken marriage, a couple kids, and a trashy trailer somewhere with a mortgage."

I squeezed Jill's hand. "You're overthinking this. You can't save the whole world."

"No, but I can leave a good tip when I feel like the server needs and deserves it."

We walked into the hotel lobby and Margot, the concierge, hailed us with a wave. "How was the restaurant?"

Jill let go of my hand and walked to Margot's table. "It couldn't have been better. We had a server named Krista who was excellent! The food was incredible, and the prices were okay."

"I'm glad it worked well for you. I've got another seafood place closer to Miami I'd suggest for tomorrow. I could make a reservation for you."

"Krista said they're getting some red snapper tomorrow and she already made a reservation for us."

Margot laughed. "Oh, she is good! By the way, the desk clerk asked me to watch for you. Someone called and left a message for Mr. Fletcher."

Jill smiled and put out her hand. "We're Jill and Doug."

Margot shook her hand. "It's nice to have you staying with us. I noticed that Doug's got a gun under his shirt. I assume he's a cop of some kind and not a bank robber."

"We're park service investigators."

"Ah, I read about the woman's body found in the park. It sounded like an alligator attack."

Jill nodded. "It does, doesn't it."

I went to the desk and the clerk looked up. "Can I help you?"

"Margot said you have a message for Doug Fletcher."

The clerk picked up an envelope from the counter behind him and handed it to me. "The caller tried your room and left the message when you didn't answer."

I tore open the envelope as we walked to the elevators. "Who knows we're in this hotel but doesn't have our cell phone numbers?"

I handed the note to Jill, who laughed. "I guess our boss is displeased with your habit of turning off your phone while we're eating supper."

I turned on my cell and it powered up while we were in the elevator. Jill was unlocking our room when Matt Mattson answered. "Damnit, Doug. Why is your phone off every time I try to call you?"

"Why do you call me during supper when I turn my phone off?"

"I'm not kidding around, Doug. I got a call from Washington. You guys stuck your foot in a beehive, and I'm making calls to calm the waters."

"That would be Jill calling park service human resources and getting the law enforcement ranger fired."

"It never occurred to you that I might want to know when something like this happens?"

"Hang on, I'll hand the phone to Jill."

"No! Tell me what happened. I want a third-party view of the conflict before I talk to Jill about it."

"We're together in our hotel room and she's going to hear everything I say so I'll just put you on speaker." I activated the speaker function before Matt could protest. I set the phone on the small desk. "Okay, what do you want to know?"

"What precipitated Jill's call to HR?"

"Nobody down here wanted us. Both the superintendent and the law enforcement ranger were happy to leave the investigation as an alligator attack. We started asking questions and the ranger became an ass. Jill jumped on him, and he pushed back. Shortly after that, we were going to meet in the superintendent's office, and we overheard the ranger talking with his wife and he referred to Jill as 'the dyke' and that's when everything went to hell."

"Geez," Matt said, then paused. "Did he apologize?"

"He said he was sorry Jill had heard that, not that he was sorry he'd said it."

Matt let out a deep sigh. "Okay. It all makes more sense now. Jill, are you there?"

"Yep, right here."

"What's the situation now?"

"I'm pissed, but the ranger is trying to play nice, although it seems like a stretch. We got the superintendent to put a note in his file and let the termination process play out. I said if he played nice for a few days and bought in, we'd pull his termination back before it made it to the final approvals."

"You'd better make that happen quickly. You and Doug have high visibility and what you do and say carries a lot of weight. That termination is moving swiftly, and HR is behind you one hundred percent. They wouldn't tell me exactly what had been said, but it was clear that whatever happened was way out of line and unacceptable behavior."

"That's reassuring."

"Human resources is with you, but the park superintendent is fighting it. Watch your backs."

Jill glanced at me. "Thanks for the warning, but we're pretty sure the ranger will stick it to us if given the chance."

"Hang on, Mandy wants to say something."

Mandy Mattson was Matt's southern belle wife. "Hey, girlfriend. I heard some

Yankee ranger was calling you names. Good on you for sticking up for yourself."

"It wasn't so much sticking up for myself as reacting to the jerk while in a rage. At least I didn't punch him."

"You use your words. I know you can swear with the best of 'em, but it hurts jerks like that more if you just seem calm and cut 'em to pieces."

"Thanks for the encouragement. You're always there to talk me back from the edge."

Mandy laughed. "If that boy needs a cussing out, you give me his phone number and I'll take care of that for you. His ear will be smoking by the time I'm done with him."

"I think we've got it under control. Goodnight."

Jill ended the call and sat on the bed. "Matt's right. I've kicked the hornet's nest."

"I think that's what it took to get Larry's attention."

"But still, it's not how I like to operate."

I sat next to her and put my arm around her shoulders. "Honey, you use all the tools you've got, and I've never seen you deal with any situation improperly."

Jill leaned into me. "You're so full of shit."

"What?"

She pushed me away. "Go brush your teeth and put your weapon away."

"What are you going to do?"

"I'm going to get naked, climb in bed, and have my way with you."

"Have your way with me? What's that mean?"

Jill laughed. "Maybe you'll be begging for mercy when I'm done with you."

Chapter 6

We were eating the self-serve breakfast in the hotel lobby alcove when Larry walked in and sat down with us. I looked up. "How did the ballgame go?"

"The kids are only six, so they're just past the point of knowing which end of the bat to hold. The whole team runs after a ground ball and none of them can catch a fly ball. That's not true: We have one kid who can catch. He's the first baseman."

"Did they win or lose?"

"It's not really relevant. If a team bats all their players, they take the field whether they've had three outs or not. At this age, we're teaching them the basics."

Jill nodded. "Like hitting and fielding."

Larry laughed. "Hell, I've got one kid who's still not sure if he should run to first or third base when he hits the ball."

"I take it he hasn't had many hits."

Larry shook his head. "He'll get there. He's the runt."

I stood up. "Would you like a cup of coffee? I'm going for a refill."

"I'll walk with you." When we got to the coffee pot Larry looked back at Jill, who was scanning the newspaper. "Has she cooled off?"

"I thought she was pretty cool yesterday afternoon."

Larry put his paper cup under the urn's spigot. "She was pretty hot for a while. You know, I didn't mean anything by what I said. I was just blowing off steam."

"Calling my wife a dyke is hardly an appropriate way for you to blow off steam."

He glanced back at Jill and was close to saying something but bit off his comment. Instead saying, "I should probably apologize."

"That'd start the day off on the right foot."

Larry sat down and stared at Jill until she noticed the silence. "Yes?"

"I was out of line yesterday. I had a long talk with my wife last night, and she told me there were probably very few words I could've chosen that would've been more hurtful than what I said. I'm sorry."

Jill's eyes darted to me, then back to Larry. "You can make up for it by proving what a great law enforcement ranger you are and treating us like colleagues instead of an annoyance."

"Sure. What's the plan for today?"

Jill raised her eyebrows. "What would you do if we weren't here?"

"I'd written this off as an accident, so that's not a relevant question. Now that we think Jane Doe may have been murdered, I suppose I'd be trying to figure out how she got to the park and who she was with."

"Good thoughts," I said. "She didn't walk there from a bar."

"That trail is busy all the hours we're open, so whatever happened to her, took place between closing and opening. There aren't any security cameras, so no video. I guess I'm at a loss."

Jill put her Styrofoam plate and plastic utensils in the garbage can. "What did you find when you checked the area around the body?"

"It was just on a hummock where a gator had dragged her after he ripped off her arm. Where we found her wasn't where she went into the swamp."

"Did you check along the trail with a metal detector?"

"There wasn't anything on the trail when I got there."

I nodded. "And the sides of the trail?"

"You mean, in the water?"

Jill's look wasn't kind. "You didn't see her watch, cell phone, or keys on the boardwalk. So yes, in the water."

"The bottom is...well it's not like a sandy beach and the water isn't crystal clear. The recovery team went in by airboat to pick up the body."

84

"What did you see at the site where the body was recovered?"

Larry looked sheepish. "I wasn't on the airboat. I was watching the alligators from shore to make sure they didn't get aggressive with the recovery team."

I nodded, trying to look upbeat and lead him to offering solutions instead of roadblocks. "Okay. Tell us how you would check the area with a metal detector."

"Whew. I suppose a guy could take a two-man kayak in with an underwater metal detector. One person paddles while the other swings the detector. We might find some cans and such."

"How would you pick up something off the bottom if you found it?" Jill asked.

"Anything heavy, like a cell phone, would sink into the muck. It'd be impossible…" Larry looked at Jill, who wasn't impressed with that response. "Well, it'd be challenging to scoop something out unless you used a backhoe or something."

"There's nothing you could use by hand out of the kayak?" Jill asked.

Larry shook his head immediately. He paused and I could see the wheels turning. "I suppose a fish landing net or something like that could reach into the slop and get something like a cell phone out."

"How do we make that happen?" I asked.

Larry looked interested. "Let's talk to Jack and see if he can free up a couple rangers to paddle the swamp near the boardwalk." He started to get up, but we remained seated. "What?"

"How about the wedding ring?" I asked.

"What about it?"

"It had initials and a date. We should look for a marriage license."

Larry rolled his eyes. "That wedding could've taken place anywhere in the United States. People come here to honeymoon from everywhere. I'm not wasting my time..." Larry froze waiting.

"How aren't you wasting your time?" Jill asked.

"I wouldn't even know where to start. I bet every state has a database...if not every county. A guy would have to call a thousand counties and ask if they had a marriage license for that date and matching those initials. Hell, we don't even know what the last initials are, only the first initials."

Jill leaned close. "Where would you start?"

Larry drew a deep breath and blew it out. "Well, if they were tourists on a destination wedding, I'd call the prime tourist locations, like Miami, Palm Beach, Sanibel Island, St. Pete and Orlando."

Jill got up. "Great! You and Doug can start making calls while the rangers are checking with the metal detector. I'll see if there's a way to trace the woman's DNA other than the CODIS law enforcement database."

Larry got up and looked at me, hoping I was going to argue the suggestion. I raised my eyebrows. "I imagine you've discovered that cop work is hours of boredom and seconds of terror."

Larry threw his paper cup into the wastebasket. "Yeah, but there are levels of boredom." He took out a keyring and tossed it to me. "I'll call the park while you drive."

Jill followed me to the driver's side of the SUV. She waited until Larry was inside, then whispered, "Apparently you need testicles to drive a park service vehicle in Florida."

"Don't go there," I warned.

Jill smiled evilly and got in the backseat.

Larry punched a number in his cell phone and turned on the speaker function. "Jack, hey, I had coffee with Fletchers this morning and they..." Marconi glanced at me, "we want to check the swamp around where the woman's body was found with a metal detector. We need to look for her cell phone and keys." The pause was so long I thought the call had been dropped. "We brainstormed and I think we could put a couple rangers in a kayak, one person paddling and one swinging the detector. If they have a landing net, they could sweep the bottom if they get a signal."

Jack sounded less than enthused. "Geez, they'll find more soda cans than anything else."

"Jack, this is Doug Fletcher. That may be true, but we need to make the effort. If we recover anything, we might be able to identify the woman."

"What's that going to gain us?"

I pulled to the shoulder and picked up the phone. "Jack, this may be a murder. That's what we do, we investigate suspicious deaths. It's our duty to do our best to determine who the victim was, what happened, and who else was involved. We bring closure to the victim's family."

Jill leaned over the seatback. "Listen, if you don't trust or want us, we'll turn this over to the FBI. None of us want to do that at this point, but this *will* be investigated, and we owe it to the woman's family, if not the justice system, to give this our best effort. If you don't agree, I can call..."

"Geez, you've made enough calls! If you have to look for her phone in the swamp, go ahead."

Larry turned the phone toward him. "Jack, I'd like a couple rangers experienced in kayaks to take a metal detector into the swamp."

"I thought you guys were handling this..."

I picked up the phone. "Jack, we have a list of things that need to be done. If you'd rather assign a half dozen rangers to call every county in Florida, Georgia, Mississippi, and up the coast to try and find a marriage license, we'd be happy to paddle a kayak. Jill's going to see if there are civilian agencies who do genetic tracing since the woman's DNA isn't in the federal CODIS database. Again, if you've got rangers to assign to that, there are dozens of other avenues she could be investigating."

There was a pause. "Sounds like you guys are chasing a wild goose."

"This is how investigations go. If there aren't eyewitnesses, we beat the bushes and look for other ways to identify the victim and the events leading to her death. It's what we do…all the time. This is what it means to be a cop."

Jill took the phone. "I'm sure you've watched cop shows on television. Well, the things they accomplish in an hour, take weeks of tedious work. It takes investigators making calls, following leads, and being stubbornly invested in understanding what happened. Time is slipping away. Delaying the investigation only reduces our chances of finding the facts and the people involved."

Jill set the phone on the console and listened to Jack sigh. "*The First 48.* I've watched the clock ticking down as the detectives struggled to sift through the things they discover on that television show."

I looked at Larry, who was nodding. "It's like that. We have two pieces of evidence: A body and a wedding ring. We need to try to find the other pieces, and to jump on the DNA and wedding ring. The woman didn't walk here from Miami or drown in the swamp."

Adler paused. "I assumed she'd drowned in the swamp."

Larry leaned toward the phone. "She didn't drown, Jack. She died before the gator got her."

"Sonofabitch. Okay, I'll grab the rescue/recovery team and get them into a kayak this morning and have someone with a rifle watch the gators. It sounds like you three have ideas on where to chase the other things, so I'll leave you to them. Let me know if there's anything else you need from me."

Larry gave me a thumbs up and shut down the call.

Jill slid back and buckled her seatbelt. "I think Jack's bought in."

I looked at her in the mirror. "For now. We have to make progress or he's going to lose interest. Larry, where do you stand?"

He thought for a moment. "You two are the real deal. I've never worked a murder investigation and I have no idea where to go with it."

Jill put her hand on his shoulder. "You're with us?"

Larry looked over his shoulder. "Yeah. Sounds boring, but Doug made it clear, that's what an investigation is. I was a patrolman, and we hadn't had a murder in our New Jersey town in as long as anyone could remember. I took a few burglary reports and car thefts, but the sex crimes were handled by detectives and so were most of the burglaries."

I pulled back onto the highway. "Why'd you move down here?"

Larry was obviously uncomfortable with the question. "I kind of liked the idea of being a park service cop. I don't work nights and very few weekends, the pay and benefits are better, and…my wife liked the idea of being farther from my family. It was a good move for us."

"Then we showed up and messed up your nice, neat life,' Jill said from the back.

"There's some of that. But there's also the part where I didn't want to admit the woman's death was anything but a gator attack. I wanted to believe that…maybe because I didn't know what to do."

"That's not an excuse. We're sworn to uphold the law and that includes diligently investigating every crime. If we don't know what to do, we find resources who can help."

"That seems like admitting incompetence."

Jill leaned forward. "None of us know everything. There are specialists in every area of law enforcement and it's up to you to access them when you're stuck."

Larry thought about that a second. "Kind of like my doctor referring me to a specialist or surgeon."

"That's a great analogy," I said.

Larry was still mulling that when I pulled into the visitor center parking lot. We got out of the SUV and I started walking toward the entrance. Larry motioned for Jill to step aside with him. I decided to keep walking and let things play out between them while watching from the doorway.

He was animated, gesturing with his hands as he spoke to Jill. She stood with her arms crossed and listened. They went back and forth for a few minutes, and I watched Jill slowly relax, then uncross her arms. Larry eventually put out his hand and Jill shook.

I held the door open for them. When Jill passed, she mouthed, "Later."

The two rangers in the break room looked up when we walked in. Larry nodded to them and went right to the coffee, pouring for the three of us. "I'll talk to Jack and see where we can settle in to make our calls. Why don't you guys have a seat for a couple minutes while I get us set up."

We sat next to the rangers, a man and woman, both dressed in their gray and green uniforms. They were young, and apparently more than co-workers based on the guy's deference to the woman. Both were from Florida and neither had worked in any other park. They mined Jill for information when they found out how many different park service assignments she'd had. Neither were particularly interested in my history once they heard I'd been a cop.

Marconi walked into the break room and nodded toward the coffee pot. Jill and I excused ourselves and joined him.

"My boss has two rangers getting a kayak. They'll be on the water in half an hour. I've got my own office and Jack's going to a meeting in Tampa, so we can use his office, too." He looked around the now empty break room. "I suppose one of us can make calls from here. It's usually pretty quiet until noon."

Jill pulled out her cell. "I'll make my calls from here. I'll go out and watch the kayak after I talk with the genealogist. You guys take the offices."

Jill was punching a number into her phone as we walked out. Larry looked over his shoulder as we exited the break area. "I think Jill and I are okay now. I really apologize for that comment. I was mad but that's no excuse. I was out of line, and I told her so again."

I nodded. "She seems to be okay with the situation. I'd limit my comments and language to our investigation. You don't want to scratch that scab."

"I'm not good at being 'politically correct.' If someone ticks me off, I go right back to New Jersey mode. If they say something, I respond, and louder."

We stopped outside the superintendent's office. "Salty language isn't foreign to Jill. She grew up on a ranch. That said, she's accustomed to rangers being professional on the job and she's sensitive about her appearance. She's worked a long time in a man's world and has carved out a niche as a seasoned professional. Calling her a dyke struck a nerve."

Larry closed his eyes, drew a deep breath, and blew it out. "I'm sorry about that. Jill carries herself like a professional and, well, I'm not used to seeing strong, confident women like her. It's an adjustment for me."

"Just wait until you work for someone like Jill."

"You worked for her as a law enforcement ranger, right?"

"I did. She drafted me to investigate a murder."

"And that apparently went okay."

I put my hand on Larry's shoulder. "I treated her as my boss, and she treated me professionally. I was one of the first men who looked past her appearance and dealt with her as a manager who liked to be kept informed. I gave her daily updates, explained what I was doing, and why I was doing it. She appreciated being kept informed and enjoyed learning about the cop side of the investigation. She's smart, a quick study, and polished."

"Do you know anyone in Dade County you can call to search for a marriage license?"

"Don't you think there's a state database of licenses?" Marconi asked.

"You make some calls and find out. I'll try Mississippi and Georgia."

A quick online search directed me to the Mississippi State Department of Health as the depository of marriage records. It took two calls to get past the bureaucracy and to an actual person.

Mamie Edwards had a charming deep voice and southern accent. "I understand you're with the park service and looking for marriage license records. I'd be happy to help you out…tell me why the park service is making this search?"

I explained the discovery of the body and wedding ring.

"And you hope to find someone married on that date with those initials. Okay. Hang on."

I heard computer keys clicking. "Ranger Fletcher, I've got six marriages on that date, but no pair of initials matches. I wish you well."

The first person at the Georgia Department of Health was informative. "Got it. If the marriage was less than six months ago, I have to get that record from the county."

"Thanks."

Larry walked in. "Miami-Dade County came through for me. Andrea Arnot and Juan Castro got married nine days ago at the Catholic Church in Little Havana. They could be the A and J on the ring."

I smiled. "And you thought this would be hard."

Larry grinned. "Let's be real. This was luck and they might not be the right people."

"Good cops use common sense and make their luck. You started with the place you thought was most likely and it worked."

"I can't imagine the church has a security camera, so no image to compare to Jane Doe. Now what?"

"Were they from Miami?"

"Juan listed an address in Cuba. Andrea was from Youngstown, Ohio."

"Did you call her home?"

Larry smiled, indicating he'd correctly anticipated that question. "If she has a landline, it's unlisted."

"Did you ever do a wellness check in New Jersey?"

Larry nodded. "You're thinking I should call Youngstown. They can search for her driver's license, get an address, and have a cop check her home."

"That'd be the next thing I'd do."

"I'll call. I wonder if she's got a roommate?"

"Hard to say. The Youngstown PD can check with her neighbors. Maybe someone knows where she works or her family. They might be able to get into her home and find a photo."

Larry's eyes lit up. "Ahh, her driver's license will have a photo. That'd help."

"They might even find someone who knows if Andrea's got a tattoo on her back."

"I'll make the call. Then what do you suggest?"

"I think we should check on the rangers with the metal detector."

* * *

Jill leaned on the railing, talking with a uniformed ranger who had a rifle slung over his shoulder. He was apparently the gator guard for the kayak team. They were watching two rangers in an ocean kayak, the rear ranger paddling slowly while the front ranger swept a metal detector slowly through the water with one hand, holding a fishing net in the other.

Larry and I walked down the pathway and joined them at the railing. "How goes the search?"

Jill didn't look up. "Three pop cans and a man's watch so far."

"A man's watch?"

"It was right next to the railing. I suppose someone from another time zone was changing their watch to eastern time and lost their grip."

I glanced at the armed ranger. "Have the alligators been threatening?"

"They're not usually interested," responded the blond ranger in his mid-twenties.

The ranger with the metal detector reacted to beeping about six feet from the railing and signaled for the paddler to stop. The kayak glided a bit, then backed up and the paddler tried to hold position. The ranger in front swept a fishing net through the water. "If it gets much deeper, I'll need a net with a longer handle."

The first two sweeps yielded nothing, so the man in front used the metal detector to recheck the spot. Having apparently drifted laterally, they adjusted their position and swept the net again.

"I've got car keys!" The rangers paddled close to the railing and held the net out to Jill. "They're not covered with algae, so they haven't been in the water very long."

Jill donned a pair of purple gloves and reached into the net. She fingered through the keys as the kayak paddled away to continue their search.

"There's a VW fob with a built-in remote and three other keys. At least one of these must be for an apartment or house."

Larry looked over her shoulder. "Some apartments have a separate key for the pool and workout rooms as well as a little key for the mailbox."

Jill spread the keys in her hand. "The little key is stamped, 'do not duplicate'. I assume that's a mailbox key. The others are larger Schlage keys that could be for a door or deadbolt."

Larry looked at me. "So, what do we do, cruise the streets from here to Miami, pushing the car remote until a VW beeps at us?"

I took the VW key from Jill and wiped the thin film of green algae from the black surface. "I don't think these electronic key fobs do well in the water."

Jill nodded. "In my limited canoe and rafting experience, everyone used a dry bag to protect their cell phone, wallet, and car keys. I think you have to assume the key electronics are toast."

Larry opened a small folding knife and used the blade to separate the halves of the key. Green muddy water ran out. Holding it out to us, he pointed to the now milky and dull button battery. "I think Jill's right. This isn't going to open any doors." He put the halves together and flipped the fob. "There are numbers on the back. Maybe the dealer can use the code to tell us the year and model of the vehicle."

"How aggressive is the parking enforcement in Florida City?"

"What are you thinking?" Larry asked.

"It's been nearly a week. The car may be in an impound lot."

Larry shrugged. "In New Jersey it'd be impounded the next day. Around here, I'm not sure how closely the cities monitor parking."

"Can you find a number for the local impound lot on your smartphone?" I asked.

"I'm sure it's listed so people can find it easily. Nothing makes people angrier than someone towing their car." He walked to the shade of a tree and fingered his phone.

Jill dropped the keys into a plastic evidence bag and sealed it. "We don't know if these keys have anything to do with the dead woman."

"I'd say it's 50:50 that they're hers. Maybe they fell out of her pocket when the gator dragged her."

Jill grinned. "Maybe some angry divorcee was getting even with her husband by throwing his keys in the swamp."

I laughed. "In my experience, anyone who was that angry would drive the whole car into the swamp, not just throw the keys."

"That's some level of anger I've never experienced."

Larry was back a minute later. "The Florida City PD towed a VW Jetta the day before yesterday and a Tiguan SUV last week. Anybody want to take a ride?"

Jill handed me the bag with the keys. "I'll stay here and cheer the kayak team on. You guys go ahead."

* * *

Larry drove the park service SUV. "I called the VW dealer in Miami. The parts department said we might be able to dry out the key fob and get it to work. The battery is probably hopeless, but the RFID tag is in a waterproof capsule, so if we find the car, we should be able to start it even if the doors and trunk release on the fob don't work."

"Where can we get a replacement battery?"

"There's a Batteries and Bulbs store in Florida City that specializes in replacement batteries for anything from watches to

101

computers. They're on the outskirts of town."

The battery place was a standalone green building with one car parked in the lot. Inside was a maze with racks of every battery I'd ever seen from a AAA to cell phone replacement batteries. Half the shop was lightbulbs, tiny to spotlights. In the rear of the store a stereotypical nerdy guy, with glasses sliding down his nose, was working on the guts of a computer. He nearly jumped when we appeared at the window. He set his screwdriver down and rushed to help us. "What can I do for you?"

Larry removed the keyring from the bag and took the VW key off the ring. "This has been in the water for a while. I'd like to know if it will ever work again."

In seconds, the technician had the VW fob apart and the battery out. "It kinda depends. If it was in salt water, it's probably dead. If it was in freshwater, there's a chance..."

"It was in a freshwater swamp," I said.

The tech touched the tester probes to the battery and shook his head. "I might be able to polish this up, but a new one only costs a few bucks." He searched through a couple plastic drawers in a small parts cabinet, then pulled out a plastic sleeve containing a new battery. I was amazed as his fingers opened the sleeve and manipulated the battery into the fob. He flipped the fob and pushed a button. "No go. Let me try something else."

He carried the fob away from the window and spread a rag on the counter. Selecting an aerosol can from an overhead shelf, he sprayed the fob, then wiped it with the rag. "I tried an electronics cleaner. It dries and cleans the contacts." He reinstalled the battery, snapped on the cover, then pressed the unlock button. A tiny red light flashed. He smiled and handed the fob back to Larry. Pushing his glasses up his nose he smiled and said, "That might do it."

I read his name tag and took out my wallet. "What do we owe you, Ken?"

Ken scanned the battery package barcode. "Seven thirty-nine, including tax."

I handed him a twenty-dollar bill. "What about your time and the cleaning?"

He put the twenty in the register and counted out my change. "It's part of the service we provide."

I pushed the change back to him. "I don't like having all the coins jangling in my pocket. You keep it."

Ken looked at me nervously, then took the ten-dollar bill off the pile and held it out to me. "Okay. Here's your ten."

"Put it in your pocket."

Larry held the door as we walked out. "You probably doubled that kid's hourly pay."

"Don't you think it was worth it?"

"Well, yeah, but you're not going to get reimbursed. You didn't even get a receipt."

I got in the SUV. "It was the right thing to do. He did something special for us. I appreciated it."

Larry digested that as we pulled away. "My dad never did anything like that. He would have negotiated Ken down to five bucks for the battery and told him to include the tax."

"Why do that to a kid, Larry? What I did was so little, and it made him feel so good."

"My dad likes seeing people squirm. He brags about it to his buddies."

"I don't see much point in beating up a kid who's making minimum wage over a buck or two. He's driving a twenty-year-old Honda with bald tires and is probably living with his parents. Did you see his smile when I told him to stick the ten in his pocket? I made his day and he'll probably tell his girlfriend about it."

Larry glanced at me. "I doubt a nerd like him has a girlfriend. He'd tell his dog about dealing with my dad."

I shook my head. "Maybe it's a Minnesota thing, but I sleep better by making somebody happy."

We drove in silence for a few miles before Larry said, "If the key opens one of the impounded vehicles, we'll be able to run the plates and get a local address."

"Let's hope it works."

I could tell Larry was mulling something. "I read through more wire service stories about your arrests in Arizona, Wyoming, Iowa, and Texas. That's some fine police work."

"Trust me, Larry, I wasn't working alone. I was happy to be part of the team that made those things happen."

"You and Jill even rescued a kidnap victim."

"Don't believe everything you read on the internet."

"A reporter from New Mexico said you were the most humble, sharing, cop she'd ever met."

"That was very kind of her and a gross exaggeration."

"Nothing explained how you got hooked up with the park service in the first place. You said Jill hired you, but you never said how that happened."

"I'd retired from St. Paul PD and was working as a seasonal ranger at Walnut Canyon National Monument. I saw a guy who was pushed over the railing. The Flagstaff office didn't have a law enforcement ranger and the superintendent asked me to take on the investigation."

"That was the case with the Kokopelli in the guy's pocket?"

"That was it."

"Sounds like a hair-raising chase along the Grand Canyon rim."

"It was pretty humorous, in retrospect. I commandeered a car from an old Navajo woman, not realizing it had a big V-8 engine and bald tires. I was either squealing my tires when I accelerated or squealing my tires when I locked up the brakes. The woman demanded to ride along, then screamed at me about ruining her car. Halfway around the rim she told me to stop and let her out because I was scaring her."

"Did you let her out?"

"I ignored her. If she'd been hurt or killed there would've been hell to pay."

Larry waited a minute, then asked. "So, Jill was the park superintendent who hired you. How'd you get from employee to husband?"

"We got to be friends, then realized we were best friends and lonely."

"She gave up her Arizona superintendent job to follow you to Texas."

"The park service helped. There was a wrongful death lawsuit against the park, and someone decided that Jill, the superintendent, should take the fall. She was officially on leave during the investigation, so it was convenient for her to get away from the Arizona mess and hide out in Texas until the dust settled. She eventually took a ranger position in Texas. Does your wife work?"

"She's a dental assistant in Florida City. It's pretty low pay without benefits, but she feels useful and fulfilled. We rely on my benefits and pay. Her salary barely covers daycare."

"How many kids?"

"My son is six and my daughter is three, just past the terrible twos."

"Is your wife happy in Florida?"

"She's happy to be a long way from my relatives and sad to be so far from hers. It's a trade off. Overall, we argue a lot less if none of the parents are meddling in our lives. How about you and Jill? Are your families in Texas?"

"Jill's family is still on their ranch in western South Dakota, the Black Hills. Right now, that's where my mother is, too. She's nursing one of Jill's adopted uncles back from cancer surgery."

"Is that why you two were assigned to the Wyoming and South Dakota cases?"

"We were there for Thanksgiving and got called to Devils Tower. The park service requested us for the Wind Cave murder."

"I'd love to be doing the investigative things you're into, but my wife would kill me if I was running all over the country."

I thought, "*You have no idea what steps to take during an investigation and you want to step into my shoes?*"

* * *

Like every other impound lot I'd ever seen, this one was on the outskirts of Florida City where its back fence abutted a swampy area. My first thought was *this is mosquito heaven*. My second thought was *All these banged up cars are leaking fluids right into an environmentally sensitive area.* Neither of those issues seemed to be preying on the mind of the obese man sitting behind the desk in oil-soaked coveralls. A patch sewn over his breast pocket said, "Dewey." He was eating a sandwich with one greasy hand while flipping through *Field & Stream* magazine with the other.

"Help you?" Dewey asked, spitting pieces of sandwich as he spoke. He seemed unimpressed by Larry's uniform or the badge on my belt.

Larry stepped forward. "I called about the two VWs you towed."

Dewey gestured toward a window. "Out there. Watch your step, I saw a cottonmouth this morning."

I closed my eyes. Snakes are my greatest natural fear. I handed Larry the bag with the keys and pushed him ahead. "You take the lead."

The weedy, crushed oyster shell and gravel lot was filled with banged up and abandoned vehicles, reminding me more of a junkyard than an impound lot. The Tiguan wasn't far from the office, but nothing happened when Larry pressed the unlock button on the fob. "Well, either this isn't the one or the remote is dead."

Walking farther down the crushed-shell paved driveway, I avoided patches of potentially snake-infested grass and peeked under vehicles along the way. Larry pressed the remote at the end of the row and parking lights flashed, and a Jetta's horn beeped. "I think we have a bingo!" He pulled on a pair of purple gloves as he walked through the deep grass alongside the car and opened the passenger door. He leaned inside. "I've got the insurance and registration. The owner is a woman who lives in Florida City." Larry locked the doors and walked to the shell covered driveway. "You're kind of hanging back. What's the matter?"

"I have a thing about snakes, especially venomous snakes."

Larry's eyes went wide, and he stepped farther into the shells. "A cottonmouth is venomous?"

"Very."

Larry's voice went up a half octave. "Why didn't you say something before I went traipsing through the grass?"

"I thought you knew."

"There aren't any venomous snakes in New Jersey, at least not the parts I've been in."

"We should check the car interior for blood."

Larry handed me the evidence bag and a pair of purple gloves. "Go ahead. I'll try to get more information about the woman named on the insurance card."

I unlocked the doors again, hoping the beeping would scare away any wildlife, then I gingerly walked to the driver's door, carefully checking the grass, and looking under the cars on each side. The car smelled musty, but I suspected any car sitting in a swamp for a week would grow a bit of mildew. I didn't smell the coppery stench of blood. The front seat was littered with fast-food bags, French fry bits, ketchup packets, dirty napkins, and paper cups from a variety of fast-food places. Aside from spilled soda pop and ketchup, I couldn't identify any blood stains. I checked the console and found more ketchup packets, napkins, and a strip of two condoms. Our woman was heterosexual.

Moving to the back seat, I found the same mess as in the front. It was hard to determine if there had been an assault inside the car because the scene looked like a fast-food bomb had gone off. The red stains on burger wrappers and salad containers looked more like ketchup and French dressing than blood.

I closed and locked the car. I was concentrating on the mess inside the car

110

and not being vigilant about my path when something brown moved through the grass ahead of me. Without thought, I found myself standing on the hood of the Jetta with my gun drawn.

"Holy shit. You're pretty agile for an old guy. You went from flat-footed to four feet in the air. Then you stuck the landing like a gymnast and had your gun out before I could open my mouth. What the hell happened?"

"I saw something brown moving in the grass."

"That was a rat."

I put the Sig back into the holster and struggled to get down without scratching the paint or falling off. "You could've told me it was a rat."

"I figured you could see that it was a rat."

"All I saw was brown and I reacted without thinking."

Larry smiled. "You might want to check your underwear."

"Screw you. Next time yell, 'rat,' or something so I know it's not a deadly snake."

"I figure the fat guy in the office was messing with us. If there was a big old venomous snake out here, I imagine they wouldn't have much of a rat problem."

"I think snakes only eat every couple weeks. Rats probably have two litters of babies in that time."

"I don't think they call them litters of rats."

I threw up my hands. "Whatever. You get my point."

"Did you find any blood?"

"I saw a lot of red stains, but I think they were ketchup and dressing. We should have this towed to a secure facility until we get a search warrant. A forensics team could put a blue light on the seats to see if there are any bodily fluid stains inside it."

I saw Larry smile. "If she was a sexually active South Beach bed bunny, I'm betting there are many bodily fluid stains all over the seats."

"Bed bunny?"

"The single South Beach girls are all hunting for a rich husband. They hop from bed to bed hoping to find someone who'll marry them or, failing that, get them pregnant and pay a royal sum to go away with a non-disclosure agreement."

"Are you speaking from personal experience or just spouting rumors?"

Larry was unfazed by my jab at his veracity. "I have a beer with the local cops once in a while. They see all kinds of weird stuff down here. Everything from people smoking dope while driving to humping in the back of the bar parking lots. It all happens here."

We were next to the office when I was struck by several thoughts. I waved Larry into the office. Dewey had moved on to a family-sized bag of Fritos. "Where was the Jetta parked?"

The guy looked up like he was seeing me for the first time. "Unless somebody moved it, it's in the second row."

I sighed. "I want to know where it was towed from."

Dewey shrugged. The action caused his whole upper body to rise and fall. "I don't drive the trucks. I just run the office and collect the fees."

"But you have a record of the tow location."

He glanced at a file corner cabinet covered with greasy fingerprints. "It's in a file."

"Please look it up."

Dewey licked his fingers but didn't move. "You got a search warrant?"

"I don't want to search the car. I want to know where it was parked when it was towed."

"I told you, I didn't drive the truck."

Larry couldn't handle it any longer. He stepped past me and leaned on the desk. "Get your fat ass out of the chair and find the Jetta towing record."

Dewey wasn't easily intimidated, and he slowly put his Fritos bag aside. "You ain't the boss of me. I work for the city. You got no authority here."

Larry unsnapped his handcuffs and made a show of arranging them.

Dewey watched with curiosity. "What are you planning to do?"

"I'm going to handcuff you and then haul you to the federal lockup in Miami."

That caught Dewey's attention. "Why would you do that?"

"Because you're interfering with a federal murder investigation. Now haul your sorry ass out of that chair and find the towing record or you're going to be laying on the floor with your hands cuffed behind your back."

Dewey made a show of pulling a red bandana from his back pocket and wiping Fritos fragments off his face and fingers. "I think you'd better talk to my boss. You can't leave this lot unprotected. There's posted open hours. I gotta be here to collect the money when people come for their cars and to make sure the other cars don't get vandalized."

I leaned against the door frame and watched Larry.

"I'm giving you one more chance to get the damned towing record for the Jetta. If you don't do it quickly, we'll cuff you and haul you to Miami. You'll have to go to a bail hearing in front of a federal magistrate and then you'll be able to call someone to come down to post bail for you. I don't give a shit if this place is ransacked while you're gone. That's on you. We asked you to do one simple thing, and when you didn't comply you pushed me past my limit."

"You got no right to do that. I'm a civil servant and I've got protections."

Larry pushed the phone toward the man. "Call your boss or union rep and tell him to meet you at the Miami federal lockup. I hope he's not too busy to come down now." Larry sensed the man's hesitation. "Or don't you have a phone number for either of them?"

Dewey looked at the phone, then back at Larry. I sensed something amiss, but I wasn't sure what. "The recent records are in the bottom drawer."

I stepped toward the desk to keep an eye on the man as Larry pulled open the bottom file cabinet drawer and looked at the mess of slips, apparently jammed randomly into the files.

"How do I find the Jetta record? What's it filed under?"

"It's filed under wherever I found an opening. If you want it, you just gotta dig through them."

Larry pulled out the first file and dropped it on the floor. Dewey's eyes went wide. Larry pulled the second file and took a different approach, turning it upside down and shaking all the slips onto the floor.

"Do you see the Jetta slip yet?" Larry asked Dewey.

"Hey! You can't do that. You're going to have to pick all them up and put 'em back."

Larry lifted out the third and fourth files and shook them onto the floor. "Filing isn't in my job description. Besides, I might not get the slips in the right order." He paused. "Are you ready to find the slip I want, or do I keep going?"

Dewey waved his arm. "You're not even a real cop. Get the hell outta my office before I call the county."

Larry picked up two more file folders. "I think your files are already a mess. I might be helping you." He dumped them on top of the growing pile of paper.

Dewey couldn't take it anymore. "Hang on! The new ones are on the computer. Them is the old ones."

I shook my head. Dewey was king of his own filthy kingdom, and we weren't letting him exert his usual control. "What's the problem? We're not letting you make us squirm like the people who come in here begging for you to release their cars?"

Dewey sneered, then spun his chair. He opened computer files without entering a password, leaving me to wonder about his computer skills and the security of his files. Using one fat finger on the keyboard he scrolled through the files. "It was over on Krome Avenue. Says it was parked in the Caribbean restaurant lot overnight and the owners complained to the local cops."

I motioned to Larry. "I assume you know how to get there."

Larry smiled, looked at the pile of towing slips on the floor and followed me out the door. "He'll probably spend all afternoon filing those slips."

"I bet they'll be in the wastebasket in five minutes."

Larry leaned on the top of the SUV and glanced back at the office. "Do you think any of the towing fees make it into the county bank account, or does he pocket them?"

"I'm sure any fees paid with a charge card will go to the county. I've got a feeling that a cash payment might go into his pocket and the towing record would just disappear from his computer."

Larry unlocked the SUV. "I saw dates on towing slips from the 1980s when I dumped the first folder. He's a model civil servant at work."

I got in the passenger side of the SUV and waited for the air-conditioning to start. "Our friend Dewey wasn't civil or a servant."

Larry laughed. "I gotta write that down."

Chapter 7

The Caribbean restaurant was gearing up for lunch when we arrived. We sat in the SUV while Larry called the Department of Motor Vehicles. After four calls he got someone to look up the Jetta's license plate and give him the name of the owner.

Larry disconnected and raised his eyebrows. "The owner is Madison Wirth. They're sending me an email with her address and driver's license photo." A moment later his phone chimed, and he opened the email attachments. "Here's her picture."

It was a typical DMV photo, like a mugshot taken without expression. Madison looked like she was in her early twenties, with an almond-shaped face and short, dark hair. The information said she was five-six and weighed one hundred ten pounds.

I handed the phone back. "She's a skinny thing."

Larry nodded. "So is Jane Doe."

"The initials in the ring were A&J. The car owner was named Madison. Something doesn't add up."

The restaurant's front door was still locked, but there were cars in the back of the lot. We walked in the back door, surprising a cook who was stirring a huge pot that smelled like jerk seasoning. The cook was dark-skinned and spoke with a Caribbean accent that sounded like honey. "You can't be back here, mon. You got no hair covering."

I stood back, near the door to not infringe further on the cook's space. "We need to talk to the bartender."

The cook nodded toward a set of doors. "Up front. He's setting up for lunch."

The bartender was counting money into the cash register. Seeing us out of the corner of his eye, he reached for something under the counter as he turned to face us. His look of anger melted away when he saw Larry's uniform and my badge and gun.

"You guys scared the shit outta me."

"Sorry," I said as Larry pulled out his cell phone and held out Madison's driver's license photo. "This woman's car was towed out of your lot a few nights ago. Do you know if she was drinking here that night?"

The bartender glanced at the picture and shook his head. "She's not a regular. If she was here, I didn't notice her."

"She has a dolphin tattoo on her lower back."

The guy shook his head as he broke a roll of quarters and dumped the coins into the cash register drawer. "They're everywhere. I think Zodiac Tattoos has cornered the market on dolphins, stars, and butterflies." He paused. "Is she in some kind of trouble?"

Larry put his phone away. "She's missing. We're trying to find out who she was with when her car was towed."

The bartender checked the clock, signaling his impatience. "Can't help you."

"Do you think any of the waitresses might recognize her?"

The bartender arranged currency in the register. "I can't say what they might've seen. You'll have to ask when the evening staff is here at suppertime or later."

The bartender closed the cash register and stepped from behind the bar. "I've got to unlock the door for lunch. You're welcome to go out this way instead of going through the kitchen."

Walking to the SUV, Larry turned to me. "Did you feel like you just got the bum's rush?"

"Yeah, he didn't look very closely at the picture and was in a hurry to get rid of us. On the other hand, we caught him when they were trying to open. He was busy."

Larry pulled out of the parking lot as lunch customers walked past.

"That guy suggested Madison's tattoo might've been done at Zodiac Tattoos. I'd like to talk to them."

Larry glanced at me. "Tattoo shops aren't morning places. They get a lot more business later at night, after people have a few drinks and have lowered their inhibitions."

"Is there a coffee place along the way?"

Larry smiled. "Coffee and a sweet roll. Now you're speaking my language."

* * *

The Zodiac Tattoos logo was an unimaginative circle of zodiac symbols. The shop windows were darkened so no passersby could see inside. A buzzer sounded when Larry opened the door.

Inside were two reclining chairs with arm supports. A small stainless table and a rolling stool sat next to each chair. A dark-haired bearded man was leaning over a young woman's exposed lower back. He was focused on filling in the wings of a butterfly. Another eight or nine butterflies, each larger as they moved up the woman's back, were outlined in patches of inflamed skin.

The man's arms were a mélange of colors. He had so many tattoos and themes it was impossible to pick out any one theme. An eye here. A skull there. A heart on his upper arm. Nothing seemed to tie the pieces together.

The young woman glanced at us, then put her head down. Grimacing in pain, she bit her lower lip as the tattoo pen buzzed above the towel tucked into the waist of her shorts.

"You need an appointment. I don't do walk-ins," the tattoo artist said without looking up from his work. "Call and leave a message. My number is on the business cards by the cash register."

"We'd like to show you a tattoo."

"I don't redo other people's mistakes and I don't give refunds for regrets."

I looked at Larry to let him know I was going to try the "nice" approach. "We'd like your help."

The tattoo pen stopped humming and he turned his head. A hint of surprise flashed in his eyes when he saw Larry's uniform. "That'd be a first. A cop who needs help."

"We're park service cops. We don't know everything like local cops."

Larry smiled. "Yeah, my specialty is ticketing litterers."

Larry's comment was perfect, disarming the man. A flicker of a smile curled the corner of the artist's mouth. He leaned down and said something to his subject, then he set the tattoo needle aside and stripped off his purple gloves. "What've you got?"

I held out the autopsy tattoo picture. "I've got a dead woman. This art was on her back. I heard that you do a lot of dolphins, and I was wondering if this is your work."

The man handled the photo carefully by the edges and turned it to get the best light. "This is the best picture you've got?"

"It's the only picture we've got." The woman on the table seemed to ignore us. "The subject had been dead a few days before this was taken."

He nodded. "Got it." He handed the photo back. "Yeah, that looks like my stuff."

"Do you have a record of who got this art? Did she come in alone or with a friend?"

Larry smirked. "Was she sober?"

The artist smiled. "I only work on sober adults who sign a waiver. I do a dozen dolphins a week. There are a few variations, so nobody gets exactly the same art, but they're all similar and I don't keep photos of them. Sorry, but I can't give you a name or who was or wasn't with her."

The artist looked tough, but his language was polished. He seemed genuinely sad he couldn't help. "If we're done here, I need to get back to the butterflies flying out of her butt."

I nodded. "Thanks."

After the door closed, Larry looked over his shoulder. "She wanted butterflies flying out of her butt?"

"Different strokes…"

"Yeah, but butterflies flying out of your butt is pretty far out there." Larry led the way back to the SUV. "Now what, boss?"

"What's Madison Wirth's address?

* * *

Madison Wirth lived in a sprawling apartment complex filled with three-story buildings. The building with her address was near the end of the complex. Larry parked among the resident's vehicles which ranged from beat up American cars to some expensive foreign makes. I followed Larry to the front door. A keypad alongside the door barred entry. Alongside the keypad was a list of apartments with the last name of the occupants listed alongside a three-digit number. A phone hung next to the listing so visitors could call to get buzzed in.

I was looking through the list when a blonde pushed the door open and held it for us. She was dressed for a trip to the beach, wearing a gauzy cover over her bikini top and a sarong around her hips. "You're cops. Who's in trouble?"

I smiled and put my hand on the door. "One of your neighbors lost her keys and we found them."

"Cool," the young woman said as she breezed past and sped down the steps.

Larry watched her for a second. "Hell of a security system if the residents let strangers in the locked door."

I walked into the atrium. "In all fairness, she knew we were cops when she opened the door."

Larry shook his head. "She knew we were dressed like cops. But I think she would've let anyone in who was standing at the door."

"The resident listing showed Allen/Wirth living in apartment 311." I pushed the elevator button. "What's your bet? Is Allen a boyfriend or female roommate?"

Larry considered the question while we waited for the elevator. "I'm thinking she has a female roommate. I think our victim was cruising the bars looking for guys."

The elevator doors opened, and a young man dressed in the blue and white uniform of a fast-food chain pushed past us, rushing to get into the elevator. When the doors closed, Larry shook his head. "He must have six roommates to afford a place here on what he's making flipping burgers."

We walked to apartment 311 and I knocked on the door. The apartment seemed unoccupied, no television or other sounds coming from inside. Larry took out the evidence envelope and chose the key that looked like it matched the deadbolt.

125

"We can't unlock and walk in."

Larry paused. "If the roommate's not around, what difference does it make? It's not like we're going to search the place."

I knocked again. "No, we're not using the key to enter unless we get a warrant."

The words were hardly out of my mouth when the deadbolt clicked, and the door opened against a security chain. A single eye appeared under brown bangs. "Yeah?"

"We'd like to talk to you about Madison."

"Who are you?"

"We're park service investigators. Could we come in and talk?"

"Show me your ID."

I held my laminated credentials up to the crack and waited. The door closed and the chain rattled.

The woman who opened the door was chunky. Her hair was brown, and piercings penetrated her left eyebrow and nostril. She wore headphones with a mic. Behind her, a computer screen glowed on an IKEA desk. Most of the other furniture was cheap or second-hand.

The woman didn't invite us any farther in than the entryway. "What about Maddie?"

"When did you last see her?" Larry asked.

The woman cocked her head. "I don't know. A couple days ago."

"Does she often disappear for a few days at a time?"

The woman shrugged. "Depends. If Josh is off, she sometimes spends a couple days at his place."

I nodded toward the desk. "Do you work from here?"

She looked at me skeptically. "Why do you care?"

"Do you have some ID?"

"What? I live here. I don't need any ID. What's up with you two?"

"Can I see your driver's license, please," I said.

The woman walked to the living room and pushed aside a pile of papers to pull out a compact wallet.

Larry leaned close. "What's up?"

"I'm just making sure she's really Wirth's roommate."

The woman pulled out a driver's license with a photo of a younger, angrier version of Britney Allen. The address matched the apartment. I handed it back to her.

"What's going on?" she asked as she put the license away.

"Show her the keys, Larry."

Marconi held the evidence bag flat on his palm. "Do these look familiar?"

"They might be Maddie's. She owns a Jetta." Britney stopped. "Why do you have Maddie's keys?"

Larry was ready to answer when I cut him off. "Does Maddie have a tattoo?"

Britney's eyes went wide, and her hand flew to her mouth. "Is she in the hospital?"

"We need to contact her next of kin. Do you have a phone number for her parents or siblings?"

Britney shook her head. "I know they live near Sarasota. Their numbers would be in Maddie's cell phone." She looked at Larry. "You have her cell phone, right?"

"Does Maddie have a tattoo?"

Britney's eyes looked all over the room as she tried to process the information. She paced away from us and then back. "Yeah. She has a dolphin on her back. Tell me what's going on."

"We found Maddie's keys and her car. We need to contact her relatives."

"I don't know who they are. I mean, I've never met them. She just calls them Mom and Dad, so I don't even know what their names are."

"Where did Maddie work? Maybe someone there will have her contact information."

Britney started pacing again. "No. Something bad happened to Maddie. Tell me what's going on."

"I'm afraid we need to contact her family first," I said.

Larry couldn't stand it anymore. "Maddie's in the morgue. We need her parents to identify her remains."

Britney deflated. She reached out for the wall and sank as her legs folded under her. I caught her arm in time to break her fall. Tears streamed down her face, and she shuddered with sobs. I knelt beside her.

"We'd like to look through Maddie's things to see if we can find something with her parent's names and address."

Britney pointed to a closed door. "In there."

Maddy's room was like the inside of her car, clothing strewn on the floor where it had been dropped. While a clothes basket appeared to hold clean clothing, most of the items on the floor were previously worn shorts, jeans, towels, t-shirts, bras, and thong underwear. We stood at the door for a second, taking in the enormity of the mess.

Larry shook his head. "I think we should ask Britney if this room has been ransacked or if this is the pigsty Maddie lived in."

I glared at him. "You saw her car. You know the answer. Go talk to Britney and get Madison's boyfriend's name."

I waded through clothing on the floor to a dresser that was equally strewn with stuff. I pulled on a pair of purple gloves and picked through the items on the top until I found a small wooden box with an assortment of rings and earring studs. Inside was a class ring from Riverview High the class of 2016. There was nothing personal on the dresser or in the half-full drawers. I found a Paxil prescription in the nightstand and pocketed the bottle, thinking we might be able to find family through the pharmacy or prescribing doctor. Alongside the Paxil were baggies of marijuana buds and white powder.

Larry looked around the doorframe. "Britney says her boyfriend is an EMT named Josh Baxter who works for FCFD. The station is only a few blocks from here." Larry paused when he realized I had been looking into the nightstand. "Did you find anything interesting in there?"

"Marijuana and some unidentified white powder. A couple charge cards."

Larry nodded. "Cocaine is still big on South Beach." He surveyed the mess, then opened the closet. "Maddie appears to be more of a cowboy bar girl than a South Beach bed bunny. Lots of shorts, tank tops, and jeans. No short, tight dresses."

"That's a thing? Being a cowboy bar girl?"

Larry nodded. "There are still ranches around here and bars that cater to the cowboys and wannabe cowboys. They play country music and serve more beer than martinis."

I close the nightstand. "Girls who want to meet cowboys instead of rich playboys?"

"Girls who are looking for someone more genuine than a guy pretending to be a playboy and stringing them along as long as…"

Britney stepped into the doorframe. Her eyes and nose were red. "Maddie was into Josh. She wasn't into the hook-up scene."

"The hook-up scene?" I asked.

"Drinking in bars hoping to find Mr. Right. It's hard on the self-esteem hooking up with guys who never call back."

I nodded and felt sick. Larry nodded like it was a fact of life and maybe a place he'd been.

* * *

My phone rang as we drove to the fire station and I answered, assuming it was Jill, without looking at the caller ID. "Hey, how's the gator hole search going?"

"What are you talking about, Doug?" My mother sounded rightfully confused.

"I thought Jill was calling to update me on something she had going on. What's up?"

"Jill's not there with you?"

Larry looked at me, smiling. "Mom?" he mouthed.

I nodded. "I'm riding with the Everglades ranger. Jill's working on something else."

"But what happens if she gets in a shootout? Who's going to have her back?"

"Mom, Jill's supervising two rangers who are trying to find a lost cell phone in a swamp. She's not going to get in a shootout."

"You said shootouts occur when you least expect them."

I closed my eyes. "That's true, but the odds of Jill getting in a shootout while searching a swamp is very low."

"I don't find that reassuring. You get back there and make sure you take care of her."

"I'm on my way."

"Douglas Fletcher, don't lie to me!" Mom's voice was loud enough for Larry to hear, and he swerved over the centerline while laughing. "Who's laughing? Is he laughing because I'm chewing you out?"

"Yes, Mom, he's laughing because you're yelling loud enough for him to hear you."

"Good! Other ranger, whatever your name is, take Doug back to Jill and make sure he's watching out for her."

Larry leaned toward me. "Yes, ma'am. I'm on it."

"He didn't sound sincere."

"I'm sure he'll be sincere once he stops laughing."

"This is *not* humorous! I'm worried about Jill, and you're out galivanting around while she's in danger! This is not funny!"

"She's not in danger, Mom."

"You said she was trying to find a cell phone in a swamp. She could drown! Reassure me that she's at least wearing a lifejacket."

"She's watching from shore. She won't drown." I paused. "Did you have something in mind when you called?"

"Of course, I did, but I got rattled when I heard you'd abandoned Jill."

Larry had tears running down his cheeks as he laughed.

"What was it?"

"What was what?"

I closed my eyes. "Why did you call me?"

"Oh, I called to ask you a question about Chet. Are you somewhere I can ask you a sensitive question?"

"Sure. My partner doesn't know Chet, so ask away."

"I don't want to ask this with a stranger listening."

"Mom, Larry's laughing too hard to be listening."

"Is he still laughing at me?"

"Mom, ask your question."

"Well," she paused, "Chet's having a male problem and we wanted some advice."

"Okay, what do you need to know?"

"Well, to be frank, he's dribbling."

Larry broke out laughing again.

"Tell that man to stop laughing. This is serious!"

"Tell me about the dribbling. Are we talking about Copenhagen dribbling out of his mouth, or are we talking about incontinence?"

"This has nothing to do with his snuff chewing! He's dribbling when he…pees."

Larry pulled off the road and stopped the SUV. He motioned for me to hold the phone so he could hear the conversation.

"Why are you calling me about this? It's a question for Chet's doctor."

"He's too embarrassed about it to talk with the nurse who takes messages. He asked me to call you."

"He's embarrassed to talk with a nurse, but he's willing to have you relay a question to me?"

"Yes."

"Ask him if this is something that's continuous, so he needs Depends, or just with urgency."

"I don't have to ask. I already know."

"Mom, stop right there. This may be too much information. Call the doctor."

134

She cut me off. "It's when he's trying to…"

"Stop! Do. Not. Tell. Me. More. You call the doctor and speak to the nurse since you seem to be able to explain it."

"But she's a cute little thing who smiles at him when he sees the doctor. He doesn't want her to know that…"

"Mom. I will not get involved in this. I'm hanging up."

"You are so bull-headed."

"Goodbye, Mom."

I ended the call and looked at Larry, who was smirking. "This is what I have to look forward to when I'm your age?"

"Probably."

Larry shifted the SUV into gear and pulled onto the road. "I'm getting an unlisted number. I'm not discussing Mom's boyfriend dribbling after prostate surgery."

"I'm afraid that's not an option. And this isn't the most embarrassing conversation I've had with her."

"Really? You've got one to top that?"

"She visited us in Texas and told me over breakfast that our bedroom walls were paper thin and didn't block the sound of our lovemaking."

Larry snorted. "Oh, man. Your mom must really be something."

"Especially since she moved in to take care of Jill's Uncle Chet."

"Your mother moved in with Jill's uncle?"

"Aren't we at the fire station yet?"

"I've been circling the block for five minutes while you finished your call."

"Stop circling."

My phone rang again as Larry pulled into the "police vehicles only" parking spot in front of the fire station. I swiped the screen and was prepared for another conversation with Mom when a male voice asked if I was Fletcher from the park service.

"Yes, this is Fletcher."

"Ken Parks, the assistant medical examiner. I got the toxicology scan back. Jane Doe had rohypnol in her tissue. She'd been roofied."

I froze, unprepared for the call or the information. "We found a set of keys in the park, near where the body was recovered and identified the likely owner as Madison Wirth. Her roommate confirmed that Ms. Wirth had a dolphin tattoo on her lower back. We're going into an interview with her boyfriend in a minute."

"Is he a suspect?"

"Everyone's a suspect at this point."

"Is he a *likely* suspect?"

I thought for a second. "I doubt a boyfriend would roofie his girlfriend."

"Have you located her next of kin?"

"We haven't. Her roommate didn't know her parents and only knew she was from Sarasota."

"Spell her name for me. I'll have one of my people try to locate her parents."

* * *

Except for the two fire trucks and an ambulance, the first floor of the fire station was empty. Voices drifted down the stairs, so we walked up and found six guys sitting around a table in a kitchen area. The aroma of food lingered in the air, reminding me we'd missed lunch. Four men were playing bridge with two watching.

When we walked in the door, one of the firemen watching the bridge game got up. He appraised Larry's uniform and my badge as he walked toward us. "Hi, guys. What can I do for the park service?"

"Is Josh around?"

A fireman with his back to us turned his head. "Yeah."

"Could we have a few minutes with you?"

Frowning when he saw Larry's uniform, he handed his cards to one of the other firemen and stood. Nodding toward the door, he said, "It's quiet downstairs."

We walked downstairs with Josh behind us and stopped alongside a firetruck. Larry wasn't schooled in interviews and led off with, "Madison Wirth is dead. Do you know how to contact her parents?"

I glanced at him, letting him know he'd screwed up. He gave me a look that asked, "*What*?"

Josh looked like he'd been punched and any questions I had about him as a possible suspect evaporated as he went from stunned to teary. He was either genuinely surprised and sad, or he should be on Broadway.

I let Josh process the information for a moment, then delayed while he composed himself. "When did you last see Madison?"

"I…she…what happened?"

I cut Larry off, not wanting him to reveal everything we knew. "When did you last see her?"

"Last week, like Tuesday. We were supposed to meet the next night, but I got a call out and didn't get back to the station until after the bars closed. She hasn't been returning my calls or texts, so I figured she was pissed."

"Did you talk the night you stood her up?"

Josh shook his head. "We got called to a bad accident on I-95 and I was preoccupied, then I was driving and filling out stuff at the hospital."

"Do you often go for days without seeing her?"

"Not usually, but she's been unhappy about my work, and it's been causing friction. I've stood her up a couple times, but she usually cools off in a day. This has been extraordinary."

"Have you spoken with her roommate?"

"You mean Britney? Nah, she gets so caught up in her online trading she doesn't hear her phone or the door. I just leave messages for Maddie and wait for her to get back to me." Josh paused. "What happened? We didn't get a call out for an accident or anything. I'd know if she'd been hurt at home. One of the guys would've told me."

"We found her body in the Everglades National Park."

Josh's eyes went wide, and he glanced at my badge. "Ah, that's why the park service is involved. What…?"

"We don't know yet. Someone tried to make it look like she'd been attacked by an alligator, but it appears she was murdered."

"Murdered? Maddie?" Josh stared at us, awaiting a reply. "Why? Was she sexually assaulted or robbed?"

"It doesn't look like those were the killer's motives."

"Then why?"

"Did Maddie wear a wedding ring to ward off unwanted guys at the bar?" Larry asked.

"Maddie? No, why do you ask?"

"The body we recovered was wearing a wedding band with the initials A and J. The wedding date was a week ago."

"Maddie was wearing a ring?" Josh was stuck on the ring and not the initials.

"Do you know a couple with the initials A & J?"

"No." Josh ran a list through his head. "Nope, none at all."

"Where were you planning to meet her?"

Josh shook his head. "I always texted her when I got off. She liked the music in the cowboy bars."

Larry was ready to leave and looked at the door. "Josh, do you know Maddie's parents?"

"I've never met them. Her father manages a grocery store. Her Mom works part time for a cleaning service."

"What are their names?"

Josh drew a breath and thought. "Ed. Her father is Ed Wirth. Her Mom's name is Alison."

"Where do they live?" Larry looked at me like I was nuts, but I cut him off.

"They live in Bee Ridge, southeast of Sarasota."

"Do you have an address?"

140

Josh shook his head. "Like I said, I've never met them. Maddie never told me their address."

I put my hand on his arm. "Are you going to be okay?"

Josh nodded. "I've got to tell the guys." He took a step, then turned back to us. "Do you need me to identify the body?"

I shook my head. "The medical examiner will use dental records."

Josh blinked back tears. "Her body is badly decomposed?"

I nodded and he turned away, bracing himself against the wall.

Larry held the door, then followed me to the SUV. "That was slow. Geez, I was ready to fall asleep."

I got in and Larry started the engine. "Interviews are tedious and that wasn't slow. It was the pace we needed to let Josh get his head around Maddie's death. I've spent a whole night with murderers, letting them talk until they start contradicting their own stories, then letting them unravel."

"I couldn't do that," Larry said as he backed into the street. "I'd be cracking heads or just walking away."

"Lots of cops have that problem. Patience is what separates the great investigators from the guys who spend their careers chasing speeders."

Larry digested that in silence. "So, you consider yourself a great investigator."

141

"I'm average at best."

Larry glanced at me to see if I was kidding. "You're serious."

"I am."

"Fletcher, you're the strangest cop I've ever worked with. You've got no ego. Yet, you seem to get things done."

I punched in the number for the medical examiner's office and asked for Ken Parks. Larry pulled into a fast-food restaurant. "Burgers okay with you?"

I pulled out my wallet, but Larry waved off my offer to pay. "Great, with a diet Coke."

Parks answered as Larry walked out of the restaurant. "Dr. Parks, I have the names of Madison Wirth's parents. Ed and Alison Wirth. They live in Bee Ridge."

"Thanks. I'll call them."

"Anything new for me?" I asked as Larry got in the truck.

"I'm afraid not. We know everything I'm going to get."

"You said she had rohypnol in her tissue. Would that and the alcohol be enough to kill her?"

"I'm looking at the tox report. In my opinion, that's unlikely. She probably would've come around the next morning without any memory of the previous night."

I watched Larry set my drink in a cup holder. He opened a bag, and the smell of burgers filled the SUV. "Thanks, Doc."

Larry took out his burger and handed me the bag. "Nothing new with the medical examiner?"

"Nothing. He's going to call the parents and give them the bad news."

Larry took a bite of burger and thought. "That's a shitty job, telling folks their kid is dead. The detectives always handled that."

I unwrapped my burger. "First, there's disbelief, then come the tears and anger. There's not much to be done except offer condolences and try to get background."

"Background?"

"Who were they with? Where had they been? Who were their friends?"

"Why ask all that?"

"If we're dealing with a murder, we need context and the people who may have known what happened."

Larry nodded as he jammed fries in his mouth. "I was thinking of car accidents. You don't need a lot of context to tell someone their kid died when they rolled the car or hit a light pole."

"Sure, you do. You've got to know if they were drinking and if they were, where they'd been. There are a lot of insurance issues that need answers."

Larry thought about that. I became more aware of Larry's lack of experience the more we talked. My cell phone rang before Larry was out of the parking lot. Jill's name was displayed in the caller ID. "What's up?"

"I'm done for the day. Come take me away."

"Hang on." I turned to Larry. "You're burned out and Jill's ready to be picked up. Let's go back to the park."

Larry looked relieved as he turned west.

"We're on our way. Would you mind stopping at a couple bars on the way back to the hotel?"

"I need a shower, but if you don't mind riding around with a sweaty ranger, let's do it."

I disconnected and we drove in silence for a few minutes. Larry glanced at me. "That comment about spending hours talking to a murder suspect. You were exaggerating, right?"

"I've spent a whole night in a hot interview room with a murder suspect. We drank coffee and went over his story again and again until he tripped over his lies."

"No shit. Just like that? No rough stuff? No rubber hoses? He just couldn't keep his story straight and admitted he'd done it?"

"He had to work through it, but eventually he talked himself around in a circle and couldn't remember what he'd told me earlier so invented a new storyline. When I confronted him with the inconsistencies he nodded, knowing he'd messed up."

Larry blew out a deep breath. "I haven't got the patience to do that. It's as hard on you as it is on the guy you're grilling."

"I've spent a lot of hours in little rooms with lying idiots who were the scum of the earth. It's part of the job."

"I'll have to think about that for a while."

Jill was standing just inside the visitor center and walked out when Larry pulled up. "Hi guys. Are you making any progress?"

Larry nodded. "A little. We've identified the woman who owned the car, and she is probably Jane Doe. We went to the bar where the car was towed and showed the staff her driver's license picture, but no one recognized the dead woman." He looked at me. "I'm burned out. You guys will be back tomorrow, right?"

"Unless we find the murderer."

Larry rolled his eyes. "Good luck with that." He walked into the visitor center without looking back.

Jill walked with me to the rental car. "What's he going to do for the rest of the day?"

I unlocked the car and let the heat rush out before climbing in. "I don't know. I suppose he'll do whatever he does when we're not here."

"What's he like when you have him alone?" she asked as I drove away from the park entrance.

"He's the same with or without you. He's loud, impatient, and mouthy."

"Sounds like my day was better than yours."

I started the car. "Honey, anyone's day has been better than mine."

"What are we doing the rest of the day?"

"My gut says someone other than the owner moved the Jetta to where it was towed."

"Why?"

"I'm not sure. The place where the Jetta was found didn't look like a hangout for a twenty-something crowd and no one there recognized the woman's picture. The puzzle pieces aren't coming together for me. I think there's a bar somewhere that'll say, 'yeah, that's Madison. She hangs out here.'"

"Someplace other than where her car was parked before it was towed."

"Yeah."

"Is something making your 'Spidey sense' tingle."

I glanced at her. "Something like that."

"I guess that means we're talking to bartenders."

"Do you have something more pressing?"

"Not unless you're going to buy me a swimsuit so I can work on my tan by the pool."

I snorted. "You can't sit still long enough to read a book unless you're trapped in an airplane seat. You wouldn't lay by the pool working on your tan."

"Then we'd better go bar hopping."

Chapter 8

The bars around the west side of Florida City were quiet in the afternoon, populated by only a few hardcore drinkers. Jill and I showed the driver's license picture to a half dozen restaurant owners, four bartenders, and two dozen waitresses. None of them recognized Madison's picture. Most said they served so many faces that all but their regulars ran together. Three or four waitresses looked at the picture for a second. One stared at Madison's face. "She might've been here a couple months ago with a guy." I gave her my card and told her to call if she remembered any names.

The Reef Restaurant reminded me of a Port Aransas eatery that served the best shrimp on the island. The interior was weathered wood. The walls were covered with old portholes and glass balls from Japanese trawler nets. Wooden slatted crab traps, hung from the ceiling. The décor seemed odd for a place an hour from the nearest salt water. Two men sat together at the bar drinking draft beer and the rest of the bar, assorted tables, and booths were empty. The bartender was washing glasses and hanging them from an overhead rack. He turned and threw a drying rag over his shoulder when we walked in.

"What'll you have?" he asked with a thick southern drawl.

I set my park service ID on the bar and handed him Madison's picture. "We're trying to identify the woman in this photo."

He studied the photo for a second and handed it back. "She looks kinda familiar."

Jill perked up. "When was she here?"

The bartender smiled. "I get some rangers in here drinking after their shift, but I've never had Yankee Park Service investigators. What's up?"

I took the picture back and put it in my shirt pocket. "We found a woman's body in the park a couple days ago and we think it's this woman. We're trying to determine when she died and if she was with anyone the night she was killed."

"You'd best talk to Carol, my Yankee waitress. She probably served her and would know more about that than me. Besides, she might be able to understand your accent. Are you from Wisconsin or something?"

I smiled. "I'm from Minnesota and my partner is from South Dakota."

"I saw that Fargo movie, 'yah sure, you betcha.'"

Jill smiled. "You know that we don't really talk like that."

The bartender leaned on the bar. "You didn't say those words, but you sure as hell have that accent. Eh!"

Jill shook her head. "Eh is a Canadian expression."

"And how far from Canada did you live?"

Jill smiled. "North Dakota is in between."

The bartender laughed. "And what's there, honey, two cows and a wheat field? And your partner is from Minnesota. That touches the Canadian border. I've heard that northern Minnesotans speak Canadian."

"The Canadians speak English, just like you and me," I said, getting into the discussion.

The bartender shoved my ID back to me. "Whatever. You can talk about it with my waitress. She's from St. Paul and can probably understand you. Her name is Carol Martin."

I froze for a beat. "Carol Martin, from St. Paul? I might've known her."

"Somehow, I'm not surprised. What's the population of St. Paul, four hundred?"

"How did you hire a waitress from Minnesota?" Jill asked.

The bartender smiled. "If you're around here very long, you're going to see a whole lot of self-absorbed people who are trying to look young, rich, or both, trying to hookup with someone else who is rich, young, or both. They don't make reliable workers and quit, or just stop showing up, just about the time they know enough to be useful. I've had a few employees from the Midwest, and they understand what work is, and that they need to show up at the same time every day and work all the way to the end of their shift. Carol is a little older than my clientele and crusty, but she's reliable and good. She's worked here for five years, and that's about four and a half years longer than anyone else. I pay her five bucks an hour more than my competition pays because she's that valuable to me."

"When is she scheduled to work again?"

"She'll be back for the afterwork rush."

I glanced over the top row of bottles and saw a tiny hole with a wire sticking out. "No security camera?"

"Nah, I've never seen the value. Anyone who's ever robbed me was wearing a cap and face cover. The cops never caught them. When the last camera broke, I didn't replace it."

We walked to the car in silence. Inside Jill turned to me, "Why did you arrest this Carol person?"

"I never arrested her. If it's the same woman, she hung out at a bar I used to frequent when I was a young cop. I think she was a waitress at a hamburger joint and she'd walk over to the bar to unwind after her shift. The odds of me running into a waitress I knew from St. Paul are infinitesimal."

"A big word to divert me from the fact that we're probably going to meet one of your bar buddies. Is she cute? Did you more than hang out at the bar with her?"

"Hey, she was at the bar. So was I. We didn't date." I paused. "Am I detecting jealousy?"

"No. What you did twenty years ago has nothing to do with who you are today. I'm simply curious about what we're walking into."

"It's probably not the same person. If it is, she's spent her whole life somewhere else and there was nothing between us."

* * *

The bartender at The Reef gave us vague directions to an older area of south Florida City. The streets narrowed until they were unpaved and barely wide enough for two cars, then so narrow we had to edge onto the thin grass of the yards to meet an oncoming car. As the bartender promised, we found a distinctive aging Chevy Citation, painted lime green, parked beside a tired white trailer with rusty streaks running down from each screw. The car made me flashback to my early years as a cop. There weren't any cars of that vintage left in Minnesota, all the rest having succumbed to the salt used to melt the ice on the winter roads. The Citations in Minnesota had all crumbled into rusting junkyard heaps.

Jill looked around as we got out of the rental car. "I understand how tornadoes wipe out communities like this. There are hundreds of old trailers here that'd blow away in a South Dakota blizzard. If not for the palm trees, this place would be trailer hell."

I led her to weathered wooden steps and knocked on the door. The murmur of televisions came from inside and from a neighboring trailer. Further down the road a drunk man and woman were yelling at each other, their slurred words echoing through the trailers and mingling with the hum of dozens of window air-conditioners. My knock sounded like I was hitting an empty tuna can with my knuckle.

A short gray-haired woman pulled the door open, "What?" she asked as the smell of cigarette smoke hit my nose. She was no-nonsense and quickly glanced at my badge and sidearm. Her eyes focused past me, sizing up Jill.

"I'm Doug Fletcher." I paused, looking at the woman's face, lined prematurely by decades of cigarettes and hard life. "You're

Carol Martin. We hung out together at the Golden Gopher Bar when I was a rookie cop."

Carol studied my face for a moment, then she smiled and pushed open the door. She nodded toward a small kitchen table straight ahead of us, then walked into the living room and turned off an old television. She stubbed out a cigarette in an ashtray on the table next to a recliner. We sat on vinyl covered chairs built on chrome tubes that were another throwback to my youth. The green vinyl matched the Formica tabletop. When we were seated, Carol went past us into a tiny, neat clean kitchen. Carol was short, maybe five-one, and she slid a footstool over to the cabinet and took down a tube of three plastic Solo cups. From a different cupboard came a bottle of Jameson's Irish Whiskey.

"Sorry, but I don't get many guests, so my hospitality is limited." She turned and hacked into her elbow. The cough sounded like a piece of lung would fly out at any second. Catching her breath, she popped ice cubes out of an aluminum tray and threw a few into each cup. Carol set the cups and whiskey on the table and brought three cans of diet Coke from the humming refrigerator.

The sound of the fighting neighbors drifted in through open windows. Jill glanced at the screen door. "Should we go over and break up the fight?"

Carol glanced at the door. "Nah. They always fight when they can afford to get drunk. They do this all the time, honey. Everyone does. They'll yell and curse, but one of them will pass out and it'll be over.

"This place is a shithole and depressing as hell. We cope and eke out a living. When we get a few spare bucks, we buy a bottle of booze and get drunk to forget about having to live in a trailer park full of cockroaches as big as your hand and a yard with snakes as big around as your leg."

Carol poured two glasses more than half full of whiskey and slid the bottle to Jill. She popped a soda can and splashed a tablespoon of diet Coke into two glasses, then pushed one in front of me. "The Doug Fletcher I knew drank like a fish."

They say aromas from your past can evoke memories stronger than any visual stimulus. Jill's mother baking bread takes me back to my youth, the happy time before my father died when Mom used to bake every week. The smell of Carol's whiskey took me back to a smoky bar just outside of downtown St. Paul. The owner, George, was a gruff guy who knew the local riffraff and ran them out with a string of profanity learned at Marine Corps boot camp. The aroma of his homemade chili dogs drifted

155

into my mind, along with the laughter of drunks shrouded in cigarette smoke haze.

Carol picked up her plastic cup and drank down a quarter of it. She looked at me, then my cup, visually laying down the challenge.

Jill reached out and took my cup of Jameson's and drank a swallow. She set the cup down, then poured diet Coke over the ice in the third cup, setting it in front of me. "That Doug Fletcher doesn't exist anymore." She picked up her drink and took another swallow. "I'm Jill Fletcher, the one who loves him and helps him stay sober."

Carol stared at Jill for a second, then picked up her cup and held it like a toast. "I wished I'd met someone like you, someone who could've taken me away from this stinking place and straightened me out."

Jill lifted her cup and touched the rolled plastic edge to Carol's. "Amen."

Carol looked at me. "Are you going to drink that soda?"

I lifted my cup and touched it to hers, then to Jill's. "How about a toast to George, the Golden Gopher Bar, and chili dogs."

Carol started laughing, which precipitated another round of coughing. She spilled some of her drink. Jill jumped up and got a sponge from the sink to mop up the puddle on the table.

"Honey, you look like quite a woman," Carol said. "I bet you don't take shit from anybody."

Jill smiled. "Doug has a pretty good line of B.S. that I've been taking for a couple of years."

Carol nodded. "I had a husband like that for a couple years, but Ovid had a heart attack in '98 and died. I decided if I didn't remarry, I wouldn't have to share my booze with another drunk." Carol took a third drag on her drink, draining the glass. She poured more whiskey and skipped the diet Coke, then slid the bottle toward Jill. "You two didn't come down here from Minnesota to reminisce about the bad old days."

I drank some soda from the sweating red cup. "A woman's body was dumped in Everglades National Park last week. Jill and I are park service investigators. We know who she is, but we're trying to find out what happened before she died." I pulled Madison's license photo out of my shirt pocket and handed it to Carol. "Do you recognize her?"

Carol glanced at the picture and shook her head. "I don't know."

"Please look again. We're trying to solve her murder."

Carol slid the picture across the table and looked at it again. "She's dead?" She shuddered and took another drink from her cup.

"The woman we found in the swamp was dark-haired and in her early twenties."

Carol continued to look at the picture. "Can't you tell if it's her from the picture?"

Jill shook her head and the meaning hit Carol. "Oh. She was…" She slid the picture back to me. "She came in a couple nights with a date, then didn't show up anymore. They're not regulars, just folks hitting the bars."

"Did you see him alone after that?" I asked.

Carol swirled her drink, the ice cubes long gone. "No, but I saw her alone one night. The last night before they were gone."

Jill glanced at me. "You saw *her* alone?"

"Yeah. It was strange. She was alone in a booth. She kept looking at the door, like she was meeting somebody. The nights she came in with him she was pouring down expensive Scotch on the rocks, and he was drinking Coors Light." Carol looked between us. "I serve drinks and I get tips based on remembering what people drink."

"And the guy didn't show that last night?"

"No, the woman just sat there looking around and sipping Scotch."

Jill sipped at the drink Carol had mixed; a cup of whiskey on two ice cubes and a splash of diet Coke. She looked like the one drink was going to put her under the table. "What time did she leave the bar?"

"Close to last call. Maybe one or so. I remember her ordering one last drink and giving me a twenty."

"Then she walked out alone?" Jill asked.

Carol stopped and stared at her cup for a moment, thinking. "No, another woman who'd been drinking alone at the bar joined her in a booth for a couple of minutes. I thought they might order again at last call, but they waved me off. They talked for a while, downed their drinks, and left together."

Jill pushed the last of her drink away. "Describe the other woman."

"I remember people by their liquor. The woman at the bar was kind of looking around like she was hoping for a hook-up. Over the years I've developed intuition about the people who are sitting alone. Some are hard drinkers and just want their booze and aren't into the social scene. Others are drowning their sorrows and want to talk. That woman was looking for a hook-up, eyeing the people coming and going like she was measuring them up."

"Physically, what did she look like?"

Carol thought. "Dark, short hair. Medium height. She wasn't movie-star pretty, but cute. She wasn't wearing a lot of makeup."

"How old do you think the two women were?"

"The Scotch drinker was early twenties, and the boulevardier drinker was thirty or so. Old enough so I didn't need to card her." Carol thought about what she'd said, then clarified her comments. "Both women were cute. They might've been sisters—dark-haired and attractive."

"What's a boulevardier?" Jill asked.

"It's a bourbon drink with dry vermouth and Campari. They're pretty and a little sweet, with a lot of booze. Our younger crowd is into them. The woman at the bar had been nursing one drink all evening."

Jill had consumed more alcohol than she was accustomed to and was rambling, asking about the drinks and not the women. Then I realized she was taking Carol into familiar territory, comfortable memories. Carol knew people by what they drank.

"So, they had a drink together. Then what?"

Carol shrugged. "They left. The bar was closing."

"Did they leave together?"

"Yeah," Carol said, the memory coming back. "They left arm in arm. I thought maybe they'd switched teams," Carol

160

looked at us to see if we'd understood her euphemism for going from heterosexual to bisexual or lesbian. "The woman drinking boulevardiers was leaning on the younger woman like she was 'into' her, and they were going somewhere for the night."

Jill nodded. "So, they were happily leaving together."

Carol considered that thought. "You know, the younger woman, the Scotch drinker, staggered a bit. She was leaning into the other woman like she'd had too many drinks."

"Do you think she was drunk?"

Carol frowned. "She'd been with some friends earlier and had like four or five drinks over a couple hours. I would've told the bartender if I thought she was too drunk to drive, and he would've paid an Uber to take her home."

"Why would she stagger?" I asked.

"I don't know. Maybe she was a short-hitter who couldn't hold her booze."

"Was she alone or in a group the other times you saw her?" Jill asked.

"She was in here a couple times with a guy in uniform who drank Coors Light. They seemed like a couple."

"In uniform, like a cop?" I asked.

Carol shook her head. "No badge. Maybe like a paramedic or fireman."

I steered the conversation back. "So, they walked out together, the younger woman staggering. Did you go out and see them get into a car?"

"It was last call, and I was busy. The drunk seemed like she had a safe ride with the other woman, so I kept working."

Jill frowned. "The younger woman, the one drinking Scotch, hadn't consumed enough to be drunk. Do you think the woman from the bar slipped something in her drink?"

Carol looked at me. "You know, I've seen a few guys hanging with women who were suddenly too drunk. I have the bartender call the cops and we keep them from leaving together." Carol paused. "Shit. It never crossed my mind that a woman would roofie another woman. But you're right, she acted too drunk. I wonder."

Jill put her hand on Carol's arm. "Describe the younger woman again."

"I don't know. She was taller than me, but most people are. She was maybe five-six, with kind of long dark hair. She was slender, cute, you know, not a knockout, but she had a nice figure and caught a few eyes."

"Did you notice if she had a tattoo? A Panama Beach license plate."

"Phew! Every other woman has one of those, so no, I don't notice any of them unless they're really pretty or unusual."

"Jane Doe had a porpoise jumping out of her waistband."

Carol laughed. "Tramp stamp. I see a dozen of them a night. All the younger women seem to be into jumping dolphins and swarming butterflies on their lower backs."

Jill leaned forward. "Can you remember anything else? Did she have keys, a cell phone, a necklace, piercings, earrings, nose rings, other jewelry?"

Carol thought. "Everyone has a cell phone and car keys. Their shorts and jeans are too tight to keep them in their pockets, so they set them on the tabletop or bar. They all have pierced ears. I don't notice earrings unless they're like five carat diamonds, and every third woman has a piercing of some kind: belly buttons, noses, eyebrows, titty rings. They all run together in my mind unless they're really gaudy, infected, or distasteful." Carol paused. "The other woman, the older one, was wearing a wedding band. I remember because she'd been cozy with a Latin guy early in the week and I thought they were probably a couple. She's wearing what I figured was his wedding ring, then he doesn't show up that one night, and she's hooking up with a younger woman. I remember thinking that was odd."

I perked up. "A Latin guy? Anything special about him?"

"He was a looker. I mean the kind of guy who turns women's heads. Dressed nicer than the average drinker."

"Did they come in together the night she left with the other woman?"

"I was waiting on a table and saw them sitting at the bar. He had one top-shelf rum on the rocks and was gone."

Jill went back to the woman in the booth. "But the younger woman, the one drinking Scotch, wasn't wearing a ring?"

Carol shook her head. "No ring. That was what made me think they were hooking up for the night. I see that happen a lot. Married guys picking up single women or cougars trolling the young studs."

"Have you seen the younger woman's boyfriend since she hooked up with the other woman, the guy who drinks Coors Light?"

Carol emptied her drink. "Not since then."

Jill tipped her plastic cup toward Carol. "You said those two weren't that different in age."

"Like I said, they looked like sisters and were both in their twenties, and no more than thirty."

Jill's eyes lit up. "Did you card them?"

"The younger one, I did. We can lose our liquor license if we serve underaged people."

"Do you remember her name?"

"I don't look at names, just birthdates. I check to make sure she was born after 2001. She pulled her license out of her back pocket with a debit card and some cash. She was old enough to be served. That's all I remember."

I got excited. "Did she pay for her drinks with a debit card? Is there a slip with her name?"

"Cash. And she was stingy with her tips."

"Does her boyfriend, the paramedic, come in regularly?"

"He sometimes comes in with his crew."

"Describe him."

"He's tall; over six feet. Blond with a crew cut. Wears a blue outfit," Carol paused, then got a look of remembrance, "He has a paramedic shoulder patch and pants with all the side pockets for carrying medical stuff. Good looking kid. He and his buddies are good tippers, so I give them really good service. He has a patch on his shirt that says, Baxter. His buddies call him Josh."

Jill stood, using the table to steady herself. "Thanks."

I got up and steadied Jill. "Are you working tonight, Carol?"

She glanced at the kitchen clock. "Oh hell, I've got to be there in ten minutes. You guys get out of here so I can change."

I stood and hugged her. "It's nice to see you again."

Carol held the hug a beat too long, then released me. Her eyes misted over. "Doug, honey, you might've been the one who got away." She turned and hugged Jill. "You treat him right. He's a hell of a nice guy. He drove me home from a bar a few nights and never even hinted at coming up for a nightcap."

"I didn't want to take advantage of an inebriated woman."

Carol pushed us toward the door. "You were too much of a straight arrow anyway. I liked bad boys."

Jill touched Carol's arm as we stepped out. "I'm happy with my boy scout. I'm glad you threw him back into the pool."

The car was blistering hot in the afternoon sun. We sat with the air-conditioning running, waiting for the steering wheel to cool off enough to touch it without burning my hand.

Jill leaned back. "You talked to the boyfriend, Josh."

"Larry and I interviewed him at the fire station."

"All the pieces fit."

I turned toward her. "So, I'm a boy scout?"

Jill leaned over and pulled me close. "You are."

"What makes me a boy scout?"

You drove Carol home when she was drunk, and never tried to take advantage of the situation. I threw myself at you in your townhouse and you offered to turn on an old movie if I was getting cold feet. That's a boy scout."

I put my arm over her shoulders and pulled her close. "That's being a gentleman."

"I imagine it's cost you a few hookups over the years."

"The bars are full of badge bunnies. I tried to avoid them."

"Badge bunnies?"

"Women who want to hop into bed with a cop."

"I wasn't a badge bunny."

I shook my head. "No, you played hard to get. I found that irresistible."

Jill snorted. "I wasn't playing at anything. I had to sort out my feelings from my head." She paused and took a breath. "I passed up a few propositions over the years, too."

I looked into her eyes and squeezed her hand. "I have no regrets about ignoring the badge bunnies. It got me to the important one, you." Jill slid back and buckled her seatbelt and I pulled onto the street. "Let's eat at the seafood place. Krista reserved a table for us, and tonight's special is red snapper."

Jill put her hand on my thigh. "You'd pick the restaurant special over an evening in bed with your wife."

"You're drunk."

Jill shook her head. "You are such a boy scout. You're still unwilling to take advantage of an inebriated woman."

I smiled at her. "You've helped me overcome that reluctance."

Halfway to the hotel something struck me. "The woman in the booth was Madison Wirth. Carol said she had her ID and cash in her back pocket. Her cell phone and keys were on the table. Jane Doe's pockets were empty."

Jill looked at me. "She was probably robbed when she was drugged."

"Or, whoever dumped her in the swamp didn't want us to identify her. Carol said young women wear their jeans so tight they can't put keys or cell phones in their pockets. That means her jeans were too tight for her ID and debit card to accidentally fall out."

Jill put her hand on the inside of my thigh. "I'd like to focus on something besides a dead woman and dragging stinky stuff out of a swamp."

"I'm sorry, but when the pieces start to line up…"

"Honey, they'll still be there in the morning. My lust is going to be a headache in an hour."

"A good cop runs a case hard."

"And a good husband knows how to put the day behind him and when he should hang up his gun belt."

I flashed back to my marriage to Sherry and the nights I was too engrossed in my job to come home or attend functions with her. I reached down and squeezed Jill's hand. "You're right. I'm here."

Jill patted my leg. "You're catching on. You didn't even say, 'yes dear.'"

I parked in the hotel lot and turned to Jill, who seemed surprised. "Thanks for helping me get my priorities right." I kissed her deeply. She pulled my head to her. I twisted my hips, so my pistol wasn't digging into my side and hit the horn. "Maybe we should get a room."

"Yeah, I've outgrown the stage where necking at the drive-in movie is fun."

Jill opened her car door and started to get out, then turned when she realized I hadn't opened my door. "What's the matter?"

"I have to wait a minute. It'd be a little embarrassing to walk into the lobby in my current state."

She looked at me, then her eyes drifted down to my crotch. She broke out laughing. "I'm glad I can still get your motor running."

I got out of the car and leaned against the door. "Give me a second to get back to idle."

She walked toward the hotel and looked over her shoulder. "I'll be in the room whenever you decide it's safe to walk through the lobby."

I walked into the hotel about five minutes later. Margot, the concierge, waved at me. "I scored seven o'clock reservations for you at Walton's Steak House. I hope that works. It's nearly impossible to get reservations there less than two weeks out."

The clock on her desk said 4:35. "That should be good. Is there a dress code?"

Margot smiled and shook her head. "Only a shirt and shoes."

I nodded, then remembered Krista's invitation. "Krista made reservations for us at the seafood restaurant for tonight. Can you call Krista and change that reservation to tomorrow?"

Margot picked up her phone. "No problem. Is six o'clock okay?"

I heard the shower running when I unlocked the hotel room door. Jill's clothes, usually set aside neatly, were strewn on the floor. I was under the sheets when Jill walked out of the bathroom wrapped in a towel. Her skin was pink from the hot shower, and she had a glow from the potent drink at Carol's trailer. As usual, she slipped under the sheets before pulling the towel off and throwing it on the floor.

"You're modest even when you're drunk."

"I'm not drunk! I'm mildly inebriated."

"Margot said…"

Jill ran her fingers through my chest hair. "There should be only one woman on your mind right now."

I pulled her close and said to myself, *Fletcher, the best thing that ever happened to you is lying next to you and she wants to make love. For once in your life, focus on what's important.*

Chapter 9

We ate breakfast at the hotel and drove to the park as the day started to heat up. Larry was just getting out of his car when we pulled into the nearly empty parking lot. He smiled and looked freshly pressed in his park service uniform. I felt soggy in my wrinkled khaki pants and golf shirt.

"Hey, Fletchers, what's the plan for today?"

Jill turned toward the visitor center. "I'll interview rangers while you guys play detective."

Larry seemed okay with that plan. He led me to a park service SUV in the back row of the parking lot and unlocked it. "Did you guys do any sightseeing last night?"

"Jill was feeling a little wilted, so we went back to the hotel and crashed for a while, then went to Walton's for steak."

"The heat and humidity can get to you here. We get a few Yankees with heatstroke every year. You're just not accustomed to Florida."

"You're from New Jersey, Larry. Doesn't that make you a Yankee?"

"I've acclimated."

We got in the SUV and Larry started the engine. He looked at me while waiting for the steering wheel to cool. "Are you ever at a dead end? I keep thinking we're done, yet you keep throwing out new angles to look at. You're the Energizer Bunny of investigations."

"I hit the wall on one lead, but we've got a bunch of balls in the air, and I don't give up until they're all caught or dropped."

"So, what are we doing?"

"We're going to re-interview Madison's roommate."

Larry pulled onto the road and turned toward Florida City. "We already talked to her. What was her name, Betsy or Betty?"

"Her name was Britney Allen."

Larry made a dismissive gesture.

"Listen, Larry, part of being an effective interviewer is connecting with the person you're interviewing. The first step is to address them by their name."

"I didn't think we'd ever see her again, so I blew her name off." When I didn't respond he glanced at me. "What?"

"I interview people two, three, four times. That's how you pick up inconsistencies in their stories. If they're lying to you, they'll forget their previous version. On the other hand, if someone gives you the same, pat, detailed responses each time, you know they've rehearsed and they're lying."

"You get off on this, don't you?"

"I get off on putting bad guys in jail. So, yes, I get off on it."

Larry thought about that on our return trip to Madison and Britney's apartment. Britney answered the door quickly, as if she were expecting someone. We were obviously not who she expected, and it showed on her face.

"Do you have a couple minutes for more questions?"

Britney glanced behind us. "Can you be quick?" She asked, not inviting us in. The apartment was much as it had been on our previous visit with the addition of the faint smell of marijuana smoke.

"Can we come in?" I asked.

"Listen, my boyfriend will be back in a couple minutes and…he might freak if he sees cops here."

"Guilty conscience?" I asked.

"He spent a few months in jail for computer hacking and now he's paranoid."

Larry sniffed the air. "Are you sure he's not paranoid about getting caught carrying? Possession of marijuana is probably a probation violation."

Britney frowned. "Do you have a question, or did you just come here to hassle us?"

"Madison's parents live in Bee Ridge. The medical examiner spoke with them, and they'll be in contact with you to pick up her stuff."

Britney shrugged. "That's it? You could've called."

"We also spoke with Josh, her boyfriend. He was supposed to meet her in a bar the night she disappeared."

"And that affects me how?"

Something about Britney's responses were off, but I couldn't decide if it was because she was waiting for her boyfriend who might, or might not, be bringing a stash of marijuana. Or if she was hiding something else. I decided to try a gambit. "Maddie's parents asked us to pick up her credit cards so they could close the accounts."

Britney hesitated a second too long. "She must've had them with her."

"They were in her room when we were here last time." I took a step to get around her and Britney cut me off. "I think you're mistaken, and I'd like you to leave."

A key rattled in the door behind us. I nodded for Larry, who was in uniform, to step behind the door. I stepped aside, taking Britney by the elbow. A young gaunt guy with straggling brown hair, a long t-shirt with a band logo, and surfer shorts stepped in with shopping bags in one arm and a case of Corona beer in his other hand. He

175

opened his mouth to say something to me, but Larry stepped behind him and lifted the shopping bags from his arm. "Hey!"

Larry set the bags on the floor and squatted down. He pulled out a receipt and flipped it to read the top. He looked up at me. "Madison Wirth paid for these groceries."

The guy let go of the beer and spun to go out the door. Larry reached out and slapped the guy's ankle which caused him to miss a step and catch his toes behind his other leg. I put my hand on Britney's arm and gently restrained her. Larry was out the door and cuffing the guy in one second.

"Well, Britney, would you care to explain why you're using Maddie's charge card?"

Britney was sharp. "She still owes me two months' rent."

I took handcuffs out of my back pocket. "And you thought no one would notice if you ran up a bunch of charges on her card?"

Larry lifted the guy to his feet. "Britney said no one would notice. I was just…"

"Shut up, Aaron," Britney hissed.

"Larry, take Aaron into the hall and read him his Miranda rights. I'll talk to the brains of the operation."

I snapped the cuffs on Britney's wrists. There's something about hearing cuffs click on your wrists that gives people that "come to Jesus" feeling and the need to confess and cleanse their souls. Britney was the brains and made the wise decision to throw her boyfriend under the bus.

"It was Aaron's idea. Get me a deal and I'll testify."

I smiled. "That was quick."

"Aaron's on probation. They'll revoke his probation and he'll go back to jail until the trial." When I didn't react, she tried a different tactic. "I didn't even know he had Maddie's credit cards. He must've found them in her room."

"I find it hard to believe Aaron is smart enough to do anything more challenging than lighting a joint. On the other hand, you're day-trading stocks. Have you had some setbacks? Why would you need Maddie's credit cards?"

Britney went on a rant about being abused by Aaron and making allegations about his online activities and more. I listened to her and looked at her pinpoint pupils, runny nose, and frantic search for a scenario I'd buy. She darted from one accusation against Aaron to the next. I put up my hand to stop her.

"Where's Aaron's stash?"

"You can't question me. I know my rights."

"You offered to testify against Aaron. I'd have a better case if I added drug charges to the credit card theft."

Britney froze. I could almost hear the gears turning as she ran through options. "Yeah. Um, he keeps it at his place."

"There aren't any drugs here?"

"Um, no."

"Do I have permission to search?"

"I told you, there's nothing here."

"Then you shouldn't be concerned about a search."

"I have confidential…financial stuff."

I took out my cell phone and dialed 911. Britney listened to me explain who I was, give my badge number, and request a FCPD police cruiser for an arrest.

"You need them to arrest Aaron, right?"

I shook my head. "Aaron is a patsy. They're going to arrest you, then they'll lock the apartment until they can get a search warrant. They'll keep you and Aaron separated. I imagine Aaron will be encouraged to explain the charge cards, drugs, and maybe even your online trading."

Britney broke into tears. After a few moments she looked up, surprised that I was smiling. "What?"

"I've been played by better actors than you. Keep trying. I'm curious to see what else you can dream up."

"Fuck you."

"Excuse me. That's hardly appropriate language for a young woman."

"You're a park ranger. You have no jurisdiction here."

"Really? That's your play? I'm a federal law enforcement officer who's sworn to uphold the laws of the United States. Last time I checked; Florida was still part of the U.S."

"I can say anything, and you won't be able to use it in court. You haven't read my Miranda rights and it'll be your word against mine."

"You haven't been arrested. Everything you've told me has been my discussion with a material witness to the theft of Maddie's charge cards."

"Maddie's credit cards were just sitting there. I'll testify that Aaron stole them. He used them to buy drugs and groceries. Will that get me off?"

"Tell me about Maddie's disappearance. Did Aaron have anything to do with that?"

Britney froze. "Um, I don't think so."

"Tell me about the night Maddie disappeared."

"We don't talk a lot. I mean, we didn't talk a lot. She worked, came home, changed, and left. I'd hear her unlock the door and shower when she came home after the bars closed. She went out like seven nights a week."

"Did you ever go with her?"

"I'm not into the clubbing scene."

179

"You weren't surprised when she didn't come back to the apartment?"

Britney shook her head. "She stays over at her boyfriend's place a few nights a week. So no, I wasn't concerned when she was gone."

"And you didn't know she was dead until we interviewed you?"

"No. I mean it had been almost a week and that was unusual. I thought maybe she'd gone to visit her folks."

"But you and Aaron had nothing to do with Maddie's death."

"Are you kidding? No! Aaron and I do our thing and she's got her own plans. We just share the place to split the rent."

I pushed the front door open. "Larry, bring Aaron in here and uncuff him."

Aaron rubbed his wrists. "That was harsh. What's with you guys?"

I put out my hand. "Give me Maddie's credit and debit cards."

Aaron looked at Britney, who nodded. He pulled two cards out of his back pocket and handed them to me. "Now what?"

"How much have you charged on them?"

Aaron shrugged. "Just some groceries and beer. Maybe a hundred and fifty bucks."

I put the cards in my pocket. "I'll tell Maddie's parents you owe them money."

Britney flared. "Maddie owes me like four hundred bucks in rent!"

I put up my hands. "You can negotiate that with Maddie's parents. Be happy we're not arresting you."

Larry and I walked away. I waited until I heard the apartment door close behind us. "Larry, the purchaser's name isn't on a charge card receipt."

Larry smiled at me. "They didn't know that."

I slapped his shoulder. "You're devious. Maybe you'll be a good cop yet."

"Hey, I'm already a good cop."

We opened the SUV's doors and stood outside it waiting for the air-conditioner to start cooling the interior. A FCPD car stopped behind us. "You guys called for backup?"

I walked to the car door and squatted down. I handed the stolen charge cards to the young FCPD officer and told him about Britney and Aaron.

The cop fingered the charge cards as I spoke. "You don't think they're your murder suspects?"

"I think they're small-time opportunists, not killers. You should talk to them about the smell of marijuana smoke in the apartment and see where that goes."

The cop nodded and pocketed the cards. "I'll talk to them."

Larry and I got in the park service SUV that had cooled enough to allow Larry to touch the steering wheel. "We're out of things to do now, right?"

"What did you learn from the Youngstown wellness check?"

"They haven't called me back yet."

"How long were you going to wait for the callback?"

Larry took out his cell phone and searched his call history. He was getting transferred between people when we got into the SUV. "Hang on, I'm putting you on speaker. Sergeant Harder, I'm here with Inspector Fletcher. Please repeat what happened at Andrea Arnot's apartment when you did the wellness check."

"There was no answer when we knocked, so we found the building superintendent and explained that you'd contacted us and wanted to check on her. The super said Arnot lived alone and let us in while she watched. The apartment was empty, clean, like someone had picked up before leaving for a trip, which is what the super told us was the case. There were some clothes on the bedroom floor and others neatly folded on the bed, like she'd decided not to pack them. There was a used towel hanging on the shower rod, partial bottles of shampoo and conditioner, empty toothbrush holder, partial tube of toothpaste, and facial moisturizer with the lid ajar.

"The super took us to a neighbor who was cat-sitting for Arnot. The cat sitter was mildly concerned. Arnot was supposed to return yesterday but the sitter figured there had been flight delays. That's about it."

"Sergeant, this is Fletcher. Did either the super or the neighbor mention a boyfriend, eloping, or a destination wedding?"

"Neither of them said anything about a man in Arnot's life. I gotta tell you, her place looked like a woman decorated it. There was no manly stuff anywhere, not in the decorating. No men's deodorant, shaving supplies, nor spare toothbrush in the bathroom. Everything in the whole apartment was womanly and there were only women's clothes in the closets."

"Did you look in the cabinets and dressers?"

"No. It was a wellness check, not a search. The super was behind us every step we made, and she complained when I opened the closet and refrigerator."

"Did it appear she planned to return?"

"She left her cat with a neighbor with a week's food and there was still stuff in the refrigerator freezer. So, yeah, it looks like she's coming back." He paused. "What do you know that we weren't told?"

"We recovered a body in the Everglades. The woman was wearing a wedding ring with what appear to be Arnot's initials, and we found a marriage license for Andrea Arnot, of Youngstown, and Juan Castro, of Cuba. We've identified the dead woman, and she's not Arnot, but it looks like someone wants us to think it was Andrea."

"Fletcher, there's something fishy. I got Arnot's work number from the super and asked when they expected her back from vacation. The woman who answered the phone put me on hold. Some guy answered and asked why I was inquiring, then he told me she was no longer employed there. I asked when she'd left, and he said a while ago but wouldn't give me a date."

"Has anyone reported her missing, Sergeant?"

"That's why I hadn't called Ranger Marconi. I did an online query and got nothing. Then I tried to pull up her criminal record and got a pop-up directing me to the U.S. Attorney's office."

"Did you call the U.S. Attorney?"

"Ah, no. I didn't see any upside to stirring that beehive."

I thanked Sergeant Harder, and Larry ended the call. "What do you make of that?" Larry asked.

"I think Harder put it well when he said it was strange. Her work says she's no longer employed there, but her super and neighbor thought she was coming back in a week, but is late. No one has reported her missing, but the U.S. Attorney wants to know if someone is looking for her record. It's odd that no one knew she was getting married."

"What does it mean?"

"It means Arnot was a mysterious woman."

Larry waved off my comment. "What's it mean to us? I mean in terms of our investigation?"

"Like Harder said, the pieces don't add up."

* * *

Larry left for home before I walked into the headquarters building. Jill was in the superintendent's office. Jack looked annoyed. "Sounds like my rangers scooped some stuff out of the swamp but there's no way to know if any of it means anything to your investigation."

I sat in the chair next to Jill. "That's the way it goes, Jack. We get a bunch of clues that may or may not connect to the case. We sort them, pull out the ones that fit, set the others aside, and forge ahead."

Jack wasn't convinced. "I hate to waste your time."

Jill leaned forward and put her hands on Jack's desk. "What's with you, Jack? You find a dead woman inside the park, and it seems like it's a bother to try and determine who she is and what happened to her."

Jack leaned back. "She fell in the swamp, and it was probably an accident. I don't want to waste people's time chasing their tails."

"Jack, the woman was dead. She didn't drown. She'd been drugged. She was wearing a wedding ring with someone else's initials inside it. Her car was abandoned miles away, so she didn't walk here. It looks like she was murdered."

Jill was starting to heat up, so I jumped in to de-escalate. "We're here and it's our decision to pursue or drop the investigation. We have leads to follow and if we run out, we'll sit down and discuss ending the investigation. Can you live with that?"

"Well, sure. But it seems like…"

Jill stood. "It seems like you don't want this investigated. Is there a reason?"

Jack looked shocked. "No! It's just that park service budgets are getting slashed, and I don't want to spend a bunch of money beating a dead horse. That's all."

Jill crossed her arms. "Our salaries don't come out of your budget."

Larry got up. "No, but it comes out of someone's budget and…"

I cut him off. "Jack, someone up the chain of command thought we needed to be here, and he or she, wants this investigated. Do you know why we were requested? It's obviously not your priority."

Jack stepped around the desk and closed his office door. "I had to file a report when the body was found. As you know, that goes into the database and flags pop up on dozens of desks whenever there's a death in a park. My boss called and wanted to know who was going to investigate. I told her what I knew, that it appeared to be an accident and that we weren't going to investigate it. I thought the issue was closed, but apparently Hannah spoke with her boss, and someone decided the death required further investigation and they wanted you two, despite the park having our own law enforcement people."

"Larry told me about the hikers who've disappeared, and the investigation being turned over to the FBI. He doesn't know the status of that investigation. He told me he's never even asked about it."

Jack turned red. "It was my decision to hand the case to the FBI."

Jill leaned on his desk. "So, do you know the status of that investigation?"

"I assume the FBI is pursuing it and will notify us when they close the case."

187

Jill stood and closed her eyes. "You don't know what they're doing?"

"I haven't been updated recently."

"Have you had an update since they took over the case?" I asked.

Jack glared at me. "I don't recall."

Jill closed her eyes. "Jack, that's why we were summoned. Because you already have an open case you're not pursuing. Larry isn't interested in pursuing it. And someone is embarrassed that you're already sitting on your hands and didn't want another death to go uninvestigated." Jill paused. "I assume you had a discussion about this during your last performance review."

Jack's face reddened. "My performance reviews are none of your business."

"Did it ever occur to you that we might be here to save your job?" Jill asked.

Jack was speechless.

"Jack, I was the superintendent in Flagstaff when we lost a group of hikers. The investigation was taken out of my hands, I was put on leave and eventually was assigned as a ranger in Texas. You've lost three people and weren't even going to investigate the latest death."

I opened the door. "Are you looking for a new job yet?"

Jill stepped to the door and stopped. "You'd better hope we solve this, or you might find yourself guiding tours in Dry Tortugas National Park."

We were walking away from Jack's office when we heard his voice. "I'm going to report your threat."

I smiled at Jill as I held the visitor center door. "Who do you think he's going to call?"

"Probably the person who asked for our help. I imagine his complaint will fall on deaf ears."

"Or he'll be offered a different park position. Like guiding the bear tour at Denali."

Jill held the car door open, letting the hot air escape. "The tube of peanut butter crackers from the vending machine is gone. Feed me supper."

I started the engine and pressed the button for maximum air conditioning. "Seafood again?"

Jill got in the car and smiled. "You were reading my mind."

* * *

We were seated at one of Krista's tables and she swept up to us with two glasses of water. "You missed the red snapper last night. White wine for Doug and red for you, Jill?"

Jill smiled. "Perfect. What is tonight's special?"

Krista glanced around to see who was listening, then bent down. "The chef tried a new recipe for cioppino. He let us sample it and it's to die for. He probably has a couple bowls of it, but not enough to put it on the menu."

"What's cioppino?" I asked.

Jill waved off my question. "Bring it on."

Krista put her hand on my shoulder. "You'll want red wine. I'll bring a bottle of Argentine Malbec."

"You've had cioppino before?" I asked Jill.

"If Krista says, 'It's to die for,' I'm willing to take a chance."

Krista was back seconds later with our wine, a breadbasket and butter. "He's putting the mussels and shrimp in it. I'll bring it out as soon as they're done." She uncorked the wine and poured, knowing I wasn't interested in tasting it first.

Jill buttered a slice of bread as Krista swept away. "Anything else interesting today?"

"Madison's roommate was using her charge cards. She claims Maddie owed her rent, so I told her to work it out with Maddie's parents. The Youngstown cops did a wellness check on Andrea Arnot. Her apartment looked like she was coming back, but her work office said she wasn't employed there anymore. The U.S.

Attorney wants to talk to anyone who's looking for her."

Jill took a bite of bread. "Wow, that's a lot of information. What now?"

"I'm not sure yet." I broke off a piece of bread and remembered my personal call. "Mom called yesterday. Chet has a medical situation she wanted to discuss. I cut her off."

Jill sighed. "I know. She called me today and said you weren't helpful."

"And?"

"And I told her to call the doctor. I have no reference point for dealing with post-surgical prostate dribbling."

"Anything else?"

"She said Chet's feeling better and is moving around." Jill paused. "How was Larry?"

"I felt like I was training a rookie with a criminology degree but no practical experience to go with the classroom learning. Larry's an experienced cop but apparently skirted all the tough and meaningful parts of the job."

"That's disappointing. I'm surprised the park superintendent hasn't called him on his performance."

"He hasn't had anything challenging to investigate. The one missing person case was turned over to the FBI and he hasn't followed up since. I suppose Larry does okay driving around and writing speeding tickets, but the job is more than that."

Jill stared at me. "Someone up the chain of command knows, or we wouldn't have been called in. It wasn't Jack because he was as irritated as Larry that we'd gotten the call. How are we going to deal with it?"

"The same as if Larry was a rookie: We'll take it slow and hope I don't need him to cover my back."

Jill closed her eyes. "Let's leave him in the park. I'll ride with you."

"He knows the area and I hate driving in the traffic here. Besides, you can interview the rangers in the park without sounding threatening and cover whatever else comes up there."

"Are you sure?"

I nodded as Krista delivered two giant bowls of tomato-based seafood stew with shrimp floating on the surface and mussel shells peeking out of the broth. "Enjoy!"

Jill sniffed the steaming bowl and dipped a piece of bread into the broth. She took a bite and closed her eyes as she chewed. I watched her savor the bite and dipped some bread myself. The rich tomato, garlic and seafood flavors exploded on my taste buds, and I understood her quiet delight.

We ate in silence with neighboring tables asking their servers about our dishes.

I mopped the last juice with a slice of bread. "Are you comfortable with my plan for Larry?"

Jill stared at me, apparently thinking about her response. "Just remember what your mother said about leaving me a widow."

My mind flashed back to Texas and my mother's admonition about Jill waiting a lifetime for our marriage. Mom asked me to not leave her standing next to Jill when she was handed a triangle folded flag at my funeral. "This is basically a cold case. I don't see any scenario that would end with me being shot."

Jill leaned across the table. "You were the one who told me you never know when you'll need a gun, but when you do, you need it immediately and badly."

"I think I said that the time you don't have your gun is when you'll need it."

"Same difference." She paused. "And the same can be said of a partner. Will Larry be there when you need him to back you up? You'll need him immediately and badly. Will he be there?"

"Let's hope I don't have to find out."

Krista saw the bowls we'd wiped dry with bread. "I take it you liked the cioppino," she said, picking up the bowls.

Jill smiled. "You were right, it was heavenly."

"I'll be back in a second with lemon sorbet."

I was going to say I was too full for dessert, but Krista was gone before the words were out of my mouth. Jill leaned across the table and whispered, "You'd better leave her a tip as heavenly as the cioppino."

Chapter 10

The next morning Jill and I drove to the headquarters and walked inside. Larry's office light was on, but he wasn't physically at his desk. We walked to Jack's office where he was reading email on his computer.

"Good morning, Jack."

He blanked the screen and spun around at the sound of Jill's voice. He stared at us for a moment before speaking. "Close the door."

We walked in and I closed the door behind us. "I spoke with the regional superintendent after you left last night. He…let me recall his words. He'd like the investigation pursued with 'full vigor.'"

Jill glanced at me. "How do you feel about that?"

Jack cleared his throat. "I think that would be prudent."

Jill nodded. "Your neck is on the line."

Jack crossed his arms. "He convinced me that you two are uniquely qualified to handle this investigation."

"What about Larry?" I asked.

"He's at your disposal and…it'd be beneficial if you could teach him a few of your investigative techniques."

Jill stepped to the door and put her hand on the knob. "Jack, it's not my intention to ruin your career, but if you put up barriers to our investigation, I have no reservations about making a call or writing a scathing report."

Jack was pissed but controlled his temper. "I'm aware that you two have friends in high places. You'll have whatever you need from me for the remainder of your stay."

"I'd like to talk to all the rangers who were working in the days before the woman's body was discovered," Jill said. "Can you make a list of their names?"

Jack peeled off a Post-it note and picked up a pen. "Grab a cup of coffee, Jill, and I'll have a list for you in ten minutes." He looked up at me. "Larry's waiting for you."

Larry was chatting with a group of tourists in the visitor center when I walked out of Jack's office. He nodded to me and excused himself. "What's the plan for today?"

"We're going to the county garage to look at the Jetta."

Larry led me out of the cool visitor center. The sun was quickly taking the air from warm and damp to steamy. He drove

196

out of the parking lot and turned east, toward Florida City. "You said you were going to think about our next steps overnight. What's the plan?"

"Let's see if there's anything in the car that'll give us some direction."

"Like what?"

"Blood on the seats. A bloody tire iron or baseball bat in the trunk. A note that says Tony killed me."

Larry chuckled. "A note would make things so much easier."

"I've never found a note, but I've viewed a few security videos that were better than a note. Defense lawyers hate to see video of their defendants committing the crime. Those cases rarely make it to trial because showing a jury video of a crime is hard to overcome."

Larry drove in silence on the increasingly busy highway until he turned off onto a smaller road.

"Did Jack say anything to you this morning?" I asked.

"Yeah. It was sort of odd. I was getting coffee and he steered me into a corner. He asked how the investigation was going and I said, 'okay.' He nodded and told me to help as much as I could. I thought that was strange because that was what I'd been doing."

"We talked to him this morning and he seemed fired up about the investigation."

Larry's head bobbed. "Yeah, I guess that was it. He seemed bought-in this morning. I guess he thought about it overnight and was motivated to see progress."

* * *

Larry pulled into the parking lot of a utilitarian building that had a Miami-Dade County logo on the front. He led me to the garage doors in the rear and held the door. The interior was brightly lit, and several cars and pickups were parked inside. A BMW was being dismantled just inside the door and a stainless-steel table next to it was stacked with plastic bags of white powder.

Larry chuckled. "Looks like someone's not going to get their car back."

A tall man with salt and pepper hair, dressed in white disposable coveralls backed out of the BMW's trunk holding two bags of powder. He stacked the new bags on top of the others and stepped back. "Can I help you?"

I nodded to the Jetta parked on the opposite side of the garage. "We had the Jetta towed in."

The man peeled off purple gloves and set them on the mound of drugs. "I'm Tom Simpson."

We shook hands. "I'm Doug Fletcher and this is Larry Marconi."

Simpson walked across the garage to the Jetta. "The car's here. What's your plan?"

"I'd like to know if there's any blood on the interior."

Simpson looked at the car. "Let me see your search warrant."

"Exigent circumstances," Larry said. "The owner is missing, and we need to make sure she's not trapped in the trunk or buried under the fast-food wrappers in the car."

Simpson looked around the garage like he was trying to find something. "Huh, I don't see anyone dying or in imminent danger. No one's pounding on the inside of the trunk, screaming for help. Whatever is in the car isn't in danger of destruction." Simpson ran his tongue around the inside of his lips like he had a bad taste in his mouth. "I'm reluctant to participate in your exigent circumstances search. A judge would throw it out, exclude any evidence we recover, and exclude everything that evidence leads us to. 'Fruit of the poisonous tree.'"

Larry couldn't hold back. "Our necks are on the line, not yours."

Simpson's eyes narrowed. "If I'm called to testify, I won't be able to defend the search."

Larry was ready to argue. I diverted him. "Look up Ed Wirth's phone number on your smartphone."

Larry wasn't happy but took out his phone. "What city?"

"Bee Ridge."

Simpson crossed his arms and watched silently as Larry angrily stabbed at his phone screen.

"Got it." He punched a number and put the phone to his ear.

I assumed the ME had broken the news of Madison's death to them. I put out my hand to Larry.

"What?"

"Let me talk to them."

"What?"

"The parents can give us permission to search the car."

Larry was annoyed but handed me the phone just as a woman answered.

"Is Alison Wirth available?"

"If you're selling something you can..."

"I'm Inspector Doug Fletcher, from the U.S. Park Service. I need to speak with Alison or Ed Wirth."

"The park service?"

"Are you Mrs. Wirth?"

"I'm Alison."

"Have you been contacted by Miami/Dade County about Madison?"

"I don't know what you're talking about."

I closed my eyes and pinched the bridge of my nose. I'd beat the medical examiner's call to Madison's parents. "Mrs. Wirth, I'm Doug Fletcher, an investigator with the U.S. Park Service. We recovered a woman's body in the Everglades and our preliminary investigation indicates it may be Madison."

I heard a suck of air. "How sure are you?"

"We spoke to Madison's roommate, and she confirmed that Madison has dark hair and a dolphin tattoo on her lower back. Jane Doe matches Madison's driver's license."

I let that sink in. Alison Wirth's voice got unbelievably soft. "You didn't say if the picture matches."

"We'd like to get her dental records. Do you know which dentist she went to?"

"Oh, God." Alison broke into tears, and I waited. "I thought something was wrong. She hasn't called."

"Her dentist?"

"Doctor Robinson, in South Sarasota. How soon…Can we…"

"Let us check with Doctor Robinson. The medical examiner will contact you if there's a positive ID."

"There's a chance it's not Maddie, right?"

"There's a chance, but we're ninety-nine percent sure. We recovered her car,

201

and we'd like to search it for evidence of foul play. Do we have your permission to search?"

I switched on the speaker function. "Why are you searching her car?"

"We believe her car may be a crime scene and it needs to be searched."

"Sure. Go ahead. Let us know if you find anything."

A doorbell rang in the background, and I heard male voices, then a gasp. "Alison. Come talk to these cops."

"Thank you, Mrs. Wirth. I've got your number and we'll call if we find anything." I ended the call and handed the phone back to Larry.

Simpson shook his head. "That was bad. You should've waited until after the medical examiner or local cops spoke with her parents."

I nodded. "Yeah, I screwed up. Are we good for the search?"

He nodded. "Do you have keys, or do I have to pop the locks?"

Larry pulled the evidence bag from his pocket and touched the unlock button. The horn beeped and the parking lights flashed. He was about to put the bag back into his pocket. Simpson stopped him. "Pop the trunk too."

Larry pushed and held the trunk button. The latch popped and the trunk slowly rose. Simpson walked to the trunk as he pulled on a pair of gloves. We followed and stood side-by-side, staring into the open space.

The trunk was free of the fast-food wrappers cluttering the interior of the car. Simpson picked up a workout bag, lifting it out of the trunk and holding it aside while looking inside. "No blood. No hair. No evidence of foul play. I'll put it under an ALS, but it looks pristine."

"ALS?" Larry asked.

"An alternate light source. I'll spray it with luminol, then darken the room and light the surface with a black light. Any blood or body fluids will fluoresce." Simpson hefted the bag in the trunk. "We may be able to get DNA off her workout gear. If she's got a hairbrush in here, we will probably find a hair that can be used to make a genetic comparison."

I shook my head. "We'll get her dental records to make the match. Let's check the interior," I suggested.

Simpson checked the bag's contents and put them back into the trunk. He opened the Jetta's doors and surveyed the interior. "I think the owner was a slob. I recognize logos from every fast-food restaurant in Florida City."

Larry knelt and lifted wrappers from the floor on the passenger side." This is like an archaeology dig. There are receipts attached to the bags, so we know what day she went to each place."

"It seems odd to find so many fast-food bags. She was a skinny thing," I said.

Simpson shook his head. "Lots of young people fast and binge. They don't eat for a day, then binge the next day."

Larry stood. "That's not healthy."

Simpson shook his head. "It's not, but they live by the credo, 'You can't be too rich or too skinny.' Many of them have eating disorders and systemic problems from the cycling of their eating and drinking. They're going to be senior citizen medical nightmares if they live that long."

I went to the driver's side, opened the door, then stood back. This side was less cluttered, but the console was stained around the Starbucks paper cup in the cupholder. A wire snaked out of the console. I slipped on a pair of gloves and picked up the end of the cord. "Looks like a cell phone charger cord."

Simpson peeked inside the car. "These millennials live with their phones glued to their hands."

I ran my fingers down the crack between the console and the seat but felt nothing. A similar search between the seatback and seat yielded only crumbs. I slipped my hand alongside the seat adjustment controls and hit something solid with my fingertips. With some effort I was able to push it ahead until it fell onto the floor mat. "I've got a cell phone." I pulled out the phone in a pinkish purple case and pushed the on\off button, but the screen remained blank.

Simpson pointed to the cord. "Plug it in."

I took the keys from Larry and turned on the accessories and plugged in the phone. I let it sit a few seconds then retried the switch. The phone went through the startup mode, flashed a logo I didn't recognize, then displayed a numerical keypad and told me to enter the code. "Well, I think that confirms Madison Wirth's phone isn't in the swamp. I'm done. I don't know the passcode."

Simpson nodded. "Leave it here. I'll have one of my guys look at it. He's pretty good at getting around the security on phones."

I unplugged the phone and shut down the car, returning the keys to Larry. "I don't expect we'll find much unless she took video of her attackers."

Simpson slipped the phone into an evidence bag. "I'm more curious about whose fingerprints are on the case. No millennial is going to leave her phone in her car. I'd say it's likely her killers slipped it into the car when they moved it."

Larry nodded toward the door, and I shook hands with Simpson before we walked out. Simpson called out as we got to the garage door, "Hey, Macaroni."

Larry turned and glared at him. "It's Marconi. Macaroni is a noodle."

Simpson smirked, knowing he'd gotten under Larry's skin. "Lose the gold chain. It makes you look more like a timeshare salesman than a cop."

I could see Larry turn red, preparing to respond. I pushed his shoulder to get momentum toward the door. Larry stuck up his middle finger as I pushed him out the door.

"That ass. He's got no right to comment on my chain. It's a free country and I can wear anything I want under my uniform. In Jersey, a gold chain is a sign you've made it. I can wear my chain if I want to."

We got in the SUV and Larry was still steaming. He stared out the windshield, waiting for the air-conditioning to cool the interior. He glared at me. "You haven't said anything."

"You're wearing a badge. That's all the statement you need to make." I paused while waiting for that thought to steep in Larry's brain. "I had to wear a tear-away tie when I was a patrol officer. Lots of detectives wear their badges on plastic bead lanyards that break away in a fight. I think a heavy gold chain would be a really bad thing to have on if you had to break up a domestic assault or gang fight. Someone could strangle you with it."

"There aren't many fights in the park."

I looked at him, trying not to be judgmental. "You only heard half of what I said. Your badge is a statement, and so is the gold chain. They contradict each other."

"Huh?"

"The badge says. 'I'm a professional.' It's part of wearing a neat uniform with polished shoes and leather. The gold chain says something else."

"What do you think it says?"

"It's a macho statement about your ego."

"Bullshit."

I put up my hands. "You asked what I thought, and I told you. What does it mean to you?"

Larry slammed the SUV into gear and the tires chirped and spit sand as he backed out of the parking spot. Tires squealed as a car slammed on its brakes to avoid hitting us. It swerved and honked, the driver flipping Larry the bird as he sped past.

Larry slammed the transmission into drive and reached for the toggle to turn on the lights and siren. I stopped him. "Take a breath. You nearly hit that guy."

"He disrespected me!"

"You were wrong! You backed out without looking. You're lucky he didn't hit you because I would've had to file a report saying you had violated a traffic law and caused the accident. That would've gotten

207

you a written reprimand and possibly made you personally responsible for the damage to both vehicles."

"Damn it, Fletcher! You're out of your element here. I don't need your mealy Midwest adages telling me to play nice. You've got no edge, no drive…hell, I wonder about your self-respect. This is a different world and you're soft."

"Are you done?"

"Done with what?"

"Your tantrum."

"Damn it, that wasn't a tantrum, that was setting you straight."

"Are the traffic laws different here than everywhere else in the country?"

"I don't know. Probably not."

"Then, it's illegal to back into the street without looking, and if you hit a car while breaking that law, you're at fault. Right?"

"I was mad."

"I've never read any statute that says being mad is an exemption from the traffic laws. I think that escalates a misdemeanor to a gross misdemeanor for inattentive driving. I'm not sure about Florida, but in Minnesota or Texas, they can arrest and book you in jail if you piss off the arresting officer."

Larry pulled to the curb. "You'd throw me under the bus."

"I'd state the facts as I saw them."

"I thought you were my partner."

"I've got your back if you need me, but I'm not going to lie if you do something illegal." Larry took a deep breath and glared at me. He was about to launch another tantrum when I put up my hands. "Stop. You're either a good cop, or you shouldn't be a cop. There's no middle ground. If you're going to ram around like an angry bull, hand me your badge and I'll call an Uber to drive you home."

Bracing for a punch, I tensed, preparing to block it. Then, he pulled the gold chain over his head and stuffed it into his pocket. "Better?"

"That's part of it. Lose the attitude. Put on your game face, the one that's professional and under control."

He pursed his lips and took a couple breaths. "Are you going to tell Jack to fire me?"

"Are you going to stop acting like a petulant teenager and be a real cop?"

The comment caught Larry off guard. "I'm from Jersey. It's how we react."

I lowered my voice and spoke slowly. "You're a U.S. Park Service Law Enforcement Officer, a sworn federal law enforcement officer who has taken an oath to enforce the laws of the United States. Act like one."

"You've shot people. What were they doing?"

"I shot back because they were shooting at me or my partner. Jill shot a guy who was firing a semi-automatic rifle at FBI agents and local deputies. Those shots were never taken in anger. We were protecting lives."

Larry digested that, then looked over his shoulder and pulled into traffic. "What are we doing now?"

"Let's find Andrea Arnot and her husband. I think they might hold the key to our murdered woman. Tell me what you learned from the marriage license."

"I didn't learn anything." Larry sensed I didn't like his response when I didn't answer. "I got their names, that's it."

"No home addresses?"

"I didn't ask."

I turned toward him. "You're kidding, right?"

"I didn't know what we were going to do with the names. So no, I didn't ask about addresses."

"Did you ever learn that it was better to have more information than less?"

"I told you, I didn't think we'd need it."

"Pull over."

"What?"

"Pull the damned truck over."

Larry pulled into a strip mall parking lot. "What?"

"What did you do in New Jersey, patrol the playground?"

"I was a street cop, not a detective."

I closed my eyes. "Does that mean you mentally checked out when you went to a crime scene? All you did was man the police tape and ignore what was going on?"

"What's with you, Fletcher? I told you, I was a street cop. Mostly I patrolled and made traffic stops. I didn't get into investigations."

"Did you ever use your brain?" I regretted the comment as soon as it was out.

"Listen Mr. Big Shot investigator. The world needs cops to pull over speeders and respond to domestic assaults too. Just because I wasn't investigating murders doesn't mean I wasn't a good cop."

"I was out of line. I'm sorry. We need to gather as much information as possible. Most of it won't be useful, but it's always better to have too much information than too little. Call the license bureau or whoever you contacted to get the names on the marriage license and get as much information as is available: home addresses, the minister or priest, the names and addresses of the witnesses, phone numbers. Anything that's on the license or application."

Larry stared at me without moving. "Why?"

"Because we want to find them and talk to them. Why was a dead woman wearing Andrea Arnot's wedding ring?"

Larry digested that. "Do you think they're still around?"

"I have no idea." I paused. "It doesn't matter where they are. We need to talk with her about the wedding ring."

"What will that tell us? Maybe she lost it on the beach."

"Damn it, Larry. This is how you investigate. You don't make excuses about why not to look for clues. You pursue the pieces. Anything that ties a name to the murder identifies one person who might be the murderer or knows what happened to the dead woman."

"Sounds like a lot of bullshit phone calls that won't lead anywhere."

"That's exactly what an investigation is! Tracking down loose ends. Calling and interviewing people. Chasing down dead ends in the hope of finding the one nugget that leads you to the murderer." I could see he wasn't buying it. "Take me back to the park. You walk around and glare at litterers and I'll make calls. Better yet, go home. Sit in front of your television with a beer and wait for human resources to call with the details of your termination." I put out my hand.

"What?"

212

"Give me the keys. I don't want to put you out by making you drive."

Larry took out his cell phone and scrolled through something as I got more irritated. He hit a number and handed the phone to me. "I called the woman who gave me the names on the marriage license. I'll drive. I want to hear what you ask her."

A woman with a southern accent as thick as honey answered the phone and asked how she could help me. I introduced myself and explained that my partner had called to get the names from the Arnot/Castro marriage license. "What other information is on the application and marriage license?"

"Well, there's the date, the names, and the name of the officiant. Then there's his signature and the signatures of two witnesses."

"Does it give you the address of anyone?"

"No, sir. Just their names and signatures."

"Please give me the name of the officiant."

"Father Miguel Sanchez. I believe he's the priest at St. Mark's."

"Who were the witnesses?"

"Their names aren't typed in so all I've got are their signatures and, well, I can't read them. They're kind of squiggles on the paper."

"Where's St. Mark's parish?"

"It's in old Miami, kind of in the Cuban area."

I thanked the woman and ended the call. "Do you know where St. Mark's is in Miami?"

"It's in Little Havana."

"Let's go."

Larry glanced at his watch. "It's getting a little late. Maybe we should go first thing in the morning."

I closed my eyes and tilted my head back. "Have you ever watched the television show *The first 48* that Jack mentioned?"

"A couple times."

"The whole premise of the show is that most murders are solved within forty-eight hours. The longer the murder sits, the harder it is to solve."

"We're way past that."

"Exactly! And it's getting older every day. Witnesses will be harder to find, and their memories will fade."

"That's probably true."

"I don't want to wait until tomorrow to talk with Father Sanchez. I want to talk to him this afternoon. I might be willing to wait until tomorrow to track down any leads he may generate, but I don't want to delay speaking with him."

Larry took a deep breath. "That's not a great neighborhood."

"It's not even dark. Are you afraid we're going to go there?"

"Well, no. I was just saying…"

"Will it be worse now than in the morning?"

Larry rolled his eyes. "Our wives will be waiting for us."

"They're married to cops. I think they expect things to come up."

Larry pulled out his cell phone and dialed as he drove. I was tempted to point out that it was against park service regulations and probably a violation of Florida law, but bit my tongue.

"Yeah, honey, I'm driving that investigator to Little Havana. I'll be late for supper."

I heard the woman's voice, and she didn't sound happy.

"I know that's why I went to the park service, but this is unusual. It needs to be done tonight. I'll call when we get through."

Larry ended the call, fumbling the phone while swerving between the lines on the highway. I held my tongue.

"Your wife thinks you have a nine-to-five job."

"Most of the time it is."

"Who works the weekends and picks up the slack?"

"Jack hires seasonal law enforcement rangers for the busy season."

215

"Don't you have crimes that require investigation?"

"We've never had a murder before."

"But you have had suspicious disappearances."

"A couple."

"And you led the investigations?"

Larry glanced at me as we passed through the speed-pass lane of a toll booth. "There wasn't much to investigate. We had an accidental drowning. The kayaker hit something underwater and fell out of the kayak. He wasn't wearing his life vest and he drowned. Rangers recovered his body a couple hours later."

"And the other investigation?"

"A car was abandoned in a parking lot. Rangers walked the trails and didn't find anyone. We notified the FBI, and they impounded the car."

"And?"

Larry lifted his hand. "And nothing. We didn't hear back from the FBI."

"Have you asked for an update?"

"I already told you, I've stayed out of it. It's their case now."

I looked out the side window as we drove into an area that had store names in Spanish: Panera. Tendero. Carniceria. Tortillas. Botas y Zapateos. Each store seemed to have some sort of security cover that rolled down like a hurricane shutter or pushed aside like a metal grate.

The people walking the sidewalks looked Hispanic and moved with purpose unlike the area around our hotel where walkers moved slowly, as if they were trying not to work up a sweat. The streets were lined with cars and pickups, many older models, but without the rusty fenders in Minnesota where cities covered the roads with salt in the winter to melt the ice and snow.

"We're in Little Havana?" I asked.

"For a couple blocks now."

"Where's the church?"

"I'll turn at the next light and it's down a quarter mile or so."

We stopped at the light and a group of teens glanced at us, saw the light bar and Larry's shoulder patches, then turned away looking guilty. "Is there a gang problem here?"

Larry chuckled. "They rule the streets at night."

"Drugs and prostitution?"

"Those are their big money makers. They spend a lot of time defending their turf and intimidating people. It's like any big city except they speak Spanish."

The store fronts disappeared, and we drove past aging houses with front porches. People watched us pass as they smoked while sitting on the steps. Cars parked along the curb were a decade old and not well maintained. their paint oxidized, and

217

every antenna was broken off. Some were missing hubcaps and others had cracked windshields. We passed a car whose trunk lock had been punched out and tied down with a yellow rope.

St. Mark's was a stone edifice towering over the neighborhood, ringed by a cracked asphalt parking lot. Larry parked in a spot next to the handicapped sign. Heat slapped me in the face when I opened the car door, and my shirt was damp by the time we got to the massive entrance. The building's interior was stuffy and dark, its primary lighting provided by tall stained-glass windows. Prayer candles flickered in a rack to our right and a woman knelt in an alcove in front of a marble statue of the Virgin Mary.

We approached a small gray-haired woman who was arranging brochures in a rack opposite the prayer candles. I noticed all the brochures were in Spanish. "Excuse me, we'd like to talk to Father Miguel."

When the woman turned, I saw the deep creases in her face and caught a glimpse of her gnarled hands. I guessed she'd passed her eightieth birthday. "Father is in his office. Follow me."

Our guide led us down a side aisle. I glanced at the stained-glass windows, pieces of colored glass carefully mounted in leaded framework representing the stations of the cross, Christ's progression to the final stop where he was crucified. Just past the last window were three marble steps to a dark wooden door. The woman knocked but opened the door without waiting for an answer.

Father Miguel stood as we walked in. I'd expected him to be as old as the woman who'd guided us to his office, but the priest was young with a welcoming smile.

"Father, these gentlemen wish to talk to you."

The priest stepped around a neat desk, where he'd been working with an open Bible, a notepad, and a pen. He offered his hand. "Ah, a reason to step away from the homily that's vexing me." He spoke with no hint of southern or Hispanic accent, leading me to believe he was from the Midwest.

"Father, I'm Doug Fletcher and this is my partner, Larry Marconi."

The woman disappeared behind us, closing the door as she left. Father Miguel gestured toward a worn sofa and matching upholstered chairs near a window. I stepped around a stained coffee table and sat on the couch. Larry took one of the chairs.

"How can I be of assistance to…" the priest glanced at Larry's shoulder patch, "the U.S. Park Service?"

"We have a mystery and I hope you can help us," I said. "A young woman's body was found in the Everglades. She was wearing a wedding ring inscribed with initials and a marriage date. Based on our research we think the ring belonged to Andrea Arnot who recently married Juan Castro. I believe you performed the ceremony."

The priest's face lost its smile. "Oh, dear. I hope…Are you sure it was Andrea?"

I nodded to Larry. "Father, that's a good question. We have reason to believe the body is not Andrea, but the wedding ring has us questioning the identification. Can you describe Andrea and Juan?"

I studied the priest as he listened to Larry. My interest in Father Miguel was piqued by the edge of a tattoo visible on the inside of his right wrist, hinting at some other life before the priesthood. A small, framed diploma from St. Meinrad Seminary hung near the desk.

Fr. Miguel crossed his legs and rested his elbows on the arms of his chair. "I remember them well. They approached me to discuss marriage about two weeks ago. Juan is from Cuba and Andrea is from Ohio. They were both baptized Catholic although neither has been actively attending church as adults. We had two counseling sessions, and I married them the following Saturday in the sanctuary."

"Please describe them," Larry said.

"Juan is quite strikingly handsome, with dark hair and piercing dark eyes. When we first met, I thought he might've been someone I'd seen on television. He assured me he was not a movie star but runs an import business. Andrea was attractive, but not beautiful. She had dark hair and fair skin. I guess there was nothing about her that was notable."

Larry gave me a questioning look and I nodded. He took photos out of his pocket and searched through them. "I hate to ask you to look at these, because the victim is dead and was in the elements for a few days. Could you tell me if this person is Andrea?"

Larry handed the autopsy photo to the priest. I saw his face immediately recoil from the grisly image of the decomposing woman. The priest looked at the picture, then crossed himself, uttering a prayer as he handed the photo back to Larry.

"That's not Andrea. That woman has the same dark hair, but it's longer. Even in death, this woman's face is not the same shape as Andrea's."

Larry was ready to leave, but I put my hand up. "Father, who were the witnesses at the wedding?"

"Juan and Andrea said they were vacationing when they decided to marry, so none of their friends or family were here. The witnesses were Sister Ramona, who guided you to my office, and Paco, the parish janitor."

I got up and shook the priest's hand. "Thank you, Father. We appreciate your help."

The priest shook our hands. "I'm relieved that the dead woman isn't Andrea. Are you sure the wedding ring you found was hers?"

"We have a tentative identification of the dead woman. She's unmarried and her initials don't match the A&J initials in the ring."

Father Miguel hung his head. "Has someone given her last rites? I could…"

I touched the priest's upper arm. "We've contacted her family and I'm sure they'll be making arrangements for her funeral in accordance with their religious beliefs." I looked at the wall. "You have a Midwest accent. Where is St. Meinrad's?"

Father Miguel smiled at me. "I have the same accent as you with a little less of the Minnesota 'Fargo' tendency to drag out the vowels. I grew up outside Chicago and when God called on me to change the direction of my life, I was guided to St. Meinrad's in Indiana."

"This neighborhood is quite a change from Illinois."

The priest nodded as he led us to his office door. "It's two thousand miles away, yet next door in many ways." He held the door open for us. "Let's say there are elements of my previous life that make me

222

uniquely suited to help the children of this parish."

Larry shook his head. "I wish you luck if you're trying to change Little Havana."

"I'm not trying to change all of Little Havana, but I can change a few hearts and save a few sinners. That's all any of us can do." As Larry walked down the steps, the priest stopped me. "Doug, I see both happiness and sadness in your eyes. You understand what I'm talking about, don't you?"

I looked into his eyes. "Father, you and I are working two sides of the same coin. You're trying to save souls, and I'm trying to bring peace and closure to families who've suffered the worst loss imaginable."

A smile flickered on Miguel's lips. "But you've also found happiness, not just the cynicism I see in so many policemen."

"I married my soulmate a year ago. I have a Navajo friend who said I was traveling a path to nowhere until I met Jill, my wife."

"The Cherokee have a saying that each of us has two wolves inside us: one that's evil and one that's good. We become the wolf we feed. Make sure you're feeding the right wolf, Doug. I sense that the other wolf was close to winning."

"It's been a battle, Father. But the good wolf has been winning lately."

The priest put out his hand and when we shook, he pulled me close and whispered. "I sense that Larry is feeding the wrong wolf."

"We're working on that."

Larry and I walked to the back of the church and passed the prayer candles. I turned toward the door, but Larry stepped toward the aisle and hesitated. Then he bowed his head and genuflected. As we left, he dipped his fingertips in the holy water and crossed himself.

"I didn't know you were Catholic," I said as we got in the SUV.

"I was raised Catholic and was even an altar boy. We were married in a Catholic church, but that might've been the last time I was in a church." He started the engine and hot air blasted our faces. "What did the priest say to you back there?"

"He wished me luck solving the case."

Larry looked at me. "It was more than that."

"He said he was saving souls."

"And what did you say?"

"I said we were trying to bring them justice."

Larry digested that as he drove out of the parking lot and down the street. Every person we passed looked at the park service vehicle and the two white guys inside. Most were curious and turned away. The teen boys were still on the corner, and

224

they showed open contempt with their sneers.

I stared back at them without looking away until we'd passed. "I'm glad I'm not a cop here."

Larry glanced over his shoulder. "Yeah, this isn't an easy beat." He paused. "Back to the park?"

"Yeah."

"What are we doing tomorrow?" Larry asked as we passed out of Little Havana.

"Juan and Andrea told the priest they were vacationing here. We need to retrace their trail."

Larry rolled his head like I'd punched him. "Please tell me we're not going to spend days calling all the hotels and resorts down here to see where they were registered."

"They probably rented a car at the airport. We'll call the car rental agencies first to see when they arrived and left."

Larry let out a breath. "That's manageable."

* * *

Jill was reading an email on her smartphone when we walked into Larry's office. She looked up and appeared deflated. Larry was in a hurry to go. "Are you guys good for tonight?"

225

Jill nodded and he was gone in a flash. "I found a cellphone in the weeds along the path. It was in an inch of water."

"And…"

"It was dead, so I called the cell phone company. They said it belonged to A. Arnot. It has not been reported missing, nor has Ms. Arnot replaced it."

"That's good police work." Even with praise, Jill looked sad. "What's the matter?"

Jill handed me her cell phone and leaned back. "Your mother."

"What about my mother?"

"Just read the message."

I hate reading tiny print on the phone, probably because I refuse to admit I need reading glasses. I pushed the phone to Jill. "Just give me the highlights."

She pushed it back. "Oh no. I'm not repeating any of that."

I read Mom's summary of Uncle Chet's condition and her interpretation of the doctor's words. Not being a medical professional, she mangled terms and said things that were obviously misstatements. I closed my eyes and set the phone on Larry's desk. "How did you respond?"

"I haven't. You should call her."

I stood up. "No."

Jill followed me out the door. "No? That's it?"

I held the door for her. "That's it. I'm not getting involved in her management of Chet's catheter."

"But she's struggling to balance their modesty against his need for…catheter management."

I followed Jill down the sidewalk. "Sounds like it."

"She wants our assistance."

I punched the rental car remote to unlock the doors. "I already gave my opinion."

"Your opinion is not helpful."

I started the car, and the stale hot air blew in our faces. I'd scoped out the lot when I'd parked in the morning and chose a spot in the rear that was sunny when we parked, but now put the car in the shade. "Are we going back to the hotel first or do you want to go directly to the restaurant?"

Jill glared at me as I drove out of the lot. "She's your mother." She dialed the phone and put it on speaker. Her voice transitioned from angry to soothing in an instant. "Hi, Ronnie. I read your email. And thought I'd call rather than firing off a note."

"Thanks. I hate dealing with the email app and the autocorrect drives me crazy."

"How's Chet doing?"

"Much better since we got home from the doctor. I swear, that man never goes to the doctor unless he thinks he's dying."

"Things are under control now?"

"Chet's napping and I think we're dealing with everything."

"Your email sounded rattled."

"I'm coping and Chet's overcome some of his reluctance to talk about his bodily functions with me. I convinced him I'm a big girl and have seen and dealt with a lot." Mom paused. "Jill, he treats me like a princess on a pedestal. I'm eventually going to fall off and I'm not sure how he'll deal with that."

"He's a tough old cowboy, but his heart is as big as the Black Hills. He's never lived with a woman since his mother died and you're...special to him. Enjoy the ride."

"He won't let me pay for a thing."

"It's okay, Ronnie. He can afford it."

"Yes, he can afford it. He showed me the check he received for land rent. It's more the principle of paying my fair share."

"He's enjoying your company and it's his way of expressing his appreciation. He's done the same for me his whole life."

"I've been independent..."

I leaned close to the phone. "Mom, let Chet have his moment. He doesn't know how much time he has left, and he wants to share it with you. Let him."

"But Doug..."

"You keep telling me I'm bull-headed. I didn't get that from dad."

There was silence, then a chuckle. "Yes, I suppose that's true."

"Are we okay?" Jill asked.

"Thanks for helping me talk through this."

Jill switched off the speaker feature and put the phone to her far ear, obviously hoping to keep me out of the conversation. "We're happy to be your sounding board. You can call either of us any time." She ended the call.

"Either of us, anytime?" I asked. I could feel the withering glare without looking. It was radiating from the passenger seat. "I bet you'd like to go directly to the restaurant so you can have a glass of wine."

I glanced at Jill who had closed her eyes and leaned her head back. "Maybe a whole bottle."

I drove to our favorite seafood restaurant. The hostess recognized us and seated us at one of Krista's tables. We were looking at menus when Krista swept by carrying a tray of food for the table next to us. She was setting out hot plates and charming the people at the table but reached back and touched Jill's shoulder.

With the plates delivered, Krista turned and leaned close to Jill. "You look like you need a glass of wine. Red or white?"

Jill smiled. "A big glass of red."

Krista swept away without asking what I wanted.

"What did you do today?" Jill asked.

I told her about the trip to the county garage and our visit with the priest. She laughed at the CSI tech's comments about Larry's gold chain and was relaxing when Krista showed up with a giant glass of red wine that caught the attention of the other diners as she passed. She set the goblet in front of Jill and served me a normal-sized glass of white wine.

Jill wrapped her hands around the huge glass and glanced up at Krista. "Where did you find this?"

Krista leaned down. "It's the piano player's tip jar. You've got to finish this before he comes in at seven." She took our menus. "The special is grouper. Do you want it grilled or fried?"

I smiled and shook my head. "No other options?"

"Not for you two. I suggest the grilled grouper with a side of grilled onions, zucchini and summer squash."

Jill smiled. "Bless you. I wasn't up to making a decision."

Krista swept away and Jill lifted the big glass with both hands. It was like she was drinking from a fishbowl. She sipped and set the goblet down. "There's got to be an entire bottle of wine in here."

"What happened at the park after Larry and I left?"

"I interviewed the rest of the rangers who'd been around in the days before the

230

body's discovery. Several of them remember the vultures, but no one remembers exactly which day they first showed up and none of them noticed anything that made them suspicious the birds were feeding on anything other than some wildlife the gators had dragged there."

"A dead end."

Jill nodded, took a sip of wine, then pushed the glass in front of me. "Drink some of this. I can't finish it all."

"Hey, I'm driving."

Jill sighed. "Drink a little, just so it doesn't look like I've been unappreciative."

I pushed the glass back in front of her. "I'd rather you look unappreciative than me be pulled over for a DUI."

Krista came out of the kitchen carrying two platters. Walking past several tables who'd ordered before us, she set our meals on the table. She loudly announced, "The chef said he appreciated you calling in your order ahead of your arrival. That helps spread out the rush." Seeing her unhappy customers return to their conversations, she leaned close to Jill's ear. "Did you see the looks you were getting from the people who've been waiting? I had to use that line, or I wouldn't have gotten any tips from those other people."

Jill smiled. "You know, we could've waited."

Krista patted Jill's shoulder and fled.

Jill picked up her fork and flaked off a piece of grouper, then put it in her mouth. "This is so moist and mild."

I nodded my agreement.

"So, what do you have planned for the rest of the evening?"

"I thought we'd probably be here until closing time."

Jill frowned. "Why?"

I looked at her wine glass.

"No way I'm drinking all this even if we stayed until after closing time. What's your plan B?"

"I'll take you back to the hotel and watch the news while you fall asleep in the glow of the wine."

Jill speared zucchini and nodded. "That might happen. What are you and Larry doing tomorrow?"

"I hope our lovebirds rented a car when they flew into town. Larry's going to call the rental agencies to see if they have a record of a car rented by one of the names on the marriage license. Assuming they will, we'll go look at their security video. What's your plan for tomorrow?"

Jill chewed and thought. "I'm going to call the cell phone provider to see if they'll give me a list of the calls made from the phone. I'm sure they'll refuse without a warrant, but I need to call. Then, I'll borrow the metal detector and walk the edge of the pond along the pathway."

"The guys in the kayak didn't check that out?"

"They were out farther. There's a weedy margin just over the railing. I thought there might be something there." Jill paused. "What happens if we both come up empty?"

"We'll sit down in Larry's office and write down all the things we know on Post-it notes and stick them to the wall. Then we use a different color of Post-it and put up all the unanswered questions on a different wall."

Jill slid her hand over mine and squeezed. "Have you ever hit a dead end?"

"Lots! But we're not near that point yet."

She slid her wine glass toward me. "Your glass is empty. Why don't you pour some of this into your glass?"

I poured, but the rim of her glass was wider than mine, and I spilled wine on the tablecloth. Krista was beside me with a napkin before I even dabbed at the spill. "My bad. I didn't consider what would happen when I poured a bottle of wine into that giant glass. I'll have the bartender split it between two regular glasses." She was gone before I could tell her we were done with the wine.

Jill watched Krista retreat to the bar. "I hope the owner knows what a treasure she is."

A man wearing an open-collared shirt and dress slacks leaned between us and put out his hand. "I'm Tony, the owner. Believe me, I know what a treasure Krista is."

Jill was surprised by the male voice behind her, and she spun around, coming nose to nose. "We've been here every night since we arrived and made sure we've been at Krista's tables."

The man nodded. "I've seen you. And you've tipped generously. Thanks."

"I'm a little embarrassed about the wine. I asked for a big glass and Krista..."

The man patted Jill's shoulder. "Krista told me, and I came up with the idea of using the tip jar. The wine's on me tonight."

"But..."

The man smiled and shook his head. "No buts. It's done."

Krista was back with two wine glasses, nervously watching Tony walk away. "I hope..."

"Everything is fine," I said. "Tony was just telling us what a gem you are."

Krista smiled and was gone again. "That was strange," Jill said.

"I imagine the boss keeps tabs on what's going on. He knows which of his staff are working hard and which customers are unhappy. He's good at calming the waters."

"I didn't expect him to buy our wine."

I put my hand on Jill's arm. "I'm sure Tony's made a nice profit from us over a few nights. A giant glass of house wine is probably an inexpensive gesture."

Jill looked like she didn't believe me. I watched Tony come out of the kitchen carrying two plates covered with strawberries. He set them in front of us. "Happy birthday, Mrs. Fletcher."

I grabbed Jill's hand before she could protest. "Enjoy your strawberry shortcake, birthday girl."

She got a sheepish grin and shook her head. "You're the lucky beneficiary of my birthday. I hope you enjoy it."

"Yes, dear."

Jill broke out laughing, then leaned close. "You know you'll pay for that later," she whispered.

"My ribs hurt in anticipation of the jab."

She nodded emphatically, then stuck her fork into a huge strawberry. "If you're lucky, the strawberries will make me forget your smartass remark."

Chapter 11

Arriving back to the hotel, Jill's phone trilled just as we got to the front door. I heard half the conversation as we walked through the lobby and rode the elevator.

"Hi, Mom. No, you're not interrupting supper. We're just returning from the restaurant."

I unlocked our room and held the door open.

"That's interesting. I'm glad she's making headway. How far back is she going?"

Jill sat on the bed, and I took a fresh t-shirt and boxers out of the suitcase. Jill was still on the phone when I got out of the shower and was changed.

"Hey, Doug's trying to get my attention about something. I've got to run."

I raised my eyebrows as she shut down the call and plugged her phone into the charger. "It's a sin to lie to your mother."

I got *the look*. "I've been listening to her blather on about the family genealogy for ten minutes and there was no end in sight. You were a convenient excuse." Jill dug

236

into her suitcase and took out a fresh nightie, then disappeared into the bathroom. I turned on the TV as credits were rolling for some cop show and the station ran an evening news teaser about a South Beach shooting.

"What's up with the genealogist?"

"Mom is consulting with my Maine cousin. She's decided to fill in the Rickowski family tree."

"Who cares? They're all dead old people and it's not like you and I are going to be passing on any of those genes."

"I know! But she's decided she wants to have it all down."

"How far back has she gone?"

"I guess I've got a great grandfather who emigrated from Poland. She was chugging away when she hit the wall because the area of Poland where my family originated has been part of Germany or Russia, depending on who won the last war. Mom's hoping my cousin Michele has other resources. I guess the municipal records were destroyed by one of the armies that marched through, but Michele thinks there may be some churches that maintained birth, marriage, and death records that may have survived."

"Your dad has a sibling who's into genealogy?"

"No, Mom hired Michele to do the tree. She's a professional genealogist who does family trees for people. Mom said she spends most of her time tracking down birth parents for adoptees."

I shook my head. "I'd think those records are controlled pretty carefully. Most people who put their kids up for adoption aren't necessarily interested in being found."

"Yeah, I guess adoption records are sealed in most places, and judges are reluctant to order them opened except in extraordinary circumstances."

"So, if your cousin isn't using adoption records to find the birth parents, how does she connect the adoptees to them?"

"A lot of people are sending their DNA samples to family tree companies trying to find out where their roots are. If you submit a mouth swab for analysis, they'll give you a map of where your family originated. Some also identify relatives who've submitted samples. Mom sent a swab and said she got a bunch of relative suggestions. Some have contact information and others just have a code name."

"Yes, remember that television show we watched about the forensic genealogist? There's a huge pool of DNA out there that's not in CODIS but is being used to track down rapists and murderers in cold cases."

"Okay," Jill said, obviously unaware of where I was going.

"There are people using civilian DNA data with birth and marriage records to track down criminals who aren't in CODIS. The analyst on TV identified a killer in Washington by finding matches to some of his distant cousins, then she built a family tree that led her to the suspect. I wonder if your cousin could do that if we found DNA?"

Jill had to call her mother back to get Michele's phone number. The phone in Maine was answered by a woman, who obviously had caller ID and had no idea why J. Fletcher was calling.

"If you're selling back braces, glucose monitoring devices, or checking on my credit card interest rate, you'd better hang up now or be prepared to get an earful."

Jill laughed. "This is your cousin, Jill Rickowski, now Jill Fletcher."

"Jill! I haven't seen you since your dad was roping steers at the Belle Fourche rodeo."

"Oh, wow. It's been a long time since dad competed in the rodeo."

The mirth disappeared from Michele's voice. "That was a couple years before Junior's accident. I'm so sorry."

"Thanks. There were a few tough years after that."

"It's great to hear your voice. I've been talking to your mom a lot the last couple of weeks. I think I found the area where

Rickowskis lived in eastern Poland. There's a guy in Canada who built a family tree that includes your grandparents and I'm trying to find church records to verify his tree."

"I'm putting you on speaker. My husband, Doug Fletcher, is here with me."

"Hi, Doug."

"Hi Michele, we're just talking about DNA analysis and the television show about forensic genealogy. Besides recreating family trees and finding adoptive biological parents, do you do any criminal work?"

There was a pause. "Some, why are you asking?"

"We're Park Service investigators trying to solve the murder of a woman in the Everglades. If we find something that gives us a DNA sample, but it isn't in CODIS, the national criminal database, could you track that person through civilian records?"

Michele laughed. "It's possible, but not easy. There may be family members who've submitted samples for analysis. If the data is publicly available, and if the people are willing to share their family trees, it can be easy. The difficulty comes in getting people to share. If they find out I'm working a criminal case, or searching for an adoptee's biological parents, a lot of people hang up on me."

Jill leaned close to the phone. "So, you have to cloak your questions."

"I've gotten good at convincing people I'm trying to expand an existing family tree for one of their distant cousins and dangle the possibility that I can give them some family tree branches they don't have. Most people who submit DNA samples are curious and are trying to dig back further into their family trees."

"What are the odds you'd be able to track someone's family down through your techniques if we don't get a match in CODIS?"

"Jill, I could certainly try. But if you have other ways to ID her, they'd be quicker and won't rely on an unknown relative searching for his heritage in familytreedna, Ancestry.com, or gedmatch."

I leaned toward the phone. "Thanks for the genealogy lesson. You've helped me understand what's possible and put the television show in perspective."

"No problem, Doug. The woman on the TV show is a colleague of mine and it's great to see her getting recognition for the great work she's pioneering. The show isn't fiction, but they've only got an hour to summarize days or months of research and phone calls."

* * *

I was drifting off to sleep when I felt someone grab my arm. My immediate

241

response was hardwired from my time in Iraq where we slept with a pistol under our pillows and were constantly reminded that the compound had been repeatedly infiltrated by Iraqi martyrs, intent on killing U.S. servicemen.

I grabbed the hand and rolled, flipping both of us onto the floor. I was reaching for my attacker's neck when I recognized Jill's voice shouting four-letter expletives at me. I relaxed and let go of her wrist.

"What the hell is the matter with you?" Jill asked as she crawled out from under me and sat up.

"My survival instinct kicks in when someone grabs me in my sleep."

Jill got up and sat on the bed, pulling down her nightie. "I thought you were still awake."

"No. I went to bed and fell asleep. It's what I do every night." I paused. "So, why did you grab me?"

Jill drew a breath, composing herself. "The case all came together in my mind."

I rolled onto my knees and stood. "And that couldn't wait until morning?"

"I wanted to tell you before…"

"Before I fell asleep?"

Jill blew out a breath. "It's simple. Madison Wirth was killed, and her body dumped to provide cover for someone to disappear. The wedding ring was meant to be found and tied to Andrea Arnot. We were supposed to assume it was her body, roughly matching Andrea's features and size."

"But the car keys fell out of her pocket and that pointed directly to Madison Wirth."

Jill shook her head. "I thought about the body. Jane Doe's jeans were skin-tight and didn't have pockets. The keys didn't fall out of her pocket. Someone carried them to the swamp and threw them in, assuming they wouldn't be found."

"But we found Andrea Arnot's cell phone."

I perked up. "You were going to call her cell phone company."

"They confirmed it had been purchased by A. Arnot in Ohio."

"Okay. Did they suggest how to dry it out?"

"They said it was probably 'toast.' Once they're wet...that's why they sell cell phone insurance."

"Did they offer to give you her call history?"

"You know they wouldn't. They offered to supply it to me after I gave them a warrant."

"Arnot's phone was conveniently dropped right over the railing, where it was amazingly easy to find. But in the water, so we couldn't access any of the data. The killer wanted us to find the cell phone and trace it to Arnot. They didn't want us to find Jane Doe's keys."

Jill looked like she'd connected the dots. "Yes, Wirth's cell phone was in her car."

"It was irrelevant to solving the case. They didn't think we'd find the car. And even if we found the car, the cell phone didn't provide you with any more information about Wirth or identify her as Jane Doe."

"The local cops had already towed her car and had no idea it was connected to a crime. I suppose they figured it belonged to a drunk who went home in a cab and forgot where the car was left. Or assumed it was someone who'd left it behind when they met someone at the bar."

I bobbed my head. "I'm too tired to process this information." I got back in bed.

"What are you doing?"

"I'm going to sleep."

"You can sleep? You've got my adrenaline pumping and then you just lie down and fall asleep?"

I reached out and picked up the TV remote from the nightstand. "Here, watch television until you get tired."

Jill shoved my shoulder. "Get up. You're going to entertain me until I'm ready to sleep."

I closed my eyes tight. "No."

Jill shoved my shoulder again. "Get your sorry butt out of bed. There's a cribbage board and a deck of cards in my suitcase."

I sat up. "You brought cards and a cribbage board?"

"I thought we might solve this case quickly and have a couple quiet evenings before our return flights to Texas."

I yawned. "You thought that, did you?"

"Yes."

"I thought you liked to use those evenings to take advantage of my body."

"I thought that too, but you're only good for half an hour, forty-five minutes tops. We need something to fill the rest of the evening."

"Only half an hour?"

Jill tossed the cribbage board to me. "Actually, your part takes less than that. I counted the post-coital snuggling time too."

I tossed the cribbage board aside and grabbed her hand. "Let's try for a new record."

Jill fell into bed laughing. "You'd better be trying for forty minutes and not a faster record."

"I might get bored if we drag this out."

Jill's elbow struck my ribs, gently and teasing. "I guarantee you won't get bored." She pressed her body against me and ran her tongue around my ear.

I faked a yawn. "Wake me up when you get to the interesting part."

She ran her hand across my chest. "Is this more interesting?"

"You're getting there." Jill's cell phone chirped, and she started to reach for it. I grabbed her hand. "Leave it."

She pulled away. "It might be important." She looked at the caller ID, accepted the call, and put it on speaker. "Hi Ronnie. What's up?"

"I hope I didn't wake you. I'm not sure what time it is there. Are you earlier or later than Spearfish?"

"We're in Florida, so it's two hours later here."

"Oh, dear. I thought it was earlier. I just can't get the math right on the time zones."

"What can I do for you, Ronnie?"

"Well, it's probably nothing, but Chet was bleeding a little tonight."

Jill sat up. "Did you take him to the emergency room?"

"He wouldn't go. He's not in any pain, so he said we shouldn't bother anyone. I waited until he was asleep to call you."

Jill looked at me, but the only answer I had was a shrug. I reached out and slid my hand under her nightie, and she swatted it away. "Call his doctor's office. They'll have someone on call and will get an answer for you."

"He hates to bother the doctor."

246

"He's an old bull-headed coot!" Jill swatted my hand away from her leg. "Much like your son."

"I'll call and leave a message. Thanks for helping me decide what to do. I'd rather talk to you than Doug. He wasn't helpful last time I called."

Jill grabbed my hand from her hip and glared at me. "I understand, Ronnie. He's been irritating lately." She ended the call and put the phone on the nightstand.

"Well, we're up to six minutes of romance."

Jill held me at arm's length. "That was a call from your mother. It does NOT count as romance."

I pulled her close and pressed my hips against her. "The clock started when you nibbled on my ear."

"You're a pain in the butt."

"I'm your pain in the butt."

Jill nuzzled my neck. "I wish…"

"We agreed we weren't going to change each other. We're set in our ways."

"I know, but sometimes you do things to intentionally irritate me."

"I'm being playful."

"I like being playful, but not when I'm talking to your mother on the phone."

"I told you not to answer it."

On cue, her phone trilled again. She quickly rolled out of bed and stood out of reach. "Hi, Mom. What's up?" Jill listened

247

but rolled her eyes. "Yes, I just got off the phone with Ronnie. I told her to call the doctor's office. I'm sure he has an answering service."

I sat on the edge of the bed and behaved, listening to half the conversation. "I know Chet doesn't like going to the doctor, but he's just had surgery and he's bleeding." Jill closed her eyes. "Okay, he's got blood in his urine, he's not really *bleeding.* Ronnie still needs to talk to the doctor to make sure this is not an emergency."

Jill disconnected the call.

I laid my head back on the pillow. "I'm up to nine minutes of romance."

"The clock is officially reset."

"You don't get to reset the clock once you've started it."

Jill rolled against me and threw her arm over my chest. "I'm the referee and it's just like football. The ref gets to stop or reset the clock as she sees fit."

I kissed the top of her head and was tempted to say, yes dear. I knew that would set off a round of playful wrestling but realized two calls from our parents already had Jill on edge. I rolled on my side and cupped her face. "Take a deep breath. Let it out slowly. Put Spearfish out of your mind. We're here, at this moment, and the rest of the world is a million miles away."

248

I felt her relax and take a deep breath. "I'd have been up all night pacing the floor after two calls like that when I lived alone." She snuggled into my side. "You really are my other half."

"And you're mine."

Jill lifted my hand from her face and kissed each of my fingertips. "Remember the night I came to your townhouse? The first time…"

"Yes."

"You took me a million miles away from everything. You swept away my guilt and led me to a place I'd never been. Take me back there again."

I pulled my fingers free from her hand and ran them down her neck, shoulder, and side. I stopped at her hip and gently pulled her toward me. "Like this?"

"Mmm. Exactly like that."

Chapter 12

I woke to the sound of the shower and the smell of coffee coming from the tiny pot on the counter. Jill was singing softly in the bathroom as I started a second pot of coffee and picked up the newspaper that had been slipped under our door. The headline story was about a local man who'd been arrested for destroying a shell mound while excavating for a condo development. Below the fold were a few paragraphs about the identification of the woman found in the park. A lengthy interview with the assistant medical examiner followed on an inside page. I was surprised when I saw Fletcher and Marconi identified as park service resources who aided with the identification.

Jill came out of the shower wearing only a bra and panties, as naked as she was willing to be, even around me. The coffee stopped gurgling just as she took a pair of jeans out of the suitcase. "Anything interesting in the paper?" she asked as she sipped coffee.

"There's an interview with the M.E. on the front page. He actually gives credit to park service rangers Fletcher and Marconi for assisting with the identification of Jane Doe."

"Which Fletcher?"

I held out the paper. "It just says Ranger Fletcher."

Jill snatched the newspaper from my hand. "I helped recover the keys that led to her car."

"So, it could be Jill Fletcher."

Jill snorted. "Yeah, right."

"I was the Fletcher who called with the name and contact information. I'm sure he was using our name in general."

Jill read through the article, sipping coffee. She refolded the paper and set it on the bed. "I suppose that's okay. It's not like you were trying to get your name in the paper."

I went into the bathroom to shower. "I'm just pleased he mentioned the park service. He didn't have to do that."

* * *

We walked to the hotel's dining nook and went through the buffet line. As usual, I loaded up with eggs, sausage, and bacon. Jill came back with a bowl of oatmeal and a plate of fruit. She made no comment about my arteries hardening or dying of a heart attack and leaving her a widow.

I started the newspaper Sudoku. "You and Larry are searching for a rental car today?"

"That's my plan."

"And after that?"

"I hope we'll have a security video of Andrea and Juan, and a verification of the names on the marriage certificate."

"What will that get you?"

I shrugged. "I never know. What are your plans?"

"I'll talk to the rest of the rangers." Jill paused. "I'll call Ronnie and see what happened when she called the doctor."

* * *

Larry was waiting for us in Jack's office. The newspaper was spread on Jack's desk, and he was cutting out the article about the identification of Jane Doe. Jack looked up when Jill and I walked in. He broke into a smile. "We made the headlines."

I nodded. "The M.E. was generous with his praise." I looked at Larry. "Have you

252

ever had your name in the newspaper before?"

Larry smirked. "I was in a picture of a New Jersey drug bust once, but they didn't print my name."

Jack refolded the paper and threw it in a recycling bin next to his desk. "This is exciting. What's next?"

I repeated what I'd told Jill and said she was going to need access to the rest of the rangers for interviews.

Jack was a sudden convert. "No problem! Like I said yesterday, you'll have access to whatever resources you need."

Larry and I went to his office, leaving Jill to explain her plans and needs. Larry sat in his desk chair and searched for car rental agencies. He turned the screen so I could see. "There are four big national chains and a couple locals. I'll start with the top of the alphabet if you want to start at the end."

Larry was speaking with someone at the second place he called while I was on hold with Rent a Wreck. He perked up and pulled a notepad out of his drawer. "Yes, Andrea Arnot. You had a rental in her name eight days ago?" He scribbled shorthand notes. "It hasn't been returned? Can you give me a description of the car and the license number?"

As he scribbled notes, I wrote LoJack on a Post-it and pushed it in front of him. He nodded. "Does the car have a LoJack?"

He nodded emphatically. "Have you tried to locate it?" He wrote, 'Police only', on the note pad.

Larry hung up and turned the notepad so I could read the information about the rental car. "Who can access the LoJack information?"

"I think any police agency can get it."

"Can we?" he asked.

"I don't even know which database it's in. Do you know a local cop who could get the information for us?"

Larry thought for a second. "I could call the FBI guy who is investigating the missing hikers."

"Other than the FBI?"

Larry shook his head. "Not really."

I was disappointed. Wherever I'd worked I made a point of having coffee with the local cops and sheriff's deputies. "Larry, you need to get out of the park. Find out where the local cops go for coffee and talk to them. Get to know them."

"I've talked to a couple of them. Why is it a big deal?"

"They're your backup if you get in a bind. You want them to know your name and face in case you need help."

Larry mulled that.

"Pull up the U.S. Marshal's office on your computer."

Larry hesitated, but didn't ask why I wanted it. He spun the screen so I could read the information. I punched the number into my phone. A woman with a charming southern accent answered.

"Good morning, I'm Inspector Doug Fletcher, with the National Park Service. I'd like to speak to the Assistant Director of Investigations."

"I'll transfer your call to Marshal Tschetter's office."

I was amazed that the assistant director answered his own phone. "Tschetter."

I explained who I was and gave him a brief overview of our murder and the state of the investigation. "We've found the company who rented the car to our people of interest, and I want to use the LoJack to find the rental car."

"Do you think the people are still using it, or do you think it's abandoned?"

"I assume they left the area soon after dumping the body."

"Hang on." I heard computer keys clicking. "Okay, give me the vehicle information."

I was amazed that the assistant director hadn't handed off my call. I switched my phone to speaker and read the information from the rental company to him as he keyed it into the computer.

"It's parked at the Miami airport and hasn't moved in four days. I think your people of interest hopped on a plane and left the car."

"The Minneapolis Airport Police scan the license plates and have a database of the car locations. Do you know if that's the case here?"

Tschetter chuckled. "I think every airport with international connections does that. Call the airport police and I'm sure they can tell you exactly where the car is parked." He gave me the phone number for the airport police. "By the way, if the car has been abandoned, the rental company is allowed to unlock and recover it without a warrant." He paused. "I'm just saying that because you might want to be there when they tow and open the car."

"Thank you, Assistant Director."

"You've piqued my interest. If your suspects have fled the state, it's a federal matter. Here's my direct number. Keep me informed if you need any assistance from my people."

I wrote the phone number on the notepad. "Thanks."

"Fletcher, I'm curious. Why didn't you contact the FBI?"

"Let's say my experience with them has been less than pleasant. They're already investigating the disappearance of two people from the park and haven't provided an update in the several months they've had the case."

Tschetter paused. "Ahh. I hope we can partner with you on this. Let me know what you find in the car and if you need any of my resources."

I ended the call and tore off the note with the telephone numbers. Larry was leaning back in his chair. "I wouldn't have the guts to call the assistant director of the marshal's service."

I punched the airport police number into my phone. "What's the worst that can happen? He can say no." The phone number at the airport police only rang once before it was answered.

"Miami Airport Police, Officer Page. How can I help you?"

I explained who I was, that we had LoJack information and asked where the car was parked.

"We could've accessed the LoJack for you," officer Page explained.

"We didn't know where the car was and really didn't expect to find it at the airport."

Page was silent for a moment. "It's in long term parking, section G-3. Are you going to have it towed?"

"I assume the rental company will dispatch a truck to recover it."

"I'll notify our roaming car. He'll be there to block the row for the tow truck."

Larry was already on the phone with the rental company before I ended the call with the airport police. "Yes, it's in section G-3. We want to be there when it's towed and when you open the vehicle." Larry

257

ended the call and stood. "Looks like we're going to the airport."

"I'll tell Jill. She might want to ride along."

Five minutes later the three of us were in the park service SUV with Larry driving. Jill was in the back, apparently deep in thought. "What do you expect to find in the car?"

I twisted in my seat so I could look at her. "I don't know. I suspect it may contain some evidence that Madison Wirth had been inside it. That'd be big. It'd be great if we found blood evidence—even better if we recovered fingerprints from Castro and Arnot."

"I don't suppose they'd leave behind driver's licenses, passports, utility bills, or anything that would lead us to them."

I smiled. "If you're asking, why not wish for a note that says, 'I did it,' with all the details and a signature."

Larry glanced at me. "You're starting to delve into fantasy."

Jill piled on. "And maybe Castro is really a Spanish prince, and he came to rescue Arnot who'd been kidnapped by Madison. It might be a plot right out of a Hallmark movie."

I flipped my hand. "I was trying to be serious."

* * *

The midmorning traffic was light and the trip to the airport took only half an hour. We were met at the parking lot entrance by an airport police car that led us to section G-3. A flatbed tow truck was pulling the car onto its tilted platform when we got to the aisle. We followed the tow truck to the rental car facility and watched it unload the car in an open area near the cleaning station. A manager wearing a blue shirt with the company logo walked out as the car was rolled into an open spot. I took out my credentials and handed them to her. "We'd like you to open the car so we can search the interior."

Jenette, the manager, was African American, her hair tied in a short ponytail. "You're the ones who called to get the information for the LoJack?"

Larry, who was the only one of us in uniform, stepped forward. "I called. We went through the U.S. Marshal and the airport police to locate the car."

Jenette returned my credentials. "Thanks. We would've reported it missing in another few days, but we're happy to get it back knowing it was abandoned."

"You may not be as pleased if we find evidence of a crime inside."

Jenette blinked. "A crime?"

"We think the car was used by a pair of murderers."

Jenette's hand went to her mouth. "Oh, my. I…"

"Can you unlock it for us?" Larry asked.

Jenette took a set of keys out of her pocket and handed them to Larry. Jill and I donned purple gloves. Larry unlocked the doors and popped the trunk.

I looked in the front seat. A package of baby wipes was on the floor among dozens of used wipes littering the floor. Every surface had a smudge from being wiped, from the steering wheel to the door handles and arm rests.

I backed out of the car. "Shit. We're not going to get a fingerprint off this."

Jill was in the backseat. "There's a wedding dress spread on the seat and baby wipes all over the floor."

"Look at this," Larry called from the trunk. "See what you think of this."

There were two purple suitcases and a matching carryon bag in one side of the trunk while the other half was empty. Jill looked and blew out a breath. "Looks like the man took his luggage and left the woman's bags behind."

Larry nodded. "I wouldn't be caught dead hauling around purple bags even if I was with my wife."

Jill pulled the carry-on into the empty area and unzipped it. She looked inside, then at me. "Someone left without their passport." She carefully picked it out of the bag and opened it to the picture page. "It appears Andrea Arnot didn't make her flight." She held the passport out to me.

The picture resembled the poor driver's license picture we had. Andrea's hair was different in the passport photo. I checked the date and found it had been issued a month ago. "Well, this reconfirms that the woman we found wasn't Andrea. Her hair wouldn't grow eight or nine inches in a month. Before we dig through this anymore, let's call the county crime lab and have them process the entire car."

Jenette wasn't happy. "Hang on. I need to clean this and get it back onto the lot."

"I'm sorry, but it may be a crime scene. Do I have your permission to inspect it for prints and blood?"

"Blood? Oh, hell yes. I can't rent it if it's got blood in it."

Jill frowned at her, and I winked. "Larry, call your buddy Simpson at the county garage and tell him we need him to process another car."

Larry didn't reach for his phone. "Simpson isn't my buddy."

I flashed back to the gold chain incident. "You're a professional. Call him."

Jill put the passport back into the bag and zipped it shut. We walked away from the car while Larry made his call. Jill leaned

261

close to me. "Either Andrea Arnot is dead, or someone wants us to think so."

"Whoever is behind this didn't think we'd find Madison Wirth's keys and car. Without that evidence, we'd be looking at the wedding ring and cell phone thinking we'd found Andrea Arnot's body and closing the case. Now, we have two mysteries: Is Andrea Arnot dead? Who killed Madison Wirth and dragged her body to the Everglades?"

Jill glanced at Larry, who was having an animated discussion with whomever he reached at the county crime lab. "I think we know who killed Madison. It looks like Andrea was trying to disappear. So, I think the second question is, 'Why did Andrea Arnot want to stage her own death?'"

Jill leaned close although Larry's animated call was louder than anything Jill was going to say. "What's our plan?"

"I'm going to be a mediator and try to get Simpson, the county CSI guy, to prioritize going over the rental car after Larry's got him thoroughly pissed off. Then, I'm going to stand between the two of them, so they don't come to blows."

"What happened between Larry and Simpson?"

"Didn't I tell you? Simpson told Larry his gold chain made him look like a timeshare salesman. Larry took issue with that."

Larry was walking toward us, and Jill tried to suppress her smile. "A timeshare salesman?"

"Yep."

"That's a low blow."

I smiled and nodded.

Larry's face was red. "Tow it in. They'll get to it when they have time."

I took out the slip of paper with the phone numbers I'd got from the U.S. Marshal and dialed Randy Tschetter's direct line. It clicked and rang with a second dial tone. "Fletcher?"

"We got the car and it's been wiped. A wedding dress and a woman's luggage were left behind, including her passport. We're having the car towed to the Dade County forensics garage and I need to nudge them to jump on it."

"What's your rush?"

"We may have another dead woman, and the case of the first murder is getting colder by the day."

"I'll call the head of the lab. I can get it pulled to the front of the line, but you won't be making any friends there."

"I don't need friends, I need evidence."

"You've got everything else under control?"

I looked at Jill and thought for one second. "We've got a cell phone connected to the woman missing from the car. My partner confirmed that she was the owner, but the cell phone company needs a warrant to turn over her phone records."

"Text the details to this phone, it's my cell. That should be an easy sell to a magistrate."

"One other thing, our missing woman is unknown to us. She's not in the NCIC database but something just doesn't feel right. Can you do a deep dive and see who she is?"

Tschetter laughed. "I can try, but I won't make any promises. Text me her name and address."

"Will do. She's from Youngstown, Ohio, so you may have to contact your office there."

"Did you say Youngstown?"

"I did. Is that significant?"

"It's not something I can discuss over the phone. Text me what you have. We may have to meet somewhere to talk."

Jill heard my half of the conversation and was perplexed.

I waved her off. "But you will get back to me, right? Aside from the Rapid City office, I haven't had good luck with reciprocity of information from the FBI."

"Fletcher, you'll have everything I have unless a leak would jeopardize an imminent operation. All I ask is that you be as forthcoming with information as we are."

"I guarantee that." I ended the call and handed my phone to Jill. "Text all you've

264

got about Andrea Arnot's phone and her address to the last number I called."

Jill sent the number to her phone. "Whose number is this?" She asked, composing a text and attaching the phone information to it.

"The U.S. Marshal's office. They're going to get a warrant for Arnot's phone records. The marshal seemed very intrigued that Arnot was from Youngstown. He promised to get back to me."

Larry was impatiently tapping his phone against his leg. "They're ready for the car, but it may take a while for them to get to it."

We followed the tow truck to the County garage and watched as it was backed into an open slot. There were several cars and a pickup in various stages of inspection or dismantling. The garage hummed with the sound of vacuum cleaners and rattling tools, like a commercial repair garage.

Simpson walked out of the office near the rear of the space and approached us. He glared at Larry but smiled and put his hand out to Jill. "I see they've decided to try charming me instead of twisting my arm. I'm Mike Simpson."

Jill introduced herself and seemed genuinely charmed by Simpson's homespun accent and 'aw shucks' act. She didn't let it go to her head. "So, we got this car from the airport long term parking, and it looks like a couple had driven there, but only the man's luggage was gone. We're concerned about the welfare of the woman. How quickly can you process this for prints and blood?"

Simpson looked at me and chuckled. "Hell, your husband pulled strings that got things hopping. I don't know who you called, but my boss, who hasn't been in the garage since he shook everyone's hand Christmas Eve, came running into my office and told me to drop everything and do whatever had to be done for the National Park Service investigators. Who'd you call, J. Edgar Hoover?"

"I think he's dead."

Simpson smiled. "I gotta hand it to you. I've never seen my boss so motivated."

"I can be charming and persuasive," I said.

Simpson shook his head. "I got news for you, you're not that charming or persuasive." He turned and looked at the car. "It's a rental?"

I handed Simpson the keys. "Yes. According to the LoJack, it's been in the airport's long-term parking lot for several days. The inside has been wiped down. I'm hoping you can pull a rabbit out of your hat and find us some usable prints and possibly some DNA."

Simpson popped the trunk open. "It depends on how good the person doing the wipe down is. Most people miss a few spots, like the inside lip of the trunk lid or the rear-view mirror. If your guy was good, he'll know that and clean up everything."

"So, you don't think you'll find anything?" Jill asked.

"I didn't say that. We have a few tricks up our sleeve. And the fact that the rentals are vacuumed and cleaned after each customer helps. Anything we find should be associated with the last renters. If you'll step back from the car, we'll do our thing."

Simpson brought two crime scene techs to the rental car. They donned purple gloves and started dusting the interior of the car and trunk for fingerprints. I stood behind the woman who checked the trunk and watched every surface she dusted show nothing but smears. She finished and shook her head. Then she released the gas cover and dusted the cover and the gas cap. Again, she found nothing.

"Got a print!" The male tech working on the driver's side of the car was examining the seat adjuster with a magnifying glass. "There's a partial print." He used a piece of clear tape to lift the print, and Simpson carried it to a reader on the bench.

I followed Simpson. "I'll send it to the AFIS and see if there's a match."

Jill stepped over. "What's AFIS?"

Simpson was surprised that a federal investigator was unfamiliar with the acronym. "It's the automated fingerprint identification system. The database contains the fingerprints of any person who's been arrested, screened for federal employment, or served in the military."

"Lots of people," Jill said.

"But not everyone." Simpson said as he put the fingerprint on a reader. "And the surface yielded only a partial print because it was so small."

"How long does it take?"

"We sometimes get a match in twenty seconds. Sometimes it takes up to half an hour." Simpson stared at the machine as if he were willing it to spit out a match. After a minute he turned away. "Let's see if the guys have found anything else."

The man examining the passenger side of the car was scanning the backseat upholstery with an ultraviolet light and glasses. He stepped back and shut off the light. "Nothing. Not a print, a drop of blood, or a drip of sweat. It's the cleanest rental car I've ever seen."

Zoe, the female tech was examining the luggage and wedding gown on a bench behind the car. Jill walked over and watched her lift numerous prints off the luggage and the bag covering the wedding gown. "The luggage and gown bag weren't wiped. There's even a wedding picture covered with prints."

Simpson took six of the largest, most distinct prints and scanned them into AFIS.

"Something is fishy about this. It's like we're being set up. The car is wiped, but the luggage is covered with prints."

Jill took a deep breath. "They planned to take the luggage with them, so they didn't wipe it."

I stared at the AFIS machine, this time it was me willing it to spit out a match. "Or Simpson's right. We're being played."

Zoe held up something. "We just hit gold!"

We walked over to the workbench where she had a woman's toiletry kit spread on the benchtop. "Unless this woman was using two toothbrushes, she put her boyfriend's toothbrush in her kit when they packed up."

Simpson smiled and opened two plastic evidence bags. "I'll take them to the DNA lab."

"Hey, Simpson!" The tech who found the partial print on the seat adjustment knob called out. "Check this out."

We walked to the car where the tech had removed the floor mat. "There's chewing gum stuck in the carpeting. Someone tried to cut it out, but there's enough left around the edges to run DNA."

Simpson looked skeptical. "Gum is probably the one thing the car rental company wouldn't be able to remove in their routine cleaning. That could've been left by anyone who rented the car since it was put into service."

The tech held out a small evidence bag with a tiny bit of gum embedded in fibers. "You always want everything."

I watched him mark the bag. "Hey, if that DNA matches one of the toothbrushes, you've got a sure match with one of the people in the car."

Simpson nodded, but looked skeptical. "On the other hand, I hate to spend money and lab time chasing wild geese."

Zoe joined us. "Yeah, Fletcher's right. If there's a match, you may have DNA from both the bride and groom."

The AFIS computer chimed, and we walked to the workbench. "The luggage prints belong to Andrea Arnot, of Youngstown, Ohio." Simpson turned to a different computer and started typing. "Let's see why her prints are in the system."

Jill watched in fascination. "Can you get information instantly?"

"If she's a criminal, yes." It took Simpson a minute to type in the information with two fingers. "Ms. Arnot was arrested in 2008 for pawning two stolen Rolex watches. She rolled on her boyfriend, who'd stolen them. Her two-year sentence was stayed, pending completion of public service and regular meetings with a probation officer. She completed all the requirements and never did any time."

Jill jammed her hands in her pockets, deep in thought. "So, we know Arnot lived in Youngstown and that she was a felon. Here we are a dozen years later. She's recently married, but her wedding gown is left in a rental car with her luggage. Her cell phone and wedding ring are found with a dead woman, who looks like her, in the Everglades."

Simpson nodded. "She wants us to think she's dead."

Jill gave him a strange look. "These pieces lead you there?"

"Yes. I think she was running away from something in Youngstown."

I ran my hand through my hair. "And if we find out what, it will tell us why. And that may lead us to with, whom, and where."

Chapter 13

Simpson promised to prioritize DNA testing on the two toothbrushes and gum samples and call us when the results were available. We walked to the SUV in silence. The pieces of information were swirling around in all of our minds.

Larry started the engine and turned the A/C to maximum. "Where are we going?"

Jill held up the wedding picture, carefully placed in an evidence bag after being dusted for fingerprints. "Let's show this to the priest."

Larry looked at me, waiting for direction. "You heard her. Let's go."

I glanced over my shoulder at Jill who was burning over Larry's deference to me and was shaking her head. I saw no point in addressing the slight now, reasoning it would be like punishing a puppy for a puddle left hours before.

We were on the fringe of Little Havana when Jill's phone buzzed. I caught half the conversation.

"Hi, Marshal Tschetter." Then a pause before Jill started summarizing the ongoing conversation for Larry and me. "Arnot's cell phone records weren't particularly helpful. Most of the calls were to the woman pet-sitting and to a disposable cell phone that's no longer active."

Larry glanced at me and shook his head. "Another dead end. Doesn't this drive you crazy? I'd rather be tagging litterers than dealing with this frustration."

"Shh!" Jill shushed from the backseat. "Could you repeat that, please?" She listened, then recapped. "She called two numbers in the 501-area code. Where's that?" Jill put her hand over the phone. "She called a phone in Belize."

Jill listened another minute. "Can I put you on speakerphone, Marshal Tschetter?"

Jill held the phone over the seat back as Larry drove slowly through the business district in Little Havana.

"Jill, first of all, call me Randy. The cell phone she called had a Belize country and area code. Our ability to track cell phones is limited to the U.S. and Canada, and we couldn't find any activity in that area, so it's likely it was in Belize. There's no transcript of the call, only the number."

I leaned close to the phone. "Randy, this is Doug Fletcher. Where's Belize? I think I've heard of that as a Caribbean cruise stop, but beyond that, I couldn't point to it on a map."

"It's a small country south of Mexico with a coastline on the Gulf of Honduras, in the southwest Caribbean. It's known as a politically stable nation with an economy that relies heavily on tourism. If you're looking for Belize trivia, the capitol is Belmopan."

Jill pulled the phone back. "Is there anything criminally significant about Belize?"

Randy laughed. "My research says you could live like a king in Belize on a modest pension and social security. Belize has an extradition treaty with the U.S., but they've never actually extradited anyone. The few times we've tried, the paperwork sat on some official's desk. We assume he was waiting for a bribe that would be illegal to pay under federal law."

"So, we have a meaningless treaty, and the criminal world probably knows it."

"If you Google it, you'll see there is an extradition treaty, but I'm sure anyone with a computer would discover that no one has ever been extradited from Belize to the U.S." Randy paused, and I heard papers shuffling. "I also did some research on Andrea Arnot."

I leaned toward the phone. "We ran her fingerprints and learned she has a criminal record for selling stolen watches. There have been no other convictions since 2008."

"But that's apparently the tip of the iceberg." Randy commented. "When I put her name into the federal database, I got a red flag that triggered a call from the FBI. My phone rang minutes after I searched for her name and an irate FBI agent in Ohio called." Randy paused. "I was a little obtuse with him and said we were helping the park service and had found a body with her cell phone and wedding ring."

Jill leaned back with the phone. "Doug has ruffled the FBI's feathers a few times. I hope you didn't drop his name."

"I didn't mention any names, and I left them with the impression the body may be Arnot's."

"Why did your search trigger the FBI call?"

"The agent was evasive. I got one tidbit that said she was part of a RICO investigation."

"I'm sorry, Randy, but I'm new to the acronyms," Jill said. "What's RICO?"

"It's a federal law that allows us to arrest people who are involved in racketeering and ongoing criminal enterprises."

"It sounds like something you'd use to prosecute the mafia."

"It covers a lot of things. The mafia is actually a bunch of organizations that operate independently. RICO was used for going after them, but it's been used to go

275

after groups importing drugs, operating interstate prostitution rings, human trafficking, and on-line gambling scams."

"Did you find out why Arnot's name came up?"

Tschetter chuckled. "Not from the FBI. I called a colleague in Ohio and posed the question to him. The U.S. Marshal's Youngstown office has been alerted to prepare for a number of money laundering arrest warrants. He wasn't privy to any of the names, but he found Arnot's name listed as the owner of a chain of body shops and used parts businesses. Body shops and junkyards often sell parts for cash and it's nearly impossible for the IRS accountants to track down what and where the inventory is, what's been sold, what's been scrapped, and how much was paid for the parts that were sold. It's a perfect front for money laundering."

Larry turned on the street leading to St. Mark's and the gang members standing on the corner eyed us again. One spit toward the curb as we passed.

Jill looked at the gang members and checked to see if I was nervous about the neighborhood. She locked her doors, slid her holster slightly forward, and touched the butt of her Glock pistol. Nothing in her experience, from growing up in South Dakota to working rural national parks, prepared her for Little Havana. She was out of her element and overwhelmed.

I motioned for her to hand me the phone. "Thanks for all the background, Randy. Bottom line is that Arnot may have been laundering money for someone in Ohio. We've discussed the possibility that she was creating a scenario here to look like she was dead. That may have been her only way of escaping the claws of the mob."

"I've got another scenario for you. She was skimming some of the money she was laundering. Her customer got suspicious, and she sensed it was time to permanently disappear."

Larry turned into St. Mark's empty parking lot as I answered. "That leaves us with the question of her travelling partner. We've got a picture of her with a handsome Cuban guy. He wiped the rental car they were using, leaving only a partial print that didn't get a hit in AFIS."

"Interesting. Do you have anything else on him?"

"We're checking on a marriage license between Andrea Arnot and Juan Castro of Cuba. My gut says Castro's name is an alias. The Miami/Dade County crime lab found a pair of toothbrushes in a suitcase covered with Arnot's fingerprints and a piece of gum stuck in the carpet of their rental car. They just submitted them for DNA analysis and maybe that'll give us a name to go with the face." I paused, hoping Randy had more.

"Great, Doug. Keep me informed."

I shut down the phone and got out of the SUV. Jill got out of the back and was looking around like she expected to be attacked. "Are we safe here?"

Larry led us to the church doors. "Probably. At least as long as it's daylight."

Jill followed us into the dark church. "That's so reassuring, Larry."

Larry ignored her sarcasm and walked to the last pew. Facing the altar, he genuflected and crossed himself. Jill looked surprised.

A few prayer candles were burning, and two older women knelt in prayer in the dark recesses of the sanctuary. We walked down the outer aisle to Father Miguel's office and knocked on the door.

"Come in."

Larry held the door for Jill, and we followed.

Father Miguel rose from his desk and put out his hand to Jill. "Ah, my park service friends. And you've brought this lovely young lady with you."

"I'm Jill Fletcher." Jill smiled and shook his hand. "Father, I thought lying was a sin."

The priest shook our hands and gestured toward his chairs and sofa. "Lying is a sin. On the other hand, age is relative and you're in the prime of your life, making you a young lady." Father Miguel gestured for Jill to take one of the chairs. He winked at me as I passed. He and I sat on the couch, leaving Larry in the other chair. "To what do I owe the joy of another visit?"

Jill took out the wedding picture and passed it to the priest. "We found this picture in a rental car at the airport. Can you identify the people?"

Father glanced at the picture and handed it back to Jill. "I assume you already know the bride and groom are Andrea and Juan or you wouldn't be here."

The priest looked at me, his eyes asking an unspoken question. "We've confirmed Andrea's identity, but Juan remains unknown to us. Can you tell us anything more about him?"

The priest crossed his legs, apparently weighing his response. "Juan said he was from Cuba, but I really can't say any more than that."

Larry sat up like he'd been jolted with electricity. "You took their confessions before the wedding."

The priest looked at Larry and smiled. "I did."

The priest's carefully chosen words made sudden sense to me. "You can't reveal what was said to you in the confessional."

Father Miguel looked at me, then at Jill. "The seal of the confessional is inviolate. What was said there is between Juan, me, and God, I'm sure you understand."

Jill held the priest's gaze and smiled. "Is that true even if the confessor is not who he claimed to be? Would you be violating his confidence if he lied about his identity?"

Father Miguel turned to me. "Doug, do you and Jill have mental sparring matches? She's a unique intellect and has posed a question worthy of an entire book."

I raised my eyebrows. "You haven't answered her."

The priest clasped his hands in his lap and closed his eyes. "Suppose he spoke to me as…his real self. That would make his confession true, and I wouldn't be able to comment."

Larry couldn't stand the mental parrying. "Cut to the chase, Father. Did he give you his real name?"

The priest looked annoyed and frowned at Larry. "Is your patience wearing thin, Larry?"

"Listen, Padre, I've been in the confessional a thousand times, then said ten thousand Hail Marys and Our Fathers in penance. I know about the seal of the confessional, but we're talking about a slimy jerk who killed a woman and dumped her body in the Everglades. He's not even a human being. He's an animal."

Father Miguel drew a deep breath. "My son, murderers, rapists, adulterers, and people who've committed a thousand different crimes have come to the confessional expecting the same inviolate secrecy as when you confessed your childhood sins to your family priest."

Larry threw up his hands. "But he committed murder! That's a violation of the ten commandments and is a mortal sin. It's beyond your power to grant him absolution."

"I also hear confessions from people who've committed adultery, blasphemed the Lord's name, and dishonored their parents. Those are all violations of the ten commandments, and I hold their confessions in the same confidence as the altar boys who come in confessing their inappropriate affection for their female teachers."

Larry stood up. "We're done here."

The priest looked at Jill. "Are we done?"

Jill leaned on her knees. "Did he confess as Juan, Father?"

"What faith were you baptized into, Jill?"

"My parents are Presbyterian, and I was baptized in their church as an infant. Doug and I were married in an Episcopal church."

"Have you ever spoken to your minister in confidence?"

Jill stared into the priest's eyes. "Yes, Father. I have."

"If you'd committed a grave sin, like...having a child out of wedlock, and gone to a different minister to hide your identity. Would you expect him to honor your confidence?"

Jill glanced at me. "Father, I'd never put myself in that position."

The priest smiled. "Ah, but were you as righteous when you were younger?"

"You said I was a young woman just moments ago."

The priest laughed. "I wish we had all day to parry like this. You've exercised my mind more in the past ten minutes than since I was in the seminary." He stood up, signaling the end of our discussion.

Jill put out her hand and the priest took it in both his hands. "I now understand why Doug got off his path leading nowhere when he met you. He's a very lucky man."

Jill put her left hand on top of their joined hands. "You're wrong, Father. I'm the lucky one."

The priest continued to hold Jill's hands, staring into her eyes. "Jill, may I offer you a blessing?"

"Of course."

"May you be as happy tomorrow as you are today and may those days last for eternity."

Jill's eyes teared up and the priest released her hands. "Thank you."

He shook Larry's hand and Larry was out the door before I shook his hand. "Thank you, Father."

"You'll find your answer."

We stepped to the door together. Jill paused after I walked out. When I looked back, the priest had his hand on her arm, and they appeared to be having an earnest talk. I thought about my quick words with him after our last visit and wondered what philosophy the priest was sharing with Jill.

Larry was lighting a prayer candle when I walked to the back of the church. I watched him mouthing a silent prayer as the wick caught and flared. I was touched by his reverence and startled when Jill put her hand on my shoulder.

"What did Father tell you?"

Jill nodded to a dark corner, and I followed her. "Our answer isn't in Cuba."

"What?"

"Those were the priest's words of wisdom."

"Not in Cuba? We were talking with the U.S. Marshal about Belize."

Jill nodded. "But the answer won't be found by looking at Cuba."

"Juan isn't…"

Jill shook her head and pushed me toward the door. Larry dipped his fingers in the Holy water as he passed and crossed himself.

Larry started the SUV and pulled onto the street. "Any other dead ends to chase or can we call it a day?"

Jill was still buckling her seatbelt when we passed a group of teen boys harassing a younger girl. "Larry, stop."

Larry stepped on the brakes and rolled to a stop twenty feet past the group. Jill was out of the SUV before it stopped rolling. I jumped out behind her and had to run to keep up. There were eight boys standing around the girl and one of the kids facing our direction looked up as we ran toward them. He said something to the others and one of them grabbed the girl and held her arms behind her back as she kicked and swore.

The tallest kid had his back to us and when he spun around, he had a knife in his hand. Jill stopped short of him and yelled at the kid holding the girl, using her command voice. "Let. Her. Go."

I held up my badge, but none of the boys seemed to care. They were focused on Jill and the kid with the knife. I knew Jill was too close to the kid with the knife. She wouldn't have time to draw her gun before he could slash or stab her, so I drew the Sig from ten feet away and put the sights on the middle of the kid's chest.

His face had a dark, peach-fuzz beard and moustache. His arms were covered with crudely done tattoos. He wore a black baseball cap at an angle. I didn't recognize the cap's logo.

He sneered at me. "Look, the old bitch has got an amigo with a gun."

I heard the SUV engine rev and the whine of the transmission driving in reverse. The crunching tires stopped inches behind me. The door slammed and a few of the boys looked past me, their eyes going wide. Larry stepped next to me with a shotgun against his shoulder.

Jill was intense and not reacting appropriately to the threat posed by the knife. "Let. The. Girl. Go."

"Or what? You gonna shoot me? You shoot and you'd be lucky to live until you make it to a hospital. Look around. You see anyone around here who's going to take pity on a white bitch shooting a street kid?"

Jill pulled her Glock out and aimed it at the kid's crotch. "Have you ever thought about what life would be like if someone shot you in the cajones?"

That got the kid's attention. He shifted his stance, like he was going to block her bullet with his thigh. "You can't shoot me."

Jill slid her finger off the trigger guard and onto the trigger. "Let. The. Girl. Go."

The kid holding the girl's arms released her and she ran across the street and to a distraught middle-aged woman standing on the porch of the nearest house. The mother engulfed the girl and hustled her inside the house. The motion caught the knife-holder's attention and he looked away long enough for Jill to take a quick step forward. She kicked the kid's hand, and the knife flew onto the pavement and skittered away before disappearing into a storm drain.

The move was so quick the kid looked at his hand in disbelief. He looked up at Jill and yelled, "Perra!" He took a threatening step toward Jill, then turned and sauntered away with his posse. Jill lowered her gun, drew a breath, and looked like she'd deflated.

I pointed to the SUV, and we got in the backseat together. Larry stowed the shotgun under the back seat and sped away, watching his mirrors. "What the hell, Jill? Are you trying to get us killed?"

I touched Jill's arm. "What were you thinking?"

"They were going to hurt that girl!"

"You ran within reach of a guy holding a knife. He could've slashed or stabbed you."

"Yeah. Well, that might not have been my smartest move."

"Neither was kicking the knife away."

Jill lowered her head. "What does 'perra' mean?"

Larry turned his head. "That's Spanish for female dog, a bitch."

Jill sighed. "I thought it might've been worse than that."

We drove out of Little Havana in silence, Jill watching the storefronts as we passed.

The drive from the park to the hotel was equally quiet. "Are you okay?" I asked.

"I keep thinking about that poor girl." Jill paused. "We didn't solve anything, did we?"

"Probably not. If anything, we might've stirred up the water. She lives in the neighborhood with those boys. They're not going away."

Jill looked out the window as we drove into Florida City. "I thought…"

"I know. We swore to uphold the law and we saw an assault in progress."

"Maybe if we'd arrested the boys."

"They're juveniles on their way to being real gang members. Arresting them would've helped them make their reputations, and a judge would've slapped them on the wrist and let them go home."

Jill sighed. "There's no good answer."

"We can't change the poverty, the gangs, the drugs, the lack of playgrounds and youth programs. All we can do is enforce the laws and that's only the tip of the iceberg."

We rode in silence back to the park. Larry dropped us in front of our rental car.

* * *

I parked at the hotel, and we walked into the lobby. Margot was on the phone at the concierge desk and waved frantically. Jill gave me a pleading look, but I walked over as Margot was ending her call.

"Mr. Fletcher, I just had a guest back out of Marlins' tickets. They're yours if you'd like to go to a ballgame."

I looked at Jill. "Are you interested in going to a baseball game?"

Jill smiled at Margot. "Thanks, but not tonight. It's been a long day."

Margot nodded her understanding. "I've got tickets for the afternoon game tomorrow."

"I'm afraid not. Work calls."

"Dinner reservations tonight?"

Jill shook her head. "I think I'll order a salad from room service."

Margot stood up and walked from behind her desk. She reached out and took Jill's hand. "Honey, you don't want to do that. There are a dozen restaurants within a mile that have better salads than room service. I can get you a reservation or I can get a salad delivered, whichever you want."

Jill was about to say no.

"Let's take a walk. We can get one of Krista's tables," I said.

288

Margot perked up. "I'll let them know you're on the way."

Jill gave me a sad look but walked out of the hotel with me. "We have to eat something somewhere."

"I'm not hungry."

I took her hand. "I'm hungry. You can have a glass of wine and watch me eat."

She squeezed my hand. "Sure."

The restaurant was quiet, and Krista was talking to a busboy when we walked in. She rushed across the dining room and took our menus from the hostess. "You guys are in for a treat. We have blue crab boil tonight."

"What's crab boil?" I asked as she led us to a table near the windows.

"Honey, you haven't lived until you've had crab boil." She left with the menus and without taking our drink order.

Jill leaned close. "What are we getting?"

I shrugged. "Something with crabs that's boiled."

Jill looked at the neighboring tables, apparently trying to see what crab boil is. "This sounds like something from Peg Leg Pete's, in Port Aransas."

Krista returned with two tall frosty mugs of beer. "I know y'all prefer wine, but crab boil is a beer thing." She sped away as quickly as she'd appeared.

Jill looked at me and broke into a smile for the first time all day. "Krista is a hoot."

We were sipping beer when the kitchen door swung open, and Krista carried out two steaming serving bowls. She set them in front of us, looking like she'd just given us the best gift ever. A big crab sat on top of a pile of corn on the cob, potatoes, and large pieces of smoked sausage. When we didn't react, she sat down in the spare chair at our table. "Y'all never picked crab before?"

Jill shook her head. "There aren't many crabs in South Dakota."

Krista looked around to make sure no one needed her, then she grabbed Jill's crab and pulled off the legs. "You set these aside, and then you crack open the shell like this." She pulled the shell apart, discarded some disgusting green stuff, then handed the halves to Jill. "You pull out that meat and tell me you haven't died and gone to heaven."

I copied Krista's actions as Jill pulled a piece of white crabmeat out of the shell. She examined it briefly, then popped it into her mouth. I watched her expression change from uncertain to rapture as she closed her eyes and chewed. She opened her eyes and wiped her fingers on her napkin. "I've never tasted anything like this."

Krista was already breaking the claws with a chrome-plated tool. "If you think that was good, try this." Krista pulled a large piece of meat out of a claw and offered it to Jill, who took it without reservation.

"Oh, my," she said as she chewed. "This is sweet."

I was eating my first bite of crab when Krista got up. "You're going to need more napkins." She sped off, wiping her fingers on a paper napkin as she left.

Jill picked up a corn cob and took a bite. "Thanks for getting me out of the hotel. I needed this."

I was eating my second piece of crab. I'd decided to save the claws for last after seeing Jill's reaction. "You had a tough day, and I knew an evening in the hotel room wasn't going to improve your mood."

Jill shook salt and pepper on the red potatoes in the bowl and sliced off a bite. "What did Krista call this dish?"

"I think she said it was called crab boil."

Krista was behind me, then set a stack of paper napkins and wet wipes next to each of us. "We make it with crabs, but I've had it with shrimp up in the Carolinas. They called it a beach boil. Either way, it's a treat." She paused and pointed to the sausage. "I think of the smoked links as flavoring, but they're good eating too."

I cut a piece off the sausage as Krista swept away. "This is really a simple meal, but wow, it's incredible."

Jill broke crab legs and picked pieces out, popping them in her mouth. "This would be a fun meal to make for my folks. It's simple, tasty, and they've never had anything like it. We could buy shrimp and all the other fixings and boil it up in Mom's spaghetti pot."

I wiped off my fingers and reached out for her hand. "Or we could keep it as one of our special memories."

Jill squeezed my hand, then went back to picking crabmeat out of the shell. "For being a crusty, cynical cop, you sometimes say the most romantic things."

Krista appeared again and sat in the extra chair. Although she was busy and handling a half dozen tables, she sat down and looked like everything was under control. Having overheard Jill's comments, she was smiling when she looked at me. "Sounds like someone's going to get lucky tonight."

I was sipping my beer and snorted, setting off a coughing fit. Krista handed me a napkin as Jill broke into laughter.

Tony, the owner slipped between tables and made sure I wasn't choking to death, then he knelt down opposite Krista. "Is everything okay?"

Jill smiled. "It's fabulous!"

Krista jumped up, noticing that one of her customer's had an empty beer. Tony, the owner, watched her go. "She told me you two are the nicest people she's ever waited on."

Jill wiped her mouth and watched Krista swoop from table to table, making sure everyone had full glasses and was happy with their meals. "Krista is like my mother, never too busy to care about her guests."

"She's going to own this place in a few years."

Jill's eyes went wide. "Is she your daughter?"

Tony shook his head. "She grew up down the street from us and was my daughter's best friend. My kids have no interest in the restaurant business, but Krista oozes personality and understands how to please our customers."

"Have you told her?" I asked.

He laughed and put his hand on my shoulder. "She told me that the second week she worked here."

We finished the crab and ate most of the remaining food, leaving a few potato slices. Krista swept back and picked up our bowls as we wiped our hands with wet wipes. "Was I right? Was that the best thing y'all have ever eaten?"

I pulled out my credit card and handed it to her. "You were right."

She beamed and left with our bowls and utensils. Jill leaned across the table. "You'd better tip her extra tonight."

I dug a folded hundred-dollar-bill out of a small slot in my wallet and showed the corner to Jill so she could see the denomination. She smiled, nodded, and put her hand out. "Let me give it to her."

Krista returned with a black portfolio and pen and handed it to me as Jill stood. They were hugging when I signed the credit card slip. Krista pulled me up and hugged me. "Thank you."

Jill grabbed my hand as we walked out of the restaurant. We walked the quiet sidewalk back to the hotel, Jill swinging my hand like we were school children.

Margot was talking to the desk clerk when we walked into the lobby, and she swept over to us. "How was dinner?"

Jill beamed. "We had blue crab boil and you were right; it was *much* better than eating a salad in our room."

Margot smiled. "You looked like your dog died when you came in here this afternoon. I knew you needed to get out."

Jill leaned against me in the elevator. "I don't deserve you."

"Why do you say that?"

"Because it's true." We walked the hallway to our room. "If you hadn't showed up, I'd be eating salads alone in my Flagstaff house and watching Hallmark movies that make me cry."

I unlocked the door. "This is better?"

She hugged and kissed me. "This is heaven."

I pulled her close and she pushed me away. "Hey, I thought we were having a Hallmark moment of our own."

Jill ran to the bathroom. "I've had sixteen ounces of beer and they have a higher priority right now."

I laid on the bed and turned on the TV. Jill snuggled close while we watched the evening news. I turned off the news and shut off the light. "Was Krista right? Am I going to get lucky tonight?"

Jill pushed me away. "I don't think that'd be wise."

"Oh?"

"I ate too much, and I think throwing up on you would ruin the romantic moment."

I kissed her gently with my hand on her stomach.

She pushed my hand away. "That's just a little more pressure than my stomach can handle right now." She rolled with her back to me and pulled my arm over her shoulder. "That's better."

Chapter 14

Jill's breakfast was black coffee and one slice of buttered toast. I had my usual scrambled eggs and sausage. Halfway through my plate I looked up. She was staring at me. "How can you eat anything? I'm still full from last night."

"It's an Army thing—eat when you can."

Jill flipped her hand. "Not if it'll make you sick." She took a breath. "What's the plan for today?"

"We go back to the county crime lab. Simpson said they might have DNA results."

"And we hope that Juan's DNA will be on the toothbrush and/or gum sample. Then we hope it matches a sample in the national database."

"Like Simpson said, CODIS, the DNA database, has people who've been convicted of a felony or were in the service. He might not match any of them."

"Will it help if he's not Cuban?"

I shook my head. "Eliminating Cuba only narrows it to any other Spanish speaking country and maybe two hundred million Hispanic men who aren't in CODIS."

"Let's be optimistic."

I shook my head. "It's not in my nature. I'm a cynical cop."

"Maybe it's time to change?"

"It's too late. The cynicism is encoded in my DNA."

* * *

Larry met us in the visitor center parking lot. "What's the plan for today?"

"Simpson said they might have DNA results today, so we should check in at their lab."

Larry looked less than enthused. "I flunked biology and even saying DNA makes me yawn."

Jill looked away in disgust. I looked him in the eye. "You're going back to ticketing litterers rather than learning what a real cop does?"

Larry's jaw clenched. "Get in the SUV."

I'd irritated Larry and he drove ten miles an hour over the speed limit through Florida City. Once past the city limits, he sped up even more. I bit my tongue as he passed cars and minivans, thinking it was him who'd get ticketed, not me.

We arrived at the Miami-Dade Forensics Services Bureau in record time. Larry's speeding shaved ten minutes off the fifty-minute drive to Doral. He parked near the garage, and we walked through the open garage door.

One of the techs saw us come in and yelled, "Simpson, your rangers are back!"

I heard footsteps and Simpson, in his coveralls, walked out of a hallway. He gestured for us to follow and led us silently through a maze of hallways past doors identifying the various sections of the forensics unit. He opened a door marked Forensic Biology and to an office where a middle-aged woman was typing on a computer keyboard.

"Libby, the park service folks are here."

Libby, wearing a white lab coat, shut down her computer. She stood, smiled, and beckoned us into her office where we sat at a round table.

"I'm Libby Harris, the biology section supervisor." We made introductions around the table and Mike Simpson excused himself.

"Mike brought me two toothbrushes and a chewing gum sample for expedited DNA analysis. Please give me context about the samples," Libby requested.

I explained the body discovered in the park and our identification of Madison Wirth. "We found a wedding ring and a cell phone that both belonged to a different woman, and we think she may have been trying to fake her own death. We know who the woman is, but her male partner's identity and their current location are a mystery."

Libby made notes on a yellow legal pad as I spoke. "Your objective was to identify the man by testing the DNA on the toothbrushes and gum sample."

"Yes, exactly."

Libby rolled her chair over to her desk and picked up a folder. "How much do you know about DNA testing?"

Larry stifled a yawn and I glared at him. "I'm familiar with the concept, but none of us are geneticists."

Libby put the palm of her hand on the file. "Let me explain a little of the process before I get into this information. One of my technicians was able to recover human squamous cells from all three samples. She lysed the cells to extract the DNA, then she used PCR to replicate the DNA, so she had a larger sample for analysis."

Jill put up her hand to stop the explanation. "Could you back up? Please give us a DNA for dummies primer."

Libby smiled. "Sorry. I get caught up in biochemistry and forget I'm not talking to a bunch of genetics nerds." She took a breath. "My tech got a small DNA sample and used a technique, PCR, to make millions of copies of the genes she recovered. With that sample, she used STR to break the genes into segments that can

299

be tested using an electrically charged medium that speeds the migration of the genetic segments, so we have something to read after an overnight test. Our first cut of testing is an autosomal DNA test, where we look at all the genetic material in the nucleus of the cell. We use an FBI protocol and pick thirteen specific segments for comparison. It's rather like looking at a few key markers on a fingerprint. If all thirteen points match a corresponding sample, we say we have a match."

Jill and I nodded our understanding. Larry leaned back and crossed his arms.

Jill looked excited. "And you identified the people?"

Libby smiled. "You're getting ahead of me. Once we have our thirteen points, we go to CODIS, the FBI database of DNA samples, and the computer screens for a match. CODIS found a match for the cells on one of the toothbrushes." Libby opened the file folder and took out a piece of paper. "The DNA on the yellow toothbrush matches a profile for Andrea Arnot. Her DNA was entered into CODIS by the state of Ohio after her felony arrest."

Jill looked let down. "We had her identified through her fingerprints. She was also the person who rented the car we brought in for the search."

Libby nodded. "The analysis of the green toothbrush and the chewing gum samples were interesting." She took out two sheets of paper with the tiny gray and black bars I was familiar with from past DNA cases. "The DNA on those items match each other. Based on that, you know the person who probably shared a room with Arnot, was also in the car with her."

"Okay," I said. "Was that person in CODIS?"

Libby took out another sheet. "No. The computer says the likelihood of any match with a CODIS DNA sample is less than one in a billion."

Jill leaned back. "Nothing?"

Libby smiled like she had more cards to play. "Not in CODIS. So, my tech did a quick phenotype of the genes, and we now know a little bit more about him." She took out another sheet with a rough facial drawing. "We know he's blood type "O" and is Hispanic. The rest is pretty unspectacular because it indicates he has brown eyes and dark hair."

Jill reached for her pocket and pulled out the wedding picture and handed it to Libby. "We've got his picture. He claims he's Cuban, so the brown eyes and dark hair are no surprise."

Libby glanced at the picture and handed it back. "We have one more place to look. It seems like everyone in the world wants to know where their roots are. A few years ago, National Geographic started offering home DNA tests. Their testing only gave the user a gross regional idea of their family genetics, nothing specific. Shortly after that '23andMe' started offering home tests and their analysis was more specific, and also offered the geographic ancestral information. They were the first to make connections to relatives. They were followed by Ancestry.com and others. Five years ago, those companies had tested two million samples. Today, Ancestry.com has surpassed all the other companies and the total number of completed tests has passed twenty million samples."

Larry perked up. "I watched a television show about that. They used some family tree stuff to track down the Golden State killer. They found his relatives and were able to identify him even though his DNA wasn't in CODIS."

Libby smiled. "That was one of the first cases solved using forensic genealogy. Since then, a number of states, including Florida, have been using familytreeDNA or gedmatch to develop familial relationships and trace suspects through the DNA left at crime scenes. The public information in the databases is limited to people who've volunteered their samples, so we've used companies like Parabon Nano and private consultants who tap into the public information. They go beyond the databases to track down birth certificates, marriage licenses, probate records, and more. They give us a likely match, then we have to look at other factors. Sometimes the possible matches are the wrong age, or live in the wrong geography, so we narrow the suspect list to one or two people. We pass that information to the police who get a sample of the suspect's DNA to do a definitive match."

Jill pointed to the wedding picture. "Juan Castro's name is on his marriage license. Did you find his family?"

Libby leaned back. "We struck out on CODIS and gedmatch, so I called a private genealogical consultant, Michele Daniels, who uses the databases and the other genealogical techniques I mentioned."

Jill's eyes widened. "That's who Mom's using to trace our family tree."

"Michele constructs a lot of family trees, so it's possible she's doing research for your family. She's also one of only a handful of forensic genealogy practitioners, and the only one on the East coast." Libby went on. "She found several familial connections but asked us for the mitochondrial DNA. The mitochondria are called the cell's engine and it's a tiny packet of DNA outside of the cell's nucleus. It's in the mother's egg, so it's only passed down on the female side of the family, passed by the mother to every family member in every generation, but only her daughters pass it on to their children. Michele identified your suspect's aunt in New York who'd submitted her DNA sample through familytreeDNA."

Larry was fully into it now. "New York? He told everyone he was Cuban."

Libby put up a hand. "Slow down. Just because his aunt is in New York doesn't point to this guy's origins." Libby pulled out another page with a partial family tree. "The suspect's DNA shows a strong link to Puerto Rico. The aunt moved from Puerto Rico twenty years ago. We found three cousins in the U.S. and all of them also moved from Puerto Rico. Your guy isn't Cuban."

Jill looked at me. "Not Cuban."

I looked at the family tree she'd created, which went back three generations, but was missing many people. "What can you tell us about Juan?"

Libby pointed to the family tree. "His family name is Espinoza, and his family has been in Puerto Rico forever. The good news is that Puerto Rico keeps excellent birth and marriage records, going back over two hundred years. The bad news is that it was an isolated island, and the genetic pool is relatively small with thousands of marriages between first, second, and third cousins."

Jill nodded. "A family tree that looks like a briar patch."

"Exactly. But we know his mother's and father's family names. And their tradition is using the mother's maiden name as part of the child's last name. Your missing man's last name is Espinoza de Corazon."

I turned the family tree so I could read the names right side up. "It looks like you've narrowed it down to this set of parents."

"That's the good news. The Espinoza de Corazones had four boys, and that's as far as genetics can take us."

Jill picked up the paper. "Carlos. Juan. Luis. Angel."

"None of them have ever been arrested, so they don't have DNA in CODIS. Angel's family submitted samples to Ancestry.com, and he's not a match with the suspect. Luis owns a body shop in Rincon. Carlos owns a taxi in San Juan, so Michele suggested we eliminate them because of geography."

I saw where this was going. "And Juan?"

"I spoke with his aunt this morning. According to her, Juan got in with a bad crowd and disappeared. He hasn't been in touch with anyone in the family for years."

Jill smiled. "But we have his picture."

Libby pushed the now empty folder to Jill. "You may have the only picture of the adult Juan in existence."

"We suspect he is in Belize."

Libby stood. "I think you should talk to U.S. Customs. They scan passports and may be able to do facial recognition."

Jill looked at me. "Do you think he's brazen enough to use his real name on a passport? Can we check passenger manifests to see if Juan Espinoza de Corazon flew out of Miami to Belize?"

I gathered Libby's printouts into the folder and handed them to Jill. "You have a friend in the U.S. Marshal's office who might be better able to answer that question."

We thanked Libby and wound back through the hallways to the garage. Simpson was overseeing the dismantling of an older Chevrolet. His techs were deep in the trunk and had stacked four packages that looked like foil wrapped bricks on a stainless-steel table.

He looked up when he heard our footsteps. "Hey, Fletcher, did Libby take care of you?"

I put out my hand. "My friends and colleagues call me Doug. And yes, Libby did a great job for us. I understand you submitted our items as a priority."

Simpson shook my hand. "I'm Mike, although I don't tell that to many of the outside agencies who come through here."

"I doubt we'll be back. Thanks."

Mike smiled and shook hands with Larry and Jill. "I don't hear thanks very often."

"Most folks think that comes with the territory, but I like to show my appreciation when someone helps me out."

Simpson smiled. "A bottle of Johnnie Walker would show a lot of appreciation."

"Gee, Mike, I imagine you're saddled by the same gift rules as we are. A bottle of Johnnie Walker would be way over the twenty-five-dollar gift limit."

Simpson snapped his fingers. "I could almost taste that Scotch." He slapped my shoulder. "You're okay, for a fed."

We walked to the SUV and Jill sidled up to me. "That was smooth. Getting out of buying a bottle of booze for a guy who helped you."

We got in the SUV and Larry started the engine, again blowing hot moist air in my face. "Did you see a liquor store nearby?"

"I think there was a package store a couple blocks back. Why?"

"I need to buy a couple bottles of booze."

"You just told…"

"Just drive to the store."

Larry and Jill stayed in the SUV while I went into the liquor store. I was back in less than five minutes with one large and one small bag."

"What's with the two bags?" Jill asked.

"You'll see in a minute."

I had Larry park so he was blocking the open garage door. I got out, then gestured for Jill to follow. I carried the small lunch bag inside the garage where Simpson and his crew were still digging drugs out of the Chevy.

He looked up, showing surprise. "I thought we'd seen the last of you."

I shook my head and held up the bag. "I found a way around the gift limit." Simpson smirked as his three techs gathered around. I opened the bag and handed each of them a miniature, airline-sized bottle of Scotch.

Zoe started laughing and held the bottle up to the overhead lights. "Is this real?"

"Oh, yes. Don't drink it all in one sitting."

I bent my head and whispered to Jill. "Get the other bag."

I joked with the techs while Jill walked out of the garage. She came back in, unable to conceal the bag and gathering a lot of curiosity. She held the bag out to me, the bottles clinking inside. I shook my head and gestured for her to open the sack and hand out the contents.

She handed a liter bottle of Macallan 12-year-old Scotch to each of the techs. They stared at Simpson, waiting to follow his lead. He looked at the bottle, then shook his head. "Like you said, this is over the gifting limit. We can't accept them."

I handed him the bag with another bottle still in it. "Give this one to Libby," then I turned away and led Jill by the elbow toward the door. I spoke over my shoulder. "You'd better drink them down to the twenty-five-dollar level before your boss sees them." Then we left.

Jill looked over her shoulder as we pulled out of the parking lot. "They're standing at the door holding their bottles."

"I hope they take them right to their cars."

She continued to look back. "That's what's happening." She paused. "How did you know they'd take them?"

"Who refuses a sixty-dollar bottle of Scotch?"

Larry's head snapped toward me. "You spent over two-hundred bucks on booze for those guys?"

"Three hundred, plus sales tax."

"Man alive, I need to be nicer to you."

I thought for a second. "Larry, they did a big favor for us. I imagine if you ever need their help again, you'll be the beneficiary of this gift."

Larry mulled that as he drove.

"Larry, take the next right," Jill said from the backseat.

Larry didn't have time to ask why, so he braked hard and made the turn.

"Now, turn right into this strip mall."

"Why?" he asked as he made the turn.

"There's a café advertising a salad bar halfway down this strip and I'm hungry."

"A salad bar?" Larry asked.

"Yes, a salad bar."

Larry parked the SUV and checked his cell phone as we walked to the restaurant. "It's only eleven o'clock. Why are we eating so early?"

Jill didn't say anything, so I smiled. "Someone's tummy wasn't feeling up to eating the free hotel breakfast this morning."

We were the first people in the café and took a table near the back. Larry sat so we could see the door just past a booth. Jill shook her head. "Do you *have* to watch the door in every restaurant and bar?"

Larry nodded. "If someone walks in with a gun, I want to know before it's pointed at my head."

Jill looked skeptical. "They just opened. There's probably nothing but change in the cash register."

I shook my head. "Lots of small places can't afford an armored car pick up. They make their deposits in the morning rather than walking out at the end of the day with a sack full of cash."

The very young waitress with a pierced eyebrow and a nose stud brought glasses of water and handed us menus. "You guys want a minute?"

Larry glanced at the menu and set it aside. "What's the lunch special?"

The girl paused. "Just a minute. I forgot to ask."

Jill set her menu aside and got up. "I'm having the salad bar."

Our waitress came back and watched Jill walking to the salad bar. "The special is a Cuban sandwich with fries for eight bucks." Larry and I both ordered the special with diet colas. The waitress nodded toward Jill. "Is she having anything else?"

I shook my head. "She's vegan. She'll just have the salad bar and a diet cola." The waitress nodded knowingly and left.

Larry looked at me. "Jill's vegan? I thought you guys were having seafood every night."

"Shh. Don't tell Jill that fish isn't a vegetable."

Larry rolled his eyes. A second later his phone trilled, and he got up to answer it. Jill came back with a mountain of salad topped with ham cubes and shredded cheese.

"Eat your ham and cheese quickly, before the waitress comes back."

Jill put a paper napkin on her lap. "Why?"

"I told her you were vegan."

"Why would you do that? I'm not vegan just because I prefer to have some vegetables once in a while."

"Shh. Hide the ham. Here she comes."

"Cut that out!"

Larry had taken the call on the sidewalk and was sweating when he returned. I raised my eyebrows. "Your wife wants you to pick up milk and bread on the way home?"

He let out a sigh. "It was Jack. One of the gators decided to walk down the Anhinga Trail. I guess a woman thought he was tame and was going to set her kid on his back for a picture."

Jill froze with a forkful of greens halfway to her mouth. "And?"

"The gator decided to leave and when he turned his tail swung around and knocked the woman's feet out from under her."

Jill wiped her mouth. "Is the child okay?"

Larry shrugged. "Jack didn't say anything about the kid, so I guess he's okay. The woman has a broken leg, and they called an ambulance for her. Two rangers carried her to the parking lot."

Our sandwiches arrived and the waitress asked if we wanted ketchup. She noticed the ham on Jill's salad, garnering me a glare. "Vegan?"

I shrugged. "I guess the ham was too tempting and she decided to switch back to eating meat."

The waitress snorted and walked away.

Larry yelled after her. "Hey, I'd like some ketchup." He turned back to us and stuffed three fries into his mouth. "Jack says we need to come back and do an accident investigation. He asked the witnesses to hang around or come back at one o'clock."

"Did the kid ride in the ambulance with his mom?" Jill asked.

Larry shrugged. "I dunno," he said as he picked up his sandwich and bit off the end.

Jill gave me a look like I was supposed to say or do something. I had nothing that would add to the situation, so I stayed quiet.

The waitress set the squeeze bottle of ketchup in front of Larry and gave me another *look*. "I've never had a vegan cop. I was thinking your partner was going to be my first."

I was going to make a snarky comment, but Jill anticipated my plan and kicked me hard enough to leave a bruise. "Not today," she said.

I waited until the waitress was in the kitchen before speaking. "I was going to tell her that she was still a vegan cop virgin."

Jill shook her head in disgust. "I was afraid you were going to say something like that."

Larry chuckled. "That's a good one."

We ate lunch and talked about animal attacks at the park and lost visitors. Larry was blasé about the incidents, making me wonder if he was diligent in his investigations or whether he slid through them, just gathering enough information to fill out the form. My suspicion was that he put as little effort into them as possible and they were filed and never used to learn anything or prevent any future similar incidents.

* * *

Larry drove back to the park and went to Jack's office to get background on the woman's injury. Jill and I took over Larry's office. Jill sat in his desk chair. "Let's split the calls." She chose a number on her cell phone and hit redial. "I'll call Randy Tschetter and you call your mom."

I was about to protest when she put up her finger. "Randy, hi, this is Jill Fletcher. We have a tentative identification of the man with Andrea Arnot from the Miami-Dade forensics lab."

I pulled out my phone, resigned to making the usually painful call to my mother. Jill stopped me by pointing a finger at me. "Hang on, Randy. Doug's here and I'm putting you on speaker. Please repeat what you told me."

Jill activated the speaker and set her phone on the desk. "Hi, Doug. I just got off the phone with the Youngstown police. I asked them to send a forensics team to Andrea Arnot's apartment. They went over it from top to bottom, even pulling the covers off the heat registers and checking her drains. They found a hotdog wrapped in Saran wrap in her freezer. When they unwrapped it, they realized it was a finger."

I looked at Jill, who looked green. "Was it Arnot's finger?"

"They took it to the medical examiner, and he matched it to a corpse in his morgue. That immediately set off red flags because the dead guy was a local mafioso who'd died from two small caliber bullets to the back of the head. They assume kidnappers removed the finger to prove he was alive, but that plan apparently fell apart before the finger was delivered."

"And now Andrea Arnot is on the FBI's radar."

"She was before, but now they're *really* interested in speaking with her."

I closed Larry's door. "Are you skating on thin ice talking to us?"

"I'm not skating because I'm treading water. If I weren't a fed, they'd probably have my phone tapped and I'm not certain they don't anyway."

"Shit. I'm sorry we backed you into a corner."

Tschetter laughed. "Hey, you didn't back me into a corner. I went there on my own."

"Are we putting you in a bind if we discuss the guy who's traveling with Arnot?"

"Not at all because this call never happened. Jill called my encrypted cell phone and I'm driving on I-95. Say anything you want. Ask what you want. I never heard any of it."

"The guy with Arnot is not Cuban. He's Puerto Rican. The forensic genealogy points to a family with four boys and one is unaccounted for. We got his DNA off a toothbrush in the luggage they left in the rental car."

"This match didn't come off CODIS?"

"The Miami-Dade genetics lab used forensic genealogy," Jill explained. "They used DNA tests submitted by people tracing their family trees. That data got them to a family in Puerto Rico. The family has four sons. Three are accounted for and one has been off the grid for decades."

Leaning close to the phone, I said, "Randy, this guy is a ghost. He's never been arrested. His prints and DNA aren't in any crime database. His family hasn't seen him in years."

"Hang on. I'm pulling into a rest area." We waited a few moments then he returned. "Okay, so you've got this guy's DNA. What's his name?"

I nodded to Jill. "Juan Espinosa de Corazon. We also have a picture of him. A wedding picture."

I leaned toward the phone again. "Do you have any contacts in Immigration and Customs Enforcement who could check on Miami international departures? He's been posing as Juan Castro, but he just might be using his real name and passport since he's not on anyone's radar."

"As long as I don't have to call the FBI, I can ask all kinds of questions without opening a can of worms. Send the wedding picture to my phone. I'll forward it to a friend in ICE along with the name. He'll be able to check departing people. They're using facial recognition to compare passport pictures to people who are travelling. He might be able to find this guy's picture even if he's travelling under a different name."

Jill frowned. "Customs only checks passports when you enter the country."

Tschetter laughed. "You're awfully naïve for a cop. If you think Customs is only looking at arriving passengers, you're sadly mistaken. You can't board an international flight without a passport, and they're all scanned and in the ICE database before the plane's door closes."

"Big brother is watching," Jill said, leaning back.

"Send me the photo. I'll get back to you as soon as I know anything. If you don't hear from me within twenty-four hours, it's probably because I'm in an FBI holding cell."

Jill ended the call, then took a photo of the wedding picture with her phone. She emailed it to Randy, then looked tired. "Are we done? Is this the end of our investigation?"

"A woman was killed in a national park. We don't have anyone under arrest. So no, we're not done."

"But we think they're in Belize and..."

"Let Randy do his thing. Don't throw in the towel yet."

Jill stood up. "Buy me a glass of wine, a very large glass of wine."

I laughed. "You might not want to repeat that request to Krista. Remember what happened the last time you asked for a very large glass of wine?"

Larry opened his office door and stepped in. "Are you guys done? I need to fill out an online accident report on my computer."

Jill stood. "Are the woman and child okay?"

Larry blew out a breath. "The kid has some scrapes from falling off the gator. The woman has a broken leg, so that elevates

318

the visibility of the incident. It's so much less paperwork if they only need first aid."

I followed Jill out of the office. She held her thoughts until we got outside the building. "Did you hear that? He's more concerned about the reports he'll have to fill out than the injured woman!"

"Take it easy. He's not our problem."

Jill looked over her shoulder to make sure no one was following us. "Not our problem, but his cavalier attitude reflects on all rangers."

I led her to our rental car. "He's getting better."

Chapter 15

The seafood restaurant's parking lot was nearly empty at four o'clock. We walked into the dining room where a table of businessmen appeared to be negotiating a deal. Their table was covered with papers, and everyone looked very intense.

Tony peeked out of the kitchen and came quickly to the door when he saw us. "Welcome Doug and Jill."

"Thanks," I said. "Seat us at one of Krista's tables and have her bring Jill another big glass of wine."

Tony led us to a table far from the negotiating businessmen. "Krista isn't here tonight. I'll have Marty bring you some wine."

I smiled. "You let Krista have a night off?"

Tony looked uneasy. "Actually, her boyfriend called and said she'd fallen down the stairs and needed to be off for a few days."

Tony started to turn away and I put my hand on his arm. "Her boyfriend called, not Krista?"

"Yeah. They've been together a couple years. He calls in for her whenever she's sick."

Jill caught the same vibe. "Does she fall down the stairs very often?"

Tony shrugged. "Her boyfriend says she's a klutz. Every few months she falls in the shower or slips in the kitchen. She's gone for a few days, then comes in bruised and laughing about it."

"She seemed pretty sure footed here," I said. "Has she ever fallen on the job?"

Tony sensed where this was going. "Listen, I'm not her dad or brother. She claims the falls are accidents. They don't happen all the time, so I don't pry."

Jill stood up. "Give us her address."

"What? I don't give out the addresses of my employees."

Jill took out her ID and held it in front of Tony's face. "We're federal cops. Give us her address. We're going to make sure she's safe."

Tony closed his eyes, weighing his response. "I…"

I got up. "If she's okay, we'll come back, and we'll all laugh about her being a klutz."

"If she's not?" Tony asked.

"We'll hold her boyfriend until the local cops come to arrest him."

Tony thought about it. "I'm coming with you."

Jill put her hand on Tony's chest. "No, you're not a cop and you've got too much to lose if you do something stupid."

Tony weighed Jill's comments and let out a breath. "Here's the deal. I'll give you her address, but I'm calling the Florida City PD and asking them to do a welfare check as soon as you're out the door."

I nodded. "Deal."

Tony took us to the hostess stand and scribbled a street address and apartment number on the back of a business card. "Her apartment is on the second floor almost to the end of the hall. If that sonofabitch has done something to her..." Tony hesitated. "I..."

I took the business card and put my hand on his shoulder. "We're sworn to uphold the law and our pensions and freedom depend on us doing our sworn duty. The absolute worst harm we can do is arrest him."

Tony's eyes moistened. "Maybe he'll resist arrest."

I patted Tony's shoulder. "We'll be back. Hold a table for us."

Jill walked with determination to the rental car and pinned her badge to her shirt. "Let me handle this."

I unlocked the doors and got behind the wheel. "What are you thinking?"

"I think that guy will freak out if he sees a male cop at the door. I'm pretty sure he'll underestimate me."

"And if he shows up at the door with a gun?"

Jill looked at me with steely eyes. "He'll be dead."

"Hang on. We don't know that anything's happened to Krista except an accidental fall."

"That's bullshit and we both know it. Tony laid out a pattern of an abusive relationship. I've lived through one. You haven't."

I stopped the car. "You never told me…"

"Drive."

We were a half block from the restaurant when Jill turned her head and looked out the side window. "The cowboy."

"You're ex-fiancé?"

"The son of a bitch used to hit me. Never where it'd show. He said I made him do it. I'd do things that would throw him into a rage, then he'd punch me. As soon as it was over, he'd be all lovey-dovey, but it was always my fault for egging him on."

"That's why you split?"

"Don't tell Daddy. They cross paths occasionally, and I don't want my father to run up a huge legal bill and maybe go to jail over something that's ancient history."

"How about if I kill him instead?"

Jill looked at me to see if I was joking. "Not that either." She looked at the address and pointed down the road. "I think it's the three-story building on the right."

The apartment complex looked like it had been built after Hurricane Andrew scrubbed much of the area clear of structures. The parking lot was nearly empty, and I took a spot near the entrance where a locked gate controlled access to the pool and apartments.

Jill walked up to the gate and pushed it open. "Great security here. Somebody tore the lock apart."

I looked at the rusty lock striker. "It's been gone for a while. There's a lot of rust on the strike plate."

We took an outdoor stairway to the second floor and walked to Krista's apartment. A television was playing behind the door.

Jill pointed to the hinge side of the door and whispered. "Get out of sight." She knocked and waited.

The deadbolt flipped and the door opened a crack until the security chain was taut. I was pressed against the wall so I couldn't see who'd answered the door but heard a man's voice. "Help you?"

Jill smiled. "Can I talk to Krista for a minute?"

"She's sleeping. Go away."

Jill stuck her foot out and stopped the door. "I just need to talk to her for a second. Please wake her up."

"She's sick. Go away." He tried again to close the door.

Jill held her ID up to the door. "I'm here to do a welfare check on Krista and I'm not leaving until I speak to her."

"You're no cop. You're not even in uniform."

Two Florida City cops showed up at the end of the hallway and I held my badge over my head so they could see it. The older of the two cops nodded and quickened his pace with his partner right behind him.

"Open the door or the two Florida City cops who just showed up are going to break it down."

"I don't see no city cops. Go away." The guy slurred his words, like he'd been drinking.

The older cop circled behind Jill and jammed his nightstick into the door opening. "Like the lady cop said, this door is going to open one way or another. It's up to you."

The guy in the apartment tried to close the door as the older cop eased Jill away from the opening. He nodded to his partner and the two of them threw their shoulders against the door. I heard the guy fall inside as the security chain's screws pulled out of the wooden molding. Jill was a step behind as the cops forced their way into the apartment.

We rushed into a kitchen cluttered with dirty dishes and countertops piled with take-out containers.

Krista's roommate backed away from the two uniformed cops with his hands out. Jill rushed past them, pausing at a bedroom door, she peeked through the narrow opening. Holstering her gun, she pushed the door open and disappeared, speaking softly.

The drunk man was swearing at us and gesturing with his arms as he backed into the living room. His hands were bloody, and something was off about the way he was moving. He stumbled on a dirty tennis shoe and seemed to be reaching behind himself to break his fall. I'd moved to the bedroom door to protect Jill and had a different view than the two cops, who couldn't see the pistol on the coffee table behind the drunk.

I yelled, "Gun!"

In the flurry of activity that followed I lost sight of the gun and what happened behind the two cops. I held my Sig in two hands and moved sideways, my weapon held low and ready to fire. I saw the drunk reaching for the gun, then watched the younger cop bulldoze him. The two wrestled on the floor for a minute with grunts, swearing, and yelling. I was amazed and concerned that Jill didn't respond to the scuffle and swearing.

As the two cops lifted the boyfriend to his feet and pulled his arms behind his back, I got a view of his baggy boxers and a t-shirt stained with blood, food, and beer. The older cop picked the gun up from the coffee table. He opened the cylinder and dumped the cartridges into his hand as the young cop cuffed the drunk. "I don't suppose this gun is licensed."

The drunk sniffled, a trickle of blood leaking from his nose. "Don't need a license for a gun in my own house."

The cop looked at me, nodded, and then tucked the gun in his waistband. Picking up a remote from a shelf near a big screen television, he shut off a made for television show with a fake judge meting out great ratings more than justice. I put the Sig in my holster.

The cop picked up his cap, knocked off during the scuffle. "What's going on?"

"Welfare check. We heard the woman had been injured in a domestic assault."

The boyfriend's nose was trickling bloody snot and he sniffled again. "Ain't no assault here. She fell down the steps."

I heard quiet sobs in the bedroom. I wanted to check on Jill and Krista, but the older cop put out his hand. "Can I see your badge again?"

"How about my ID? I'm a federal officer."

The older cop studied my ID, then smiled. "I've never met a park service investigator. Are you stationed here?"

"We're from Texas, investigating a murder in the Everglades National Park."

The cop nodded. "We heard something about a dead woman who'd been partially eaten by a gator. She was murdered, huh?"

"Yes. We've identified the killers, now we're trying to find them."

The cop nodded toward the boyfriend. "Is he one of them?"

I shook my head. "Our suspects are in the wind. We came here on a tip about a domestic assault on someone peripheral to the investigation."

The cop raised his eyebrows as his partner pushed the boyfriend into the hallway. "I've never heard of a fed doing a welfare check." He paused. "Your partner was trying to push the door open when we arrived."

"Exigent circumstances. We heard a woman scream."

The cop ran his tongue around the inside of his lips like he wasn't buying my story.

"Hey, can someone call an ambulance?" Jill called softly from the bedroom.

The older cop stepped to the bedroom door and looked inside. He immediately turned his head and spoke into his shoulder-mounted radio mic, announcing his unit number, the apartment address, then asking for an ambulance. He stepped toward me and closed the door behind him. "That's your partner in there?"

I nodded.

"She's not keeping it together."

"What do you mean?"

"She's holding a woman and they're both crying."

I took a deep breath and let it out. "She was abused by an old boyfriend."

The cop nodded. "I hate seeing this shit." He walked me to the apartment door. The boyfriend was swearing at the other cop and struggling against the handcuffs. "Paul, turn him around so we can see his hands."

The younger cop spun the boyfriend around, exposing the abuser's hands. They were covered with blood and his knuckles were scraped and bruised. His arms were scratched.

The older cop looked at me. "I'm going to take him into custody for domestic assault and resisting arrest unless you've got a federal crime here."

I shook my head. "We're good."

"Paul, take him to the car and read him his rights."

We watched Paul wrestle the boyfriend down the hall. I drew a breath. "I take it the girl looks like she's in bad shape."

"Yessir. She needs a hospital."

"How bad?"

The older cop paused. "I'd say she's going to be in the hospital a while."

We stood in the hallway outside the apartment talking about our park murder until the EMT's wheeled Krista past on a gurney. Her face was bruised, and the EMTs had an oxygen mask over her nose and mouth. I looked hopefully at one of the somber EMTs. He glanced at me and shrugged.

I heard a window open in the apartment as we walked in. The living room and kitchen were being examined by evidence techs, so I went into the bedroom. Jill, her face red with rage, had removed the window screen and was throwing clothes out of the window.

"What are you doing?"

Jill spun around. "I'm helping him move out." She pulled open a drawer, looked at the contents, then threw the entire drawer out the window.

I went to her and pulled her into a hug. After her anger subsided, I guided her through the apartment and out the door. I closed it behind us. "How bad?" I asked as we walked down the hallway.

"Broken fingers. Broken arm. Probably a broken jaw. Bruises everywhere. Blood everywhere." Jill broke into tears, and we stopped while she buried her face in my shoulder. "Doug, I want to kill that sonofabitch. I really do."

"But you didn't."

"Not because I didn't want to."

"What stopped you?"

She unpinned her badge from her shirt and held it in her hand, rubbing the gold surface with her thumb. "This."

* * *

We went back to the restaurant, told Tony what had happened, then refused his offer to buy our supper. Margot looked up when we walked into the hotel but saw Jill's red eyes and let us pass without comment. We ordered burgers from room service, then snuggled in bed watching Hallmark movies.

Jill was in the bathroom getting ready for bed when her phone rang. I picked it up. "Fletcher."

"Doug? I thought I dialed Jill's phone."

I recognized Randy Tschetter's voice. "You did. She's brushing her teeth. What's up? Do you need us to bail you out?"

Randy laughed. "Not at this time. Can you bring Jill to the phone? I'd like you both to hear this."

I knocked on the bathroom door and Jill opened it; her hair wrapped in a towel. "What?"

"Randy Tschetter is on the phone." I punched the speaker. "Go ahead, Randy."

"Mr. and Mrs. Juan Espinoza flew to Mexico City, then on to Belize the day the rental car was abandoned at the airport. I just spoke to the trade attaché from our Belize embassy, who happens to be on the FBI payroll. After our earlier discussion he decided to have a beer at Espinoza's bar on his way home."

Jill's eyes went wide. "You found them!"

Randy chuckled. "There were quite a few people involved, but yes, they've been located."

Jill shrugged. "What happens now?"

"There's a plane flying to Belize tonight. It'll return with the Espinozas in the morning."

"What? How? I thought Belize didn't extradite prisoners to the U.S. I can't believe the Espinozas will return voluntarily."

"I'm reasonably certain we'll be able to convince the Espinozas it'll be in their best interest to leave Belize with us."

Jill leaned close to the phone. "Will Belize go along with that?"

"I spoke with the Belize National Police. There are certain factions interested in seeing Juan Espinoza leave Belize for the U.S."

"Without extradition?"

Randy paused. "Mr. Espinoza is a suspect in a string of deaths throughout the Americas. The person I spoke with was quite interested in having him leave for the U.S."

"But…"

"We will remove him quietly. My Belize contact is concerned that there are police agencies in other countries who would be less…discreet in their arrest than U.S. Marshals. All I had to do was suggest leaking the details of one of Mr. Espinoza's 'jobs' to a friend in a South American police agency. My friend in Belize saw the wisdom in having Espinoza exit quietly. He was afraid that an unnamed South American agency would deal with Espinoza leaving a messy scene that would be bad for Belize tourism."

I closed my eyes. "Belize didn't want to deal with a bloodbath when a bunch of armed assassins came to even the score."

"That scenario was discussed."

Jill frowned. "Can I ask why that unnamed country would like to see Mr. Espinoza eliminated?"

"I can neither confirm, nor deny, that he killed a number of magistrates who were about to sit on the trial of a drug kingpin."

I suddenly understood. "That's why we were unable to locate any evidence of his existence since he left Puerto Rico. He's an assassin—a ghost who lives off the grid."

"The people in South America called him El Terciopelo, a venomous South American snake."

Nodding to Jill, I said, "That pulls together a bunch of loose ends."

"There are some very nervous people in Ohio since you identified the dead woman," Tschetter said with a chuckle. "Arnot has been laundering mob money, skimming some off each transaction. It appears the reason for faking Arnot's death was to make it appear the contract had been fulfilled so the mob would stop looking for her. Now that you've debunked that staged murder, the mob wants Espinoza because they paid him to kill Arnot, and they want Arnot so they can get the skimmed money back."

"By solving Madison Wirth's murder, we opened a can of worms?" Jill asked.

"I wouldn't put it that way. By solving that murder, you provided two witnesses who can name names and put some important organized crime people in jail, both in the U.S. and elsewhere, if we can get to them before the mob finds them."

I smiled and nodded to Jill. "That's got to be a big win for you, Randy. Thanks for the update."

"Don't hang up. Your job isn't done yet."

"What do you need from us?"

"Wear casual clothes, like you'd wear to a bar, and drive to the Homestead airport. I'll meet you at the Air Force Reserve terminal in an hour."

Jill looked confused. "Why?"

"You're taking a trip to Belize."

"Us? We're going to Belize?"

"You did the work that pulled the pieces together. I thought you'd like to be there for the takedown."

I took the phone from Jill. "Hell yes!"

Pushing the end button, I set the phone on the nightstand. Jill looked at me expectantly. "What did he mean when he said we'd be there for the takedown?"

"They'll probably let us watch the arrests from a secure location."

Jill's uncertainty turned to intrigue. "That might be cool."

Chapter 16

I drove to the airport and parked in the lot adjacent to the Air Force Reserve terminal. A short man wearing a dark suit met us in the building. "Jill and Doug Fletcher?"

I put out my hand. "You're Randy Tschetter."

We shook hands and he led us to a small jet plane parked on the tarmac. An auxiliary power unit hummed next to the plane, apparently powering the lights and air conditioning while the plane sat idle. The co-pilot circled the plane, conducting the pre-flight inspection. Entering the small business jet, I ducked my head to walk down the aisle. A pair of young airmen nodded as we passed the small galley. Past the galley, two middle-aged men sat at a table spread with playing cards.

Tschetter made introductions as the men set aside their card game. "Jim Hansen and Bob Kirby, meet our park service colleagues Jill and Doug Fletcher." Hansen and Kirby shook our hands without getting up in the cramped space. Average in every sense of the word, Hanson could disappear in a crowd of people without notice. On the other hand, Kirby was large, Black, with a shaved head. He looked like a professional wrestler and would stand out in most any crowd like an ebony beacon.

With introductions complete, Tschetter summarized our mission. "The four of you are tasked with arresting the Espinozas and bringing them back to the U.S."

Jill looked shocked. "I…we appreciate the chance to be in on the arrest, but Juan Espinoza is an assassin. We're hardly the A-team you'd deploy to make an arrest like this."

Jim Hansen smiled. "Ma'am…Jill, you're exactly the people we need to arrest Juan Espinoza. Nothing personal, but you don't look like a cop, especially dressed as you are in shorts and a golf shirt. If you two take off your badges and guns, you can walk into the bar as American tourists and not set off Espinoza's alarms. If Bob and I walked in, Espinoza would either shoot us, or be out the back door, before we got past the threshold."

Randy put his hand on Jill's shoulder. "I'll meet you here when you get back. Good hunting."

Tschetter left and Hansen gestured for us to take seats at the table across the aisle from them. I heard the airplane door close, and the engines start. Jill looked anxious

337

and watched out the window as we taxied to the runway. The engines revved up and within seconds the wheels were up, and the plane was rapidly gaining altitude.

Hansen leaned across the aisle. "Espinoza's bar is in an area called Little America, because of all the gringos who've moved there to take advantage of the low cost of living and pleasant climate. You two can pass as a married couple living in the area. Go in, order a couple drinks, and get the lay of the land."

Jill looked skeptical. "And then you arrive with the cavalry?"

Hansen smiled. "The local cops will arrive after you've been there a while. Espinoza pays them protection money, so he sees them regularly and they won't raise any alarms. They'll distract Espinoza at the bar and you two will engage Arnot. There's a bouncer, and when he sees you bugging Arnot, he's going to come over to see what's happening."

I nodded. "When he's away from the door, you make your move."

Hansen nodded. "Kirby will come in from the restrooms to cuff Espinoza with help from the Belize cops, and I'll cuff Arnot."

An airman brought us bottles of water and set a can of mixed nuts on the tables. Jill uncapped her water. "What about the bouncer? Don't you think he'll intervene?"

Kirby, who'd been silent, cleared his throat. "I hope I'm not speaking out of school, but we've heard that people tend to underestimate you, Jill. If Doug grabs Arnot, the bouncer will come running. He'll probably try to flick you aside like a fly. If you can distract him for thirty seconds, Jim can knock him down and cuff Arnot."

Jill was incredulous. "You expect me to take on a bar bouncer?"

"Ma'am…Jill," Kirby said, "We heard you took down a Wisconsin town bully without getting your shirt dirty."

Jill tried to hide her smirk. "That was a fluke."

Hansen put up his hands. "If you don't think this will work, we'll do something else. Kirby spoke with some of your colleagues who said you're scrappy and usually underestimated."

Jill looked at me and shook her head. "Liz."

Kirby tilted his head back and laughed. "You have many fans, Jill. I spoke with Jamie, Liz, and the Crook County, Wyoming sheriff."

"We'll be armed?" I asked.

Hansen shook his head. "We'll be guests of the Belize federal police and they've asked us to leave our firearms on the plane. As far as they're concerned, we're unarmed private citizens. Shooting someone in Belize would complicate...our arrangement with our counterparts there."

Jill glared at them. "We're going to arrest a murderer and a professional assassin unarmed?"

"The bouncer is unarmed, and Espinoza will be distracted by the commotion between you two and Arnot. Kirby will be on Espinoza before he can get to a weapon."

Kirby was nodding in agreement. "Espinoza has paid off a lot of people in Belize and he'll be very unhappy when an American extraction team shows up unannounced. Our plan is to get in and out quietly. Our Belize counterparts will be armed, but they're trying to avoid a bloodbath by helping us escort the Espinozas out of the country." He looked at his watch. "I suggest that we all nap during the remaining two hours of the flight."

Just past midnight, I heard the engines slow, and the flaps deploy. Hansen nodded to me, looking up from a report and mug of coffee as the wheels went down. Kirby was stretching, his arms reaching nearly the width of the cabin.

Jill was sipping from a coffee mug. She looked up from her magazine. "Welcome back to the land of the living."

"Have you slept?" I asked, stretching.

"Not a wink."

The plane slowed and an airman collected our coffee mugs, water bottles, and nut cans. He advised us to buckle our seatbelts for the landing.

We were met in a remote part of the Belize City airport by a battered Ford Taurus. Two men in wrinkled suits got out and greeted Marshal Kirby like an old friend. "These are agents Garza and Patrone of the Belize Federal Police." Jill and I were introduced as federal police colleagues without mention of the park service. Garza and Patrone addressed us as *federales*.

The gray-haired senior officer Garza spoke to us in heavily accented English. "Many of the locals have accepted the Spanish custom of eating their evening meal at ten o'clock. So, right now they're having after-dinner drinks. I suggest that we drop you two blocks from Espinoza's bar." He smiled at Jill. "Order a Panty Rippa, a local favorite rum drink. You, sir, order a Belikin Stout. You'll sound like a couple locals and won't raise any concerns."

We jammed together in the Taurus. Hansen rode in the front with the *federales*. Jill was wedged between Kirby and me in the back. Kirby had to rest his arm on the seat back so Jill's shoulders fit alongside him. "You're good to go?" he asked Jill.

Jill nodded. "It's strange. Any time I've ever had a physical confrontation it's been spontaneous. Having time to think about this is making me nervous."

Kirby chuckled, his voice deep and the laugh almost like a bass drum. "I guarantee this will be spontaneous. I've been a marshal for nineteen years, and no matter how much we plan, when it's 'go time' everything plays out in unexpected ways. As long as you're physically and mentally prepared, you'll be fine. The biggest problem is dealing with rookies who freeze up, or fall apart, when you need them most. You two are seasoned professionals. You'll do fine."

Having left our pistols on the plane, Kirby asked for our badges and IDs. "You probably won't be searched, but you don't want to be carrying these if the bouncer checks you."

We walked toward the flashing Belikin beer sign a block-and-a-half away from our drop-off point. Jill grabbed my hand and squeezed it. "I don't like this."

"Hansen and Kirby have this all mapped out. All we have to do is follow their plan."

"You're not the one taking out the bouncer."

The sidewalk wasn't busy, with just a few couples walking without urgency. Jill's pace slowed after we greeted a retired couple who were speaking English. "I expected this to be like Mexico, but it's cleaner and quieter. No hustlers like when I crossed from Texas into Nuevo Laredo and the shops here look less like tourist traps."

"I suppose safety, political stability, and the relatively low cost of living attract American ex-patriots who want to stretch their pensions."

Latin music drifted out the open door of the Camaleón Loco Salón. Jill looked at the neon sign with the multi-colored lizard. "The crazy chameleon bar?"

I shrugged and led her into the smoky bar. Half the tables were occupied, mostly by couples talking quietly, smoking, sipping drinks from red Solo cups, or drinking beer from the bottle. Espinoza's saloon wasn't a noisy singles bar, but more like a corner pub where locals gathered for drinks and talk. I nodded to the bouncer who sat on a stool next to the door. He had well-muscled arms covered with tattoos and tattooed flames ran up his thick neck from the open collar of his guayabera shirt. He nodded at us but didn't smile. I felt Jill squeeze my hand.

She followed me to a table in the center of the room. I recognized Espinoza who was talking to two men sitting on stools and leaning on the long bar. A young Hispanic woman wearing an outfit that would've made a Hooters' waitress blush, came to our table and set coasters in front of us. Her t-shirt was tied tight under ample breasts, exposing a pierced navel and several inches of taut abdomen above skin-tight shorts. "What'll it be?" she asked in unaccented English.

"Belikin stout."

The waitress looked at Jill, who was frozen, apparently unable to remember what Hansen had told her to order.

"My wife will have a Panty Rippa."

The waitress nodded and walked away. Jill leaned close. "Sorry. My mind went blank."

I looked around the bar. "Espinoza is behind the bar. I think Arnot is sitting at the table with two couples in the back corner behind you."

Jill smiled and glanced at the bar like she was watching our waitress. "Yeah, that's Espinoza. He uncapped your beer and he's mixing my drink." She picked up her coaster idly and fingered it. "Did you see the size of the bouncer?"

"He'll underestimate you."

Jill set the coaster down and flattened it with her fingers. "He'll brush me aside like he's swatting a fly."

I smiled at her. "Just pretend he said, 'yes dear.'"

Jill smiled and reached for my hand. "I'm not sure my elbow will penetrate the fat and muscle over his ribs."

The waitress delivered Jill's drink in a plastic cup and my bottle of beer. I gave her a twenty-dollar bill. She hesitated, waiting to see if I wanted change. I waved her off, assuming I'd grossly over tipped her.

Jill sipped her drink and stifled a cough. "This is sixteen ounces and it's ninety-nine percent rum. You'd have to carry me out if I drank all this."

"It looks like he floated 101 proof rum on top of the drink. It'll get smoother as you drink it down."

She slid it away, shaking her head, as two local cops in brown uniforms, walked in. They spoke to the bouncer for a second, then swaggered to the bar. Espinoza left the guys he was chatting up and brought beer to the cops. They acted like old friends.

"Nearly show time," I said to Jill.

While idly stirring her drink with the plastic straw, Jill watched the cops and Espinoza. "How are you going to get Arnot over here?"

I took a sip of beer and started choking. I looked at Arnot, conveying distress. She excused herself from the table and trotted to my side.

"Are you okay?" She asked, slapping my back.

I continued to choke and put up a finger. "Maybe in a second," I gasped.

Hansen walked through the front door, and I grabbed Arnot's wrist, pulling her into the chair next to me. "You're under arrest for murder."

Arnot was struck dumb. She looked at the bouncer desperately as Jill stood. The bouncer assessed the situation and apparently decided we weren't a great threat. He ambled toward us, elbowing aside Hansen as he passed. Jill bounced on the balls of her feet, looking nervous, but focused and ready to react. She picked up her drink and when the bouncer reached for Arnot, Jill threw the liquid into his face. While the giant was distracted by the 101-proof rum burning his eyes, Jill stomped on the arch of his foot.

Like an angry bear, the bouncer turned toward her, wiping the drink from his face, and blinking his eyes to clear the alcohol. Jill buried her knuckles into his solar plexus, the move leaving the big man more surprised than injured. When he hesitated, apparently reluctant to hit a woman, Jill drove her knee into his crotch. His eyes went wide, and he bent forward, clutching his testicles. Jill spun and used the momentum to drive her elbow upward, into his nose. The impact caused a crunching of his nasal cartilage and snapped his head back. He teetered, then slouched over as Jill prepared for his next move. Abruptly, his eyes rolled back, and he crashed to the floor with blood leaking from his nose.

Hansen stepped past the downed man and snapped handcuffs onto Arnot's wrists. Jill was bouncing, looking around the room and ready for the next threat.

Scanning the room and seeing no one else ready to enter the fray, I pulled Jill toward me. "It's over."

Jill shook her head and looked toward the bar. Kirby dragged Espinoza across the bar by his hair and the two Belize policemen stepped back, watching with apparent amusement. I didn't understand the Spanish words Espinoza was cursing but based on the expression on the policemen's faces, I assumed he was berating them for not coming to his aid. I understood enough Spanish to know when his rant went from pleas for assistance to insults of their parentage.

Before I could move to assist him, Kirby had Espinoza in handcuffs. He'd hardly broken a sweat when he pulled Espinoza to his feet. Kirby looked around the room at the patrons' gaping mouths and smiled. "Last call. This next round is on the house."

Hansen left Arnot with Jill and me and spoke with the policemen. He led them to a corner and said something that had them nodding in agreement. I thought I saw money being slipped into their hands, but it disappeared so quickly it was hard to say exactly what transpired. After shaking hands, the policemen went to the bar and quickly drank the last of their beers.

Hansen nodded toward the front door. "You guys take Arnot to the airport in the Taurus. Kirby and I are riding with the cops. We have to make arrangements for the transfer of some local financial assets." Perceiving our lack of understanding, Hansen added, "Mr. Espinoza is making generous donations to the local orphanage, the clinic, a school, and the policemen's retirement fund."

Espinoza was swearing in Spanish as Kirby pushed him to the front door. I looked back at the scene inside the bar as we walked out. The bouncer was sitting on the floor, blinking his eyes in confusion, and smearing the blood running from his nose. The saloon patrons were lined up at the bar as our waitress poured generous drinks from bottles on the top shelf behind the bar. She appeared to be garnering generous tips. I wondered briefly where she'd put the cash in her skin-tight outfit, but I didn't dwell on the thought.

Arnot was incredulous when Hansen return our badges and credentials. "You can't arrest me here! You're U.S. cops. This is Belize City, not Miami!"

Hansen smiled and put his hand on Arnot's head as he pushed her into the Taurus' backseat. "We're not arresting you. The Belize federal police are deporting you for tax fraud. You apparently brought undeclared cash into the country and they're seizing it."

Arnot looked at Jill when we were seated in the backseat. "Who are you? Are you a Miami cop?"

"We're just your escorts. We're here to make sure you don't miss your flight."

"Where's Juan?"

"He'll meet us at the airport."

Arnot turned to me. "Who are you, her bodyguard?"

I chuckled. "You saw what she did to your bouncer. Do you think she needs a bodyguard?"

"I want a lawyer."

I nodded. "I'm sure the court will appoint a lawyer for you since you won't have any money to pay for one."

Arnot's eyes went wide. "I've got plenty of money. As a matter of fact, if you let me go, I'll make sure you live comfortably the rest of your lives."

The cop who was driving looked at me in the rear-view mirror and raised his eyebrows. I shook my head. "To the airport."

Jill leaned back and laughed. "You're penniless. Juan is explaining where all your assets are in return for being allowed to leave Belize alive."

"I have my own accounts. I can make you rich."

"Accounts with the money you skimmed from the mob? Are you referring to the ones the IRS seized in the Caribbean or the ones they've frozen in Switzerland?"

"They can't…"

"We're doing you a favor. If we told your Youngstown friends where you and Juan are, you'd be tied to a chair in a dark basement, happily giving them your account information. I understand they can be very persuasive."

"I don't know what you're talking about."

"The FBI found a finger in your Youngstown apartment's freezer. It matched a body in the morgue."

Arnot went quiet while she digested that information. "I want a deal. I have information to trade."

Jill leaned forward and glared at Arnot. "Did you offer Madison Wirth a deal before you killed her?"

"I don't know who that is."

"We have the rental car you left at the airport, DNA from both you and Juan, witnesses from the Florida City bar where you drugged Madison and picked her up, and a fingerprint Juan left on the seat adjustment knob of her car. We have enough evidence for Florida to put you on death row."

Arnot closed her eyes and was silent for the rest of the ride to the airport.

* * *

We handcuffed Arnot and Espinoza in opposite corners of the plane so they wouldn't be able to develop a cohesive story during the flight. I fell asleep before the plane left the ground and didn't hear or feel a thing until we touched down.

Randy Tschetter met us at the airport and shook our hands. "Good job, guys."

Jill hadn't slept on the flight. She was emotionally drained and physically tired. "I'm glad to be done with this. We can sleep until noon, then rebook our flights back to Texas."

"I'm afraid that's not going to happen," Tschetter said as he walked us to the terminal. We stopped outside the airport waiting area entrance.

"You don't need us. The Miami-Dade crime lab can pass all our evidence to the U.S. Attorney."

"I need you two tomorrow morning for a photo op."

I blew out a breath. "Randy, I'm not photogenic."

"Doug, I was just on the phone with your boss, his boss, and her boss. I have been assured a negative response from you is expected, but unacceptable. I was told to have you two, in uniform, at the Homestead Air Force Reserve arrival concourse at eleven o'clock if I have to

351

bring you in handcuffs. We'll be taking pictures of the prisoners being transferred to the plane for transport to Ohio."

I was going to protest, but Jill grabbed my arm and gently squeezed it. "We'll be here."

Tschetter nodded. "Bring your partner Larry, too."

Chapter 17

Jill removed a pair of jeans and a t-shirt from her suitcase. "I thought our orders were to wear uniforms."

"I'm not wearing my uniform to eat breakfast." She disappeared into the bathroom.

Later, when I stepped out of the shower, I smelled coffee and heard television voices. "Anything on the news?" I asked as I pulled on jeans and tied my tennis shoes.

"There was an FBI press conference in Ohio announcing the arrest of twenty-three organized crime figures."

"Youngstown?"

"They said the federal courthouse in the northern district of Ohio."

"Who was on the steps besides the FBI?" I asked.

Jill clenched her jaw. "They didn't introduce or mention any other agencies."

I opened the door and held it for Jill. "It's miraculous how the FBI can solve cases without the help of any other agencies. They must be really good."

"You're being snarky. It's not your most endearing characteristic."

"I just get frustrated by their parochial…"

"Did it ever occur to you they were doing us a favor? Mentioning our Miami case would've tipped their hand before the Espinozas were in custody."

"Yeah, yeah. It still bugs me that…"

Jill cut me off. "You've got a burr under your saddle over the FBI. I understand that. I'm tired of hearing about it. Suck it up, Buttercup. Besides, you keep saying you don't want to stand on the podium during another news conference. You can't have it both ways." The elevator opened and Jill took one step out and looked around. With no one nearby she hooked one finger inside my shirt and turned me to face her. "And, if you say 'yes dear,' you're going to have a bruise that'll last long after we get back to Texas."

One corner of my mouth twitched while I hugged her and weighed my words. "You're wise beyond your years."

Jill let go of my shirt and pushed me toward the breakfast nook. "You know that's just an expanded 'yes dear.'"

I shrugged. "I was paying you a compliment."

We ate our usual breakfasts. I flipped through the front section of the newspaper as I ate. "Nothing here about FBI arrests." I turned to the sports section to see how the Minnesota Twins were doing.

"Randy said to meet him at the airport at eleven."

Seeing that the Twins had blown a two-run lead and lost the game, I folded the paper and set it on an empty chair. "How are we going to kill the rest of the morning?"

"We're going to the hospital."

Having seen Jill rub the elbow she'd used to poke the bouncer, I was concerned. "Are you okay?"

Jill frowned. "I'm fine. We're going to visit Krista."

I pushed my plate aside. "I...I'm not sure we're welcome. We hardly know her."

Jill leaned on the table. "Doug, we're going to see Krista and we're going to bring flowers. It's important."

I knew I'd lost the battle. "How do we determine which hospital she's in?"

Jill held up her phone. "I've already Googled it. She's in Homestead Hospital. It's on the way to the airfield."

* * *

We found a florist on the way to the hospital and Jill bought a huge bouquet in a crystal vase. The volunteer manning the reception desk in the hospital lobby was dazzled by our park service uniforms, complete with Smokey Bear hats. She looked up Krista's room number and gave us directions.

Krista was sleeping when we walked in. There was nothing personal in the room: No flowers. No cell phone. No clothing. An IV line ran into her arm and a green oxygen cannula hissed under her nose. Wires snaked from under her bedding and connected to an overhead display emitting the distinctive beeping of a heart monitor.

Her face was bruised, the eye closest to us was swollen shut. Without makeup she looked closer to forty than thirty. Her right arm was in a cast from elbow to fingertips. Every fingernail was broken off, some bandaged. Her left hand had padded splints taped to three broken fingers, making me wonder how she fed herself or dealt with bodily functions.

Our entrance must've momentarily blocked the sounds of the nearby nurse's station because her left eye opened, and she turned her head toward us. She was initially startled, but then relaxed. "Gawd, look at you two, all dressed up."

Krista's words were garbled by the wires holding her broken jaws together. Jill's breath caught and she turned away to set the vase on the table and rearrange the flowers. I walked to the bed and Krista raised her casted arm, holding her fingertips out to me.

Jill turned and watched me take Krista's hand, gently touching her bandaged fingertips. The scene overwhelmed Jill, and she let out a sob and quickly pulled two tissues from a box on the tray table.

"You look…" I was at a loss for words.

Krista nodded. "I asked for a mirror this morning."

Jill stepped to the other side of the bed and gently stroked Krista's upper arm, the only area of her body that was free of bruises. "Honey, I'm so sorry."

Krista reacted to Jill's tears and started to cry. They gently held each other while I stood aside, not knowing what to say or do.

A nurse swept in carrying a syringe. Surprised to see two rangers in dress uniforms she said, "You've got visitors and flowers! I'm here with your pain meds. Are you doing okay?"

Krista nodded as the nurse uncapped a port on the IV tubing and injected a dose of pain medicine into an IV line. "Do you need anything?"

"Not right now."

The nurse turned, looked at me, and nodded toward the door. I followed her into the hallway and down two rooms to the nurse's station. "Are you Krista's family?"

"No, we're just friends."

"Do you know how to reach her parents or husband?"

I was about to say, no when I remembered Tony saying she lived down the street from him. "I might be able to find her parents. Her now ex-boyfriend is in jail."

That news didn't surprise the nurse, who nodded. "I asked about her parents, but she didn't want me to call them."

What do you need?"

"Krista came in with nothing. She doesn't have clothes, a wallet, or insurance information. We'd like to talk to her family so they can at least bring her clothes and give her a ride home after she's discharged."

"I'll see what I can do."

I was about to turn away when the nurse asked, "Is the woman with you named Jill?"

I nodded. "Jill's my wife."

"Krista said Jill saved her, but she never said who Jill was, or what happened."

"Krista didn't show up for work, so we went to her apartment to check on her. Jill…" I stopped, because I didn't really know what Jill had done other than go into the bedroom. "I know there are HIPAA rules, but can you tell me about Krista's medical condition?"

The nurse shook her head, then stopped. "Did you arrest her boyfriend?"

"Jill and I got there before the FCPD cops. They made the arrest."

"Technically, you were one of the arresting officers."

I saw where she was going and nodded.

"Aside from what you can see, she had a ruptured spleen that was hemorrhaging. They removed it and we kept her in the ICU overnight. Aside from that, she has numerous superficial injuries like her broken jaw, arms, and fingers. She has a couple broken ribs, a lot of bruises on her arms, torso, and legs." The nurse checked to make sure no one was nearby, and she leaned over the counter. "I don't think she would've lived through another twenty-four hours without medical care. Krista said Jill saved her life, and she's probably correct."

I walked to the end of the hallway, took out my cell phone and found the restaurant's phone number. It rang a half dozen times before someone answered. "Hi, is Tony there?"

"Hang on." I heard Tony's name called out.

"This is Tony."

"Doug Fletcher. I'm at Homestead Hospital with Krista."

There was silence. "I was there last night but they wouldn't let me see her because she was in the ICU and I'm not family."

"They moved her out of the ICU. The hospital is trying to locate her parents."

"Her dad is gone, and her mom is a drunk." Tony sighed. "I'll see if her mom is awake and sober."

"Krista's going to need some clothes. In a few days, she'll need a ride somewhere safe, in case her boyfriend makes bail."

"I'll call my wife and have her get the guest bedroom ready. Krista can stay with us a while."

"Great. I'll let her know."

I was about to end the call when Tony said my name. "Doug, Krista was right, you and Jill are special people."

Jill was sitting on the edge of the bed chatting with Krista when I walked in. "I talked to Tony and he's going to bring you some clothes."

Krista nodded. "Thanks. I'm not sure where…"

"Tony's getting his guest bedroom ready for you until you sort out what happens from here."

Tears welled in her eyes. "Tony's like a dad to me."

"He thinks you're special."

Jill looked at the clock and stood. "Doug and I need to be at the airport in half an hour. We've got to go."

Krista reached her casted arm out to me. I grabbed it, touching her fingers gently. "I'm glad we were able to help…"

Krista waved Jill over with her other arm and pulled their cheeks together. I heard Krista whisper something that brought tears to Jill's eyes. Jill blew her nose as she tucked her Smokey Bear hat under her arm and walked down the hallway.

"Are you going to tell me what Krista said?"

"She thought I was an angel coming to take her to heaven when I walked into her bedroom yesterday."

I pulled Jill close. "You are an angel."

* * *

Larry, Jill, and I were standing inside the Air Force Reserve passenger lounge when a small silver and blue jet landed. A young Air Force second lieutenant walked over to us. "That's the VC-20 that'll be transporting your VIPs, sir."

The plane taxied up to the front of the building. A gray car and black SUV sped out of the gate to our right and parked next to the plane's wing as stairs unfolded behind the cockpit. I held the lounge door for Jill and Larry, and we walked across the concrete apron to the SUV. Randy Tschetter stepped out of the car wearing a dark suit. A U.S. Marshal's badge on a beaded lanyard hung from his neck.

"Good morning, Jill. I see you found your partner from Everglades Park."

"We're here as ordered," I said.

361

Randy Tschetter smiled and shook our hands. "The arraignment went as planned. Neither defendant had a lawyer to call, so the court-appointed counsel represented them."

Juan Espinoza and Andrea Arnot/Espinoza were led past us wearing the same clothes they'd been in when they were arrested. Even tired and wearing wrinkled clothes, Juan was strikingly handsome. Andrea's head was down as if hiding her face. A photographer appeared behind us, snapping photos.

Tschetter took Jill's elbow and guided her to the front bumper of the SUV, Larry and me trailing behind. "Please turn toward the building as the prisoners are led past us."

Jill turned to me. "Suck in your gut and make sure your zipper is up."

Larry looked at me as Espinoza and Arnot were led past us. "Does she say that every time you're in a picture?"

"Every time."

The last photos were of the fugitives walking up the steps of the plane, with us watching from the front of the SUV.

Tschetter shook our hands again. "You guys did a hell of a job tracking those two down. I spoke with the Assistant U.S. Attorney in Ohio this morning and she's reviewed the evidence against the Espinozas. As usual, she was wringing her

362

hands because she didn't have enough evidence to ask for a directed verdict, but I could tell she was champing at the bit to start negotiations on a plea deal that will put those two in prison for a long time."

I followed Tschetter to the SUV's passenger door and turned him aside. "It appears our victim, Madison Wirth, may have been killed outside the park. That would make her murder a Florida death penalty case."

Tschetter stopped with his hand on the door. "Actually, there are two state cases pending. Espinoza is also the prime suspect in an Ohio murder—don't forget the finger in Arnot's freezer. The state cases are the U.S. Attorney's biggest leverage. Those two won't want to be convicted in a Florida state court, where there's a death penalty. An Ohio conviction would put them in a maximum-security state prison full of murderers and rapists. Espinoza knows he wouldn't last a month in a state prison. Accepting a federal plea that includes information about his other 'jobs' would put him in a medium-security federal prison for the rest of his life, which will be much more comfortable and less risky than an Ohio prison. I'm sure he doesn't want to come back to Florida and sit on death row while appeals string out."

"And Arnot?"

"She skimmed a lot of the mob money she was laundering. She'd face the same issues as Espinoza in a state women's facility. She's smart and her attorney will negotiate her placement in a nice midwestern federal women's prison camp where she can spend her years under an assumed name in return for explaining her money laundering operation and testifying against the mob."

Jill slipped in next to me. "It seems like they should be facing a lethal injection."

"If she turns on Espinoza, I imagine that will be on the table, but unlikely. He was very cagey when he married Arnot because a wife can't be compelled to testify against her husband. A trial without her testimony would be lengthy, expensive, and would tie up the prosecutors for a long time. The attorneys would be much happier with a plea bargain putting them away for a long time."

I thought for a second. "The marriage certificate says Juan Castro and Andrea Arnot. Is it valid? Does it block Arnot from testifying against Espinoza?"

"That's a nuance in the law that's up to the attorneys to decide."

Tschetter smiled. "A plea deal would close your murder case and you two wouldn't have to testify. I have the impression you aren't big fans of the south

Florida heat and lifestyle." Randy got in the SUV without further comment.

We watched the SUV drive away, then walked back to the terminal. The heat and humidity were starting to rise, causing a low haze to develop over the grassy areas. I could feel my armpits getting damp under my coat and a trickle of sweat ran down between my shoulder blades. I took off my Smokey Bear hat as soon as we stepped into the air-conditioned lounge.

Jill turned back toward the plane where airmen were folding up the steps. "Somehow I feel like we won and lost."

Larry looked at her, mopping his brow. "I'm okay with it. We solved a murder, caught the bad guys, and they're going away for a long time."

Jill fiddled with the brim of her hat. "I keep thinking about Madison Wirth in the morgue. She was a totally innocent person who was stood up by her boyfriend. Arnot jumped on her misfortune and killed her. I don't think a long sentence in a comfortable prison is enough punishment."

Larry shrugged. "They were close to getting away with the crime. If not for us, they'd be sipping Cuba Libras in Belize and living in a big house with servants. We put them on the road to justice."

I clapped him on the shoulder. "If not for us? What was your contribution?"

Larry turned and smiled. "You've already spoken with the reporter from the Miami newspaper. Jack got a call to verify your version of the facts and he was very pleased with your characterization of my role in solving the murder, with your assistance. You've shrunken away from the spotlight once again and minimized yourselves to a supporting role."

He turned to Jill. "Thanks for giving me some rope after my stupid comments. You...could've had me fired, and instead you made me a hero."

Jill nodded. "You're an okay guy if you can keep a filter between your brain and your mouth when you lose your cool."

Larry shrugged. "It's a Jersey thing."

Jill stuck her finger into his chest. "It's not a professional thing and if you want to get ahead in the park service, you've got to keep your mouth under control."

Larry rubbed the spot on his chest as if Jill's finger had punctured his skin. "I hear you."

* * *

Jill and I walked to our rental car and laid our coats and hats in the back seat. It took a minute for the air-conditioner to catch up with the heat. Jill stared out of the windshield, obviously thinking about something.

366

Reading her thoughts, I said, "You're still not happy with the likely plea deal."

"It's not that."

"What's bugging you?"

"I'd always thought I could live anywhere in the U.S. and this is...I don't know. This part of Florida isn't a place I'd ever choose to live."

"That's okay. There are a lot of other states out there."

She turned to me. "Could you live in the Black Hills? I'm going to own a ranch there some day."

I closed my eyes. "I *could* live there. *Choosing* to live there is a different question."

"The Black Hills are pretty, and South Dakota doesn't tax income. We could live comfortably on our pensions and the ranch rent."

"The winters are cold and..." I closed my eyes and hung my head dramatically, "...you'd expect me to ride a horse."

Jill's phone trilled and she struggled to get it out of her pocket. The ringing stopped before she could accept the call.

"Who was it?" I asked as she looked at the caller ID.

"It's your mom's cell."

I put the rental car into gear and started driving. Jill waited until the message icon appeared, then called up the voicemail and put it on speaker. "Hi, Jill. Your mom just called and said they'd read an online article about you and Doug helping the Everglades park rangers find and arrest two murderers. It sounds like no one got shot this time and that's good. Chet's doing very well, and we even went out for supper last night. We need to talk about that. Call when you get a second."

Jill deleted the message and was preparing to return the call.

"Let's talk before you call Mom."

"About what?"

"There are a lot of things on the table with our families. I think they expect us to put aside our lives and move to Spearfish. Is that what *we* want to do?"

Jill cupped the phone in her hand and looked out the windshield. "Larry made an interesting comment about their lives being happier when he and his wife were away from his New Jersey parents and in-laws."

"I love your mom and dad. I think Mom and Chet are cute together. But I'm not sure I want to experience their loving affection on a daily, weekly, or monthly basis."

Jill looked at me. "Holiday visits only?"

"How about this: We'll tell Matt we'll cover every other holiday at Padre Island. We'll tell our parents we're required to provide park security for half the holidays."

Jill's eyes twinkled. "A decision worthy of Solomon."

I laughed. "You've become very Biblical since you pulled the deputy off the Wyoming interstate."

I knew I'd touched a nerve when Jill didn't laugh or smile. "I know God is with me and sometimes I realize His plans are bigger than mine."

"That's pretty heavy. What does He say about South Dakota?"

Jill closed her eyes. "I'm not getting a strong direction from Him on that. I guess that must mean your suggestion about every other holiday in Spearfish might meet His approval."

She opened the phone, touched the call back, and put it on speaker. Mom answered immediately. "Did I catch you at a bad moment, Jill?"

"We're in the car and I couldn't get the phone out of my pocket before it rolled over to voicemail. What's up?"

"Chet and I just read the Reuters story about your Florida case. It sounds like Doug ducked behind the curtain again and dragged you with him. Your ranger friend arrested the murderers without being shot at. Were you there when he made the arrests?"

Jill rolled her eyes. "Yes, we watched the arrests from a safe vantage point. You said something about going out to supper. Uncle Chet must be feeling better."

"He's perking right up. About that. Hang on while I close the door." There was a pause. "Chet asked if I'd stay with him…more permanently."

"As in…"

"He wants to marry me."

"That's sweet. What did you say?"

"I told him I had to get permission from you and Doug before I could give him an answer."

I pulled to the shoulder of the road and leaned toward the phone. "Mom, you don't need our permission to do anything."

Mom sighed. "I used you as an excuse to…think."

"And what do you think?"

"I really like it here and Chet is sweet."

Jill touched a button and held the phone to her ear. "I turned off the speaker so Doug can't hear. It's just us girls talking. Ronnie, you sound the happiest you've ever been. You have a mission in your life and Chet loves you. What else can I say?"

Jill listened, looking serious. Then her face brightened, and she nodded. "I think that's a good decision." She disconnected the call and looked at me. "Drive."

I pulled back on the highway and took the exit for our hotel. "Well?"

"There's going to be a long engagement."

I laughed. "That's the solution? A long engagement?"

"That'll give them some more time to work through some things, but it keeps Ronnie there with Chet where they're happy."

"She's happy, but not in love."

Jill nodded. "Chet's head over heels, but Ronnie isn't there yet. But she's warming."

"She's trying to get him to quit chewing tobacco," I guessed.

Jill sighed. "That and she'd prefer if he didn't wear his pistol, at least not in restaurants."

"And how does Chet feel about those things?"

"He's willing to compromise on the pistol, but it sounds like he's holding out on the chewing tobacco."

My phone rang and I pulled it out of my pocket and handed it to Jill. She answered before it rolled over, her voice surprising the caller.

"Sure, Jack. We can come back to the park." She looked at me. "Yeah, we're still in our uniforms. We'll be there in a few minutes." She ended the call and handed the phone back to me.

"What's up?"

Jill paused and looked at me. "Jack wants some pictures for the park website."

"Of us?"

"Of us with Larry."

"Uh uh. I'm going to the hotel, and we're going to pack and leave for the airport."

"It wasn't phrased as a request."

"He's ordering us to have our pictures taken?"

"The park service southeast regional director is ordering us to have our pictures taken."

My phone rang again, and Jill snatched it from my hand. "Hi Matt."

There wasn't much conversation, just a series of yesses. "We're on our way to the park now. Yes, we have our dress uniforms and would be happy to have some pictures taken with Jack and Larry."

She turned her head so I couldn't hear her conversation and I assumed she wanted Matt to pass something along to Mandy, Matt's wife and Jill's best friend. She ended the call and set the phone on the car console. "We're going to the park."

"Shit."

Jill put her hand on my arm. "Just roll with this."

"But…"

"It's bigger than your ego. This impacts you, me, Matt, Jack, and the National Park Service."

I turned and made a loop back to the highway and smoldered.

"Doug, get over it. This is part of our jobs. We made the park service look good and this is their chance to show off people who've made a difference. It's a celebration of accomplishment and recognition. It's for them more than for us."

"I don't like being the horse's ass in a dog and pony show."

Jill grabbed my bicep and squeezed. "I'm proud of what you accomplished this week. Does that count?"

"Sure."

"Then do this for me. For us."

I blew out a breath as I drove into the parking lot. "Okay. For you."

There were two news vans in the lot with their dish antennae pointed at the sky.

We put on our jackets in the stifling heat and carried our Smokey Bear hats into the visitor center. Jack, in full park service regalia, met us at the door.

He was all smiles and put his hand on Jill's shoulder. "What did you have to promise him to get him back?"

"We're picking up blue crabs on the way to the airport."

Jack smiled. "Send me the bill when you get back to Texas."

I nodded with a pained expression as Jack pointed to an array of microphones mounted on a podium near the book racks. He stepped away and engaged a pair of reporters in discussion. Jill led me to a corner away from prying ears. "We're staying in Florida until our return flight next week."

"What?"

"We're not going to rebook our Texas flights. I told Matt to mark us down for vacation until we're scheduled to return."

"I thought you didn't like it here."

Jill looked at her shoes for a second, then looked into my eyes. "We're going swimsuit shopping, then we're going to lounge around the pool until we go out for seafood and a bottle of wine."

"What are we going to do the rest of the week?"

"I'd like to walk South Beach and check out the tramp stamps on the beach bunnies one day. Then, I'd like to go on an Everglades airboat ride another day. I've heard Marco and Sanibel Islands are interesting. And I thought we'd spend the nights watching Gulf sunsets and pretending we're newlyweds."

"That's my reward for playing nice?"

Jill smiled and her dimples appeared. "No, it's your reward for having the best wife in the whole world."

The dimples always did me in. The room was quiet, and I looked around. Everyone was staring, waiting for us. I suppressed my impulse to kiss her. We walked to the podium where I stood beside Jack, with Larry and Jill on his other side.

"Ladies and gentlemen, it's my honor to introduce the U.S. Park Service investigators who helped solve a murder in Everglades National Park. Doug and Jill Fletcher teamed up with our law enforcement ranger, Larry Marconi, to solve a twisting mystery…"

The End

Readers we need you.

Please leave a review, even a one liner counts, and has a big influence on our future sales.

2020 #1 Bestselling Author
Dean Hovey

Dean Hovey is the best-selling and award-winning author of three mystery series. His scientific background, research, and travel help him create engaging characters and thrilling mysteries. One reader said Dean's characters are people he'd like to invite over for a beer and conversation.

Dean and his wife split their year between northern Minnesota and Arizona.